Broken Girl

a novel

GRETCHEN de la O

Edited by
Cassie Cox, Joy Editing

Interior Design and Formatting by
Angela McLaurin, Fictional Formats

Original Art and cover designed by
Sommer Stein, Perfect Pear Covers

PRAISE FOR

Broken Girl

"*Broken Girl* is a raw and gritty story about the ways in which we are all so very fragile. But even more so, it is a story about the ways in which love can make us courageous." ~ Mia Sheridan— *New York Times*, *USA Today*, and *Wall Street Journal* best-selling author

"With a heartbreakingly raw, gritty, yet beautiful storyline paving the way, Mrs. de la O manages to open not only your eyes but your soul to the dark, haunting truth consuming the reality of one too many innocent lives walking this earth. Gripping in every way possible, *Broken Girl* left her scars all over me. The end result is de la O's finest work yet!" ~ Gail McHugh—*New York Times*, *USA Today*, and *Wall Street Journal* best-selling author of the COLLIDE series

"This book was unlike any other I've read. Gritty, honest, and in your face! Five stars!" ~ Ellie is Uhm a Bookworm

"Gretchen de la O creates flawed characters bound by painful circumstances, creating a beautiful, stunning five-star read." ~ D. *Flirty and Dirty* Book Blog

"It's been a long time since a book has made me FEEL like this! Five huge, beautifully broken stars." ~ Adriana Locke—*USA Today* best-selling author

"This emotionally charged and gritty novel will captivate you from page one. The way that author Gretchen de la O brings to life a story of a truly broken woman is honest and authentic without exploiting the character's history." ~ *Art, Books, & Coffee*

"Every once in a while, you read a book that you know will stick with you for a long time. *Broken Girl* is one of them." ~ Kathy from *Panty Dropping* Book Blog

"Dark. Gritty. Raw. Real. All of the things I love to read. I devoured this book and relished every last word!" ~ *Up All Night Book Addict*

"A jaw-dropping, heart-pounding story that you won't soon forget. Gretchen pulls you in from the first word and holds you hostage to the end." ~ C. A. *Book Whores Obsession* Book Blog

"This story is as raw and painful as they come, but what impressed me most about the book is the absolute honesty the author uses to bring Rose to life." ~ *The Pleasure of Reading Today* Book Blog

"Gretchen de la O's words pull you into a world filled with heartache and warmth. *Broken Girl* is beautifully written story filled with depth, devotion, and love." J. *Three Chicks and Their Books* Blog

"Big O has done it again! I felt the anguish and pain ... I felt the fear and shame and guilt. Such a deep, deep read." ~ Tiffany, Goodreads review

DEDICATED TO THE LITTLE

broken girl

WITHIN EVERY WOMAN.

Broken Girl

prologue

THE ROOM'S SO dark, smells like moldy cheese and dirt. It's cold, so cold that I can see my breath. My heart's pounding in my chest, echoing in my ears. All I can see is him. He leans me back across the bed.

"Now, dirty little girls need to learn their lesson when walkin' around in the confines of men like me."

My feet are dangling off the bed.

Even though it feels like it is freezing, my skin is sweaty. His eyes are dark, narrow, filled with a look my daddy gives my mommy before they make me go to bed.

His hands are hot and sticky; the tips of his fingers scratch my waist as he pulls my pink shorts and flowery panties down and off my legs.

"You're making me do this, my little Rosalie. You give me this sickness, you see, you keep causin' all of this in my body and well, now you're gonna help me with it."

I can't talk as my voice is hiding in the back of my throat.

I am drowning.

I am scared.

More scared than any other time in my life.

I'm naked, my privates exposed.

Mom tells me that girls who let boys touch them in their privates down there are bad girls, naughty girls ... damaged goods.

I don't wanna be bad.

The heat of his hands are burning the insides of my knees as my mom's voice floods me. *"No man wants to marry a whore, Rosalie; do you hear me? Girls who let boys touch them down there are nothing but whores!"*

My tummy twists at her words and knot at his touch.

What's a whore?

I don't wanna be a whore.

His dark eyes widen, and I watch him look at my privates. His smile gets big.

The tips of his fingers are dirty, crammed with black under his nails as they touch my thighs ... I close my eyes.

He pulls my legs apart, and it seems like forever before he says something.

"You so perfect, little sunshine. We gonna take care of my sickness now."

I open my eyes just enough, still afraid to see what he's about to do to me; his stare finds me.

Globs of tears collect on the edges of my eyes.

Silently, I cry.

"Shhh, Rosalie, don't cry, you gonna fix me up. Make me all better; you's about ripe for the pickin', girl." He pushes his fingers against the tears racing down my cheeks.

My voice isn't working. I can't scream.

I wish I'd never come here to see if Tami could play. I wish I didn't have any friends with stepdads who need little girls like me.

I am like my rag doll as he pulls me to the end of the bed; my arms drag up around my head.

Why is he doing this? How long till he stops being sick?

He unzips, and his jeans drop to his ankles.

I didn't mean to look.

"You see what you do to me? I need some healin'," he growls before he touches his sickness.

I am scared.

I never saw a man's sickness before. My daddy never shows me his.

I feel my tummy shake, my muscles turn to mush. I have no control. I feel my soul leave as he begins to break me.

He pushes against my privates, too hard, too much. He hurts me down there.

Broken little girl.

I hold my breath … he huffs.

He won't stop pushing.

I am …

Torn …

Apart …

In Seconds …

one

ELEVEN YEARS LATER ...

BEER BOTTLES RIDDLED the nightstand, clanking with the tapping of the mattress wedged between it and the wall. The music that blared from the stereo was loud enough to drown out my *date's* exaggerated huffs and the squeaking of the bed frame. I held my breath as I counted the pushes, hoping he wasn't gonna take much longer. Business was time, and time was money. The faster they came, the better it made for repeat business. I threw my hips into it, tightened my cooch around his dick, and huffed out how I was about to come. I didn't want to keep the other girls waiting.

A chill of satisfaction slipped down my spine with the helpless look in his eye. One last thrust, as a long bellowing growl scorched across my skin, was proof enough for me that I had claimed another satisfied customer. I focused on the velour blood-red roses on the dark, drab wallpaper while I waited for him to pull out. *Time is money.* His breath was sour, beer mixed with cigarettes; he didn't bother kissing me, and I was fine with that. I never kissed on the lips anyway ... Never.

"Thanks, sweetheart," he spat. He stretched off the rubber

filled with his seed and chucked it next to me on the bed. "You'll take care of that, right?" He zipped his pants before he tossed two twenty-dollar bills across my chest. "And here, get yourself something pretty."

"What the hell is this? It was sixty if I fucked you," I snapped as I pulled down my skirt.

He plopped in the high-back gaudy floral chair next to the door and sucked a short breath through his shit-eating smirk before he smacked his lips together as if he had caught the smell of sex in his mouth. He dragged his filthy work boots over, pulled them on as he answered my demand.

"Is that what you call it? Laying there like a dead fish? You didn't fuck me. I fucked you ... as a matter of fact, you should be paying me," he snarled before he meandered toward the door.

"That's bullshit and you know it," I hissed.

"I can't say you weren't a tight lay. I'll tell you what I'll do for you ... I'll tell my buddies down at the shop what you're willing to do for sixty bones and let's see how many run down here to bang at your door. You want sixty for a fuck, at least make it worth it. Roll your hips against my cock or give up a little whimper every once in a while. If I wanted a dead lay, I would fuck my wife." He tossed me the same shit-eating smirk from earlier, like it was the only one in his arsenal, before he walked out, leaving the bedroom door wide open.

"I'm the best lay you've ever had and you know it, motherfucker," I hollered after him.

Every muscle in my body quaked; that dirty bastard had shorted me and there was nothing I could do, absolutely nothing. Who was I gonna tell? I was a twenty-year-old prostitute who fucked guys almost twice her age for money. As long as they filled the rubber separating them from all the worthless fucks that had come before, nobody would ever give two shits about it.

I'd learned a long time ago that nobody was willing to help the broken; they swept us under the asphalt of cracked streets and piss-drenched darkened alleys forever. Besides, most prostitutes were the unmentionable leftovers wired on crack or strung out on heroin. But not me. Even with all the demons I fought every second of my life, I'd managed to keep off that shit. I stuck to pot and always slammed a couple of fistfuls of throat-burning-gut-ripping whiskey before I punched the clock and sold my body. Damaged was one thing, even broken, but to become a prisoner of that shit other girls were shooting or snorting? No fucking thank you. I stuck to the joint and the bottle.

Sex was my vice, and it didn't take someone with a degree plastered behind a thin sheet of glass to tell me that. It was fucked up and crazy and nobody understood it; not even the nutjob psychologists could explain it. I was playing Russian roulette, and every spin of the cylinder, every pull of the trigger, and every time the hammer slammed against an empty chamber and a bullet didn't pierce my skull, I had another day and another reason to numb myself. Every time, I gained that much more control over my fucked up existence, but I knew it was only a matter of time before I took a bullet. Only a matter of time before my card was pulled and my past would catch up to me.

"Rose, we're heading downtown, you in?" Sybil said as she poked her head into the room. Her broom-bristle, fire-engine-red hair swayed across her face. Her ocher vamp-style eyes narrowed, exaggerating her thick black eyeliner and clumpy mascara. She didn't wait for my answer before she released a smile that would turn anyone into a paying customer.

"Who's going?" I asked, knowing the only thing we had in common at the moment was spreading our legs.

"You, me, and the two new girls, Crystal and Brie. I was thinking me and you could teach them a couple of things. You know?" Sybil tapped her hand on the door, pushing it open a little wider before she lengthened out her leg wrapped in fishnet stockings.

I hadn't come into this business with bells on and a party hat strapped to my dome. The idea that I had to fuck gross old men so I could eat and put a roof over my head had never crossed my mind, not until I was forced to. Although, I knew how to disconnect, fuck them before they ever had a chance to fuck me over. I was always in control and kept it business with a look, a smirk, a hum, or a whimper. It had become the way I controlled these fucks. When my body was numb, my mind would check out; it tended to dull the sharp edge of what I had to do.

"Sure, give me a minute."

I wedged my toes into my four-inch black stiletto heels, adjusted my thin red spandex skirt, and pulled my fingers through my lengthy black hair. I spent a little extra time to make sure the back of my hair wasn't natty or flattened from my last lay. I freshened up my makeup, lipstick—candy-apple red—black mascara.

Most guys were drawn to my eyes. I guess my eyes told them every detail I kept locked away in my mind. A hollow good-bye with a touch of something curious, and I never allowed tears to well over my eyelashes. I just couldn't let anything affect me that way anymore. My need to feel beyond the decay of my soul wasn't warranted and neither were tears. Call me a callous bitch, a broken woman, hell, you could even call me a slut, but don't ever call me a victim. I was exactly what my past had created. It happens. People get hurt and nobody stops their day or waits for you to catch up. Either you found your way or you got lost in the nightmares.

"Hurry up, Rose. Brie said she'll drive," Sybil said before she knocked on the bedroom door. She swung her purse across her shoulder, her florally forest perfume filling my room.

That was another thing totally messed up about selling sex ... you had to douse yourself in enough perfume to erase the smell of used latex mixed with semen.

I looked around the room; pictures of my great-grandmother were hung on the walls and propped on the tortured old furniture that had a past equal to mine. On the full-size bed, wedged between the nightstand filled with beer bottles and the wall, the dark-brown comforter was bunched up with the used rubber. *Fuck it; I'm not touching it, not for forty bucks.* I snatched my purse off the gaudy floral chair. The same chair my grandma had always sat in when she spat her judgments on me as a child.

"So this is your parents' house?" Crystal asked as the four of us collected our coats and headed out the door.

"Yeah, they're on their annual trip to *save the world*," I murmured.

"How long are they gone?" Sybil asked.

"They go every year for two weeks; they should be home any day now," I droned.

Even though it had been three years since I'd spoken to or seen my parents, they were predictable. Every year at this time, they'd take a two-week trip to some exotic place and use the excuse that they were somehow doing their part to help the world. *Always keeping up the perfect façade.*

I pulled open the huge front door and let everyone shuffle out before me … I looked around and was content that they'd know it was me who had left the house the exact way they had left my soul … dirty, used, and vacant.

two

GOING DOWNTOWN ALWAYS consisted of wrangling up a group of guys who wanted to have speed sex in the narrow alley between the Stop and Wash Laundromat and the Iron Hog Pub. It was the perfect place, filled with lonely, horny men who were willing to pay to have someone give their cocks a little attention. I called it speed sex because I didn't have to work too hard to get them lining up while they'd willingly drop a couple or three Jacksons for me to fuck 'em or suck 'em off. It was quick money, and since word had gotten around, there were more guys than Sybil and I could handle. Pick-and-choose was our best option ... *oh, and the other horny bastards, take a number, motherfuckers.*

Sybil suggested we bring Crystal and Brie in on our back alley gold mine venture and, in the process, collect a little finder's fee. I was up for anything that kept Sybil and me flush with a little extra cash. We were golden ... or so I thought.

We had had it all set. Crystal and I would take a walk around the laundromat and see if there were any potential customers, while Sybil and Brie would meander through the Iron Hog, order a couple of drinks, and show the drunk fucks what they could have if they'd come out into the back alley.

Sybil pulled open the back door of the Iron Hog, and both she and Brie slipped past a loudmouthed drunk asshole who used the opportunity to cop a feel of Brie's rack. He acted like he was trying to find the restroom, and that's when he noticed Crystal was tapping away on her iPhone. His heavy-lidded eyes narrowed, and his vision scraped up her bare legs and across her firm tits.

"Hey, you, what are you willing to do for a couple bucks?" the gawky stranger slurred at Crystal before he stumbled forward and grabbed his dick. He shook his head back and forth, clearing his long, wiry blond hair away from his sunken, wasted eyes.

I knew this wasn't the type of prick she should proposition in the back alley. Even though Crystal was only two years younger than me, she was just barely legal to make her own decisions. I'd seen girls like her before; they'd spend their days convincing themselves that they'd sell their bodies just until they'd made enough money to pay for their grandmother's operation, or back taxes, or maybe even work their way through college with a little extra money to survive. Her story was the same as all the others. When she'd made enough, she'd stop. It was always about selling themselves only long enough to pay for what they needed. Right? Then before they realized it, the sharp claws of greed would sink into their skin and never let go. It basically boiled down to the fact that they'd get too used to the lifestyle.

"Come on, whatcha willing to give up under that little sexy black leather skirt? Can the first sample of this pussy be free?" he said, towering over her; his body swallowed up her tiny frame.

"Get the fuck off me," Crystal screamed, struggling to push him away.

The disgusting odor of piss mixed with rotting garbage wafted across the narrow breezeway as a gust of wind reminded me just how wretched life could be. These fucked-up moments didn't exist for the Cinderella life most women lived on the other side of these stucco buildings. Streets where making a living wasn't lived out in a shitty alley.

"Come on, what bitch wouldn't want this inside her?" he growled as he pulled down his pants and grabbed himself.

You gonna take care of my sickness, isn't that right, little Rosalie.

Words bubbled in the back of my throat. Bile crawled up from my stomach as I opened up my mouth to scream for him to stop.

I am drowning.

I wanted to stop him from hurting her, protect her like I should've been, but the back door of the laundromat slammed shut and I recoiled into the shadows. A voice—louder, deeper, and more commanding—rang across the cracked stucco before it rolled across the weathered wooden doors.

"Hey, buddy, you heard the woman. She said no." His deep voice startled me. He stood tall, burly, dwarfing all of us, his shoulders wide, dark eyes narrowed, legs ready to launch his body if he had to pull the guy off Crystal.

"Fuck you. Find your own bitch to go balls-deep." The drunken asshole slipped his hands up Crystal's skirt.

I saw the fear in her eyes dissolve to defeat. Her shoulders rounded slightly, just enough to tell me she'd lost the internal battle of convincing herself that she didn't deserve what was about to happen. It was a moment when those of us who fucked for money were forced to pretend to be someone else. It was just another shitty part of selling your body. Men will take, when given the opportunity. Tonight was no different.

"I said, let her go!" Laundry Man barked.

"You have no idea what business I'm conducting with this whore, so if you know what's best for you … you'd get the fuck up outta here." The belligerent asshole pulled up on Crystal's skirt, giving him full access to her.

He smiled then tangled his grimy hand into her platinum-blond

11

hair before he tugged her head back, exposing her neck. Her pulse thundered under her thin skin, the muscles in her jaw tightened as she whimpered, tears clung to her eyelashes.

"She isn't doing business with you anymore." The huge virile Laundry Man slipped his arm around the front of drunken asshole's neck and pulled him off Crystal.

As he gasped for air, Crystal's attacker's feet left the concrete; he kicked, stretching for ground. His hands released Crystal, and he struggled to grab at the thick, muscular arm choking him out. His haggard face grew red, eyes bugged so large I saw the blood vessels as they began to explode and color the whites of his saucer eyes scarlet. Every gasp and soundless whisper gave way to a shade of blue that seeped around his mouth before his eyes rolled up into the back of his head. It wasn't more than a couple of minutes before Crystal's attacker was unconscious and crumpled in a pile of drunken leftover shit.

Standing in the shadows, I watched as Crystal righted her skirt and dragged the back of her hand across her cheeks. The faint glow from the single bulb that dangled above the back door of the pub lit the area around her. I was frozen, my back against the grimy stucco wall. I didn't run to her, I thought about it but decided to lurk in the background between guilt and relief. I had no idea who this man was or his motive for saving Crystal. Risking my livelihood to save her from getting pinched and thrown in jail was something I wasn't willing to do. She'd be out by the next morning anyway, ready to sell her body again to whoever was willing to pay.

Cops and the DA thought getting picked up would scare us straight. A night in jail didn't stop us. The money was too good and the hustle was too enticing.

"You okay?" he asked before he reached out to her. His giant hands hovered just below her shoulders, making her look so tiny.

"Yeah, I think so," Crystal whimpered. Her mascara blackened the delicate skin below her aquamarine eyes.

"You sure, Miss …?" he said as he lowered his head and met her gaze.

"Crystal … Just Crystal."

"Just Crystal?"

"Yep."

"Well, Just Crystal, this isn't a place you should be hanging out, all alone. You sure you're okay?" he asked again. Wisps of his dark-brown hair curved across his forehead and around his ears.

Crystal shifted her weight from one leg to the other. With the flick of her hand between them, she answered his question.

"Well, Mister …?" she said as she waited for his answer.

"Shane. Only Shane," he teased.

"Well, Only Shane, I'm not totally alone. My friends went into the pub. Wrangling up a couple of beers for me and—" She stopped as her eyes caught mine.

I shook my head and warned her to keep me out of her conversation with this guy.

"And?" he questioned.

"Just me."

"Well, Just Crystal, I can't believe they left you back here all alone. It's getting pretty late. Why don't I take you inside so you can find your friends?" He pulled Crystal out of the dark, dingy alley and into the pub. With a quick glance back, he made sure the guy he'd left in a heap wasn't moving.

The pub door slammed shut just before Crystal's attacker began to roll around on the ground, moaning.

I pushed off the bristly stucco, and it snagged my wooly sweater; the pin pricks from pressing my body tight against the wall began to fade. I took a couple of steps out of the shadows that kept me secret. I eyed the drunken asshat on the ground as he struggled to figure out what had just happened. His back was to me; his shoulders slumped, he dragged his thick black boots across the filthy ground before he struggled to his feet.

"What the hell? I'm gonna find that motherfucker and kill him and that little bitch whore too." His voice was harsh and growly. His pants hung loose around his waist; he pulled them up as he looked around. The whites of his eyes were painted wicked scarlet red. He looked like the Devil from my childhood.

I wasn't a religious person. I didn't believe that there was anything that would save me from my own fucked up life. I had been forgotten by a faith that turned its back on me and walked away simply because I didn't pray hard enough.

I had just been a kid hiding in the darkest corner of my closet, praying that God would answer my pleas and take away the rotting ache that ate at my stomach and broke my heart. Praying until I ran out of tears, begging God to take away the shitty memories that filled my mind, night after night, just so I could fall asleep. Nine, ten, eleven years old, 365 days a year, I prayed to God to take away my pain. I prayed for the strength to tell someone what had happened to me. Begged God to protect me so no other monster would force his heaviness against me and steal another little broken piece of me away. The God everyone talked about, the same God who answered the meek and gave to the pure. Well, God never listened to me. I guess he was busy helping someone who wasn't damaged, or maybe I just didn't pray hard enough.

"What the fuck are you lookin at?" the drunken asshole clipped.

I froze.

Bile rose from my stomach and lapped at the back of my throat.

Shit, I didn't want him to see me. It's too late … play the game, Rose.

"Well, I hope I'm looking at my next fuck. Sixty-five bucks and I'll let you bury balls-deep. Seventy-five, I'll include a blow job." I crawled my fingers to the bottom edge of my red skirt and pulled it up just enough before I caught my bottom lip between my teeth and methodically cocked my hip to one side.

"Are you with that skank who lured me out here just so her boyfriend could kick my ass?" he bellowed as his hands flailed out across the alley, pointing at the laundromat and pub.

"I don't know what you are talking about," I answered through a snarky grin.

"Fuck that shit. I'm done with back-alley whores. Nasty pieces of shit, every one of you," he spat before he turned away and limped his way down the alley.

Who in the hell is that bastard calling nasty?

Piss-soaked pants, bloodshot eyes with his hair matted from fighting Shane before being choked unconscious. Let me call 'em like I see 'em—the fuck was a rat; he was a cheap rat bastard who was ready to rape a girl simply because he felt he had the right to. It didn't matter if she sold her pussy for money; he wanted to violate her because he could.

The door of the pub scraped open, and the roar of many more drunken barflies floated and pounded across the night air, violating the moment I'd planned on using to take a deep breath. Shane hustled back out alone, his head down. He watched where he was going until he looked over to where he had left Crystal's attacker and froze. Our eyes met, and a chill stole my opportunity to exhale.

"Evening, ma'am. You heading into the pub? Good idea to get on in. Can't be too careful out here alone."

My voice was lodged down in my throat. The only thing I could do was nod.

He nodded in return and passed me without looking down at my body. He met my eyes long enough to tell me that he wasn't going to hurt me, just enough time to tell me he wasn't interested in what I was selling. He took a couple ginormous steps back to the other side of the alley and entered the laundromat.

My heart clung to the back of my throat, along with my pride. I wanted to tell him that I knew who he was. That I'd met him in the shadows of the alley about fifteen minutes ago when he saved Crystal. He just didn't get the opportunity to formally meet me. It was strange that I knew his name. In fact, I knew enough about him to feel safe and comfortable around him, and yet all he knew about me was that I was a woman alone in the back alley. I watched as the laundromat door swung closed behind him. He was gone, and I was an object left in the dark, dingy alley between the Stop and Wash Laundromat and the Iron Hog Pub.

three

I NEVER WOKE up before noon. Maybe every once in a while, when I had to go see a doctor or pay my electricity bill before they'd shut it off, but most of the time, my life didn't start until a quarter to one. My internal clock was all fucked up, had been that way since I was a kid. Nights had gone from something to fear to something profitably required.

I had left home at the tender age of sixteen. I decided sleeping on my friends' couches or the cold, vacant sidewalks under shabby chunks of cardboard for heat had to be better than dealing with my parents' drunken rage. My mom was unrelenting when she drank, and unfortunately for me, she was drunk more times than she was sober. A couple of sips from a half-empty whiskey bottle, and within minutes, she'd have the courage to mercilessly beat the sin out of me. When I was done bearing the brunt of my mother's burdens, I decided I had to leave, I had to get out.

I didn't start selling my body until I was seventeen. I had just been kicked out of my friend Jean's house. I guess helping myself to her parents' little stash of pot wasn't acceptable. Hell, I had just wanted to get high and pretend I was someone else, that my life meant something more than another mouth to feed. All hell had broken loose; Jean had tried to take the blame, but I couldn't let her do that for me. I grabbed my backpack, everything I owned, and I left. That was the first night I sold myself for some fast food and twenty bucks.

I watch this older, blond-haired guy park up behind the Chick-N-Flips. He gets out of one of those older Mustangs, a red one with heavy doors and a canvas black top. He seems nervous but familiarly comfortable as he approaches me.

"You waiting for someone?" he asks. His blue eyes twinkle, matching his smile.

"Yes, as a matter of fact, I am, and they should be here any minute," I answer as I balance on the balls of my feet on the edge of the curb.

I watch him as he sizes me up; he can tell I'm high and takes the opportunity to get me to talk.

"Okay, you just look a little hungry."

Our eyes meet for a moment before I answer him.

"Yeah, I'm hungry. Didn't eat much today." I feel a chill build at the base of my spine.

"Well, why don't I get you something to eat?"

And even though I'm starving and pangs of hunger twist in my gut, I give him the answer I think will curb his attention.

"No, I'm cool. I had a banana earlier, and my friend should be here any minute."

"Nobody can survive on just a banana. How about I buy you something to eat?"

You so perfect, little sunshine. We gonna take care of my sickness now ...

"Thanks, mister, but I can't pay you back."

He slips his finger under my chin and pulls my face up so I'm looking into his ravenous eyes. "Don't worry about it. We can work something out. People barter in all different kinds of ways. Use what you have to get what you need."

His words linger in my head longer than any other useless conversation I've had today. Suddenly, it's as if I know what I need to do. Maybe if I wasn't so hungry, I could walk away. If I had some sort of credibility, I could get a job, but I'm seventeen with no home, no work experience, and nowhere else to go. I know what he's implying. I'm hungry, and at this point, I have no other choice.

I follow him into the men's restroom of the Chick-N-Flips. We go into a stall and he drops his pants and I give my first blow job. When we are done, he buys me a chicken sandwich, curly fries, and a strawberry milkshake. Before he leaves, he hands me twenty bucks, starts his car, and off he goes. The twist in my stomach never goes away, but I'm fed and have some money in my pocket.

He was my first trick, my first paying customer. And three years later, still one of my most reliable. But now, instead of in a cramped stall in the Chick-N-Flips' restroom, we meet up behind the courthouse on Main Street and I fuck him for sixty bucks in the passenger seat of that same old Mustang.

Every ho out there has done what she had to do to make it. No matter my past, present, or future, I did what I needed to in order to make the work tolerable. Whether I tossed back three shots of tequila before I had to work, or smoked a little weed in order to mellow the twist in my stomach, I did what I did to make it through the night.

Tricks weren't my biggest headache. Sure, I'd get *dates* who'd get a little rough or out of hand, but my major problem seemed to be the other prostitutes who tried to fuck with the six squares of sidewalk I called my corner. That was right; I claimed eighteen feet of high-trafficked prime real estate. I'm not gonna go into the graphic details about how I inherited my pavement. Let me just say it was gifted to me after one of our own hooked herself a sugar daddy. She wasn't ever gonna have to sway her ass on a corner or worry about some John getting too rough with her or even how she was going to feed her two kids by two different fucks when the rubber broke. She'd pounded her way to the cat house. That was what she wanted.

Some girls got lured into brothels or picked up by pimps and taken up to be escorts. I'd been approached, threatened, even taken, but I'd always found a way to make it back to the Tenderloin, my six squares of real estate in San Francisco's red light district before some other ho tried to claim it. See, Sybil and I were known as renegades or out-of-pockets—hos without a pimp. I wasn't willing to give my money to some fucking asshole who never really protected me anyway. Let those girls who wanted that life take it. Selling my body wasn't something I wanted to do forever.

Get enough money to get the fuck out.

I glanced at the clock. Damn, it was two thirty and I had no motivation to get out of bed—maybe because last night had been nothing more than a total fucking loss. That drunk-ass guy, then the Shane thing with Crystal; all of it really cut into my profits. I was going to have to work twice as hard tonight, maybe even head out earlier than usual in hopes that a handful of well-to-do horny *dates* needed a late afternoon dip or blow.

My mind twisted off to thoughts about Shane, the Laundry Man. How polite he had acted last night with Crystal, jumping to her rescue. Visions rumbled through my mind as I wondered if he'd only treated her that way because she was in trouble. Would he have been so ready to help her if she was just doing her job? There weren't many men out there like him. They just never existed in our line of work. If men like Shane existed, we would've done everything in our power to keep *dates* like that coming back. But there wasn't enough hours in the day to waste time hoping for something that would never happen to us. *Back to reality, Rose.*

I pulled my phone off my nightstand and looked to see if any of my regulars needed something special today. Nope, just a couple of random texts about my data usage and a couple of missed calls from Brie. I listened to the messages she left—mostly just updates on how Crystal was doing after last night.

Those of us who had been in the business long enough had the same ol' saying ingrained into our minds. Would it be fair of me to call Brie back and recite the same fucking words? *"It's just the nature of the business. Sometimes you will be taken advantage of. Just be grateful he didn't drag you off and kill you."* Yeah, seemed harsh, almost uncaring, but the more she realized she wasn't in Nevada, the better off she'd be. We didn't have the luxury of TV's bullshit depiction of the BunnyRanch, or the *Cathouse*. I'd given up the twisted dream of some fat, bald fuck who kept me safe. It just didn't happen to girls left on the streets to make their way through the world.

I just needed to shower and get something to eat before I headed out to make up for the lost money last night. I glanced across the postage-stamp-sized studio apartment I shared with Sybil and noticed her bed hadn't been slept in. It was still made—wrinkle-free, pulled tight to where you could bounce a quarter off the blanket. She'd never come home. Actually, she hadn't in the pub either when I texted her last night. She'd said she was gonna pull an all-nighter for two hundred fifty bucks. But no matter, she should've been home by now. I shuffled over and noticed a little pink note resting on her pillow.

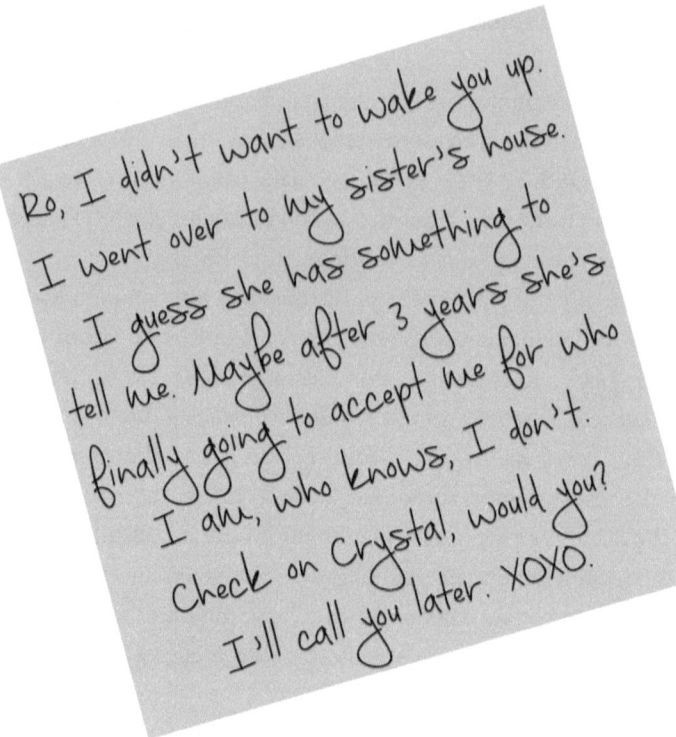

Ro, I didn't want to wake you up. I went over to my sister's house. I guess she has something to tell me. Maybe after 3 years she's finally going to accept me for who I am, who knows, I don't. Check on Crystal, would you? I'll call you later. XOXO.

I was grateful she'd had the courtesy to tell me where she was. When you lived with someone in the same business of selling sex, communication could mean the difference between life and death. Sybil and I had promised one another that we'd keep each other safe. But I'd be damned if I was gonna call Crystal and suddenly have her become my problem. I knew everyone needed someone in this fucked up business. I got that; but pullin' that girl under my wing right now was more of a hassle than anything else. What the hell did Sybil want me to do? Go over there and make sure she hadn't cried herself to sleep?

This was a gnarly business with gnarly, disgusting sick fucks who wouldn't give a rat's ass about you and whether you were gang-raped in a back alley or lying in the gutter and bleeding to death. There would always be some other girl ready to take your place.

I buried the twist in my stomach and moved the fuck on. Call it self-preservation.

The hot water pummeled my flesh, annihilating any desire I had to go back to bed. I'd be damned when flashes of Crystal's savior flooded my mind. The way Laundry Man had looked at me in the alley replayed in my head over and over again. His eyes pierced mine, the tone of his voice as he told me to get into the pub. How he had become frozen when he saw that the prick was gone. An urge swirled through my stomach, exactly what I didn't have time to get all caught up in when I thought about him. My life was too busy. *Soap up, rinse off, and get the hell out, but stay just long enough to wake up.*

I hated to do business in the late afternoon. The only *dates* who showed up on the stroll were cheap-ass motherfuckers looking for an early bird special. I ended up wasting half of my afternoon getting those stingy bastards to cough up three-quarters of my going rate ... no discounts, no exceptions. *I should actually charge them double because the risk of being pinched is so much higher.*

I had my time and price per service mathematically down and memorized. So when the cheap bastards came out for an afternoon delight, I could work the numbers to my advantage. Dip and lips ran the gamut, from the young stud construction guy needing to get his rocks off on his lunch break, to the senior citizen who wanted to pop before he hit the early bird dinner special and went to bed. Both were always hot for pussy, and for the most part, I could talk them in circles before they unzipped and ended up more than happy to pay my evening rate.

It was the uptight businessman who wanted something for almost nothing. Broken by the wits of those middle-aged pricks, it was rare that I could get them to unzip for my evening rate. Big fucking briefcases with small cocks, and if I had a dollar for every time they told me they'd never done this before, I'd be rolling up in a Benz dipped in gold. They were the stingiest fucks around and yet pulled up to the curb in eighty-thousand-dollar Porsches, walked around saturated in Armani and Christian Dior, with Rolex watches strapped to their wrists and twenty-four-karat gold rings wedged on their short, pudgy fingers. The only positive was they were so wound up, they'd blow their wads after a couple of dips. fifty bucks for a three-minute fuck wasn't so bad.

I hopped out of the shower and collected what I was gonna wear for the entire night. I slipped into my black stretchy tennis miniskirt. The same skirt that if I bent over, everyone would get a peek at my merchandise. I pulled on a tight shimmery pink halter top that made my tits look unbelievable and rummaged through the pile of heels next to my bed. I found the most comfortable pair of stilettos I could wear without having to take them off every half hour.

I blew out my hair, helping the natural wave curve around my face, before I dragged sparkling peach lip gloss across the swell of my mouth and earthy green shadow across my eyelids. I used to think there'd be a time when the life that had sparked behind my eyes would return. Come to find out that was wishful thinking, dreams of a little girl who thought the world cared. It was a mistake I'd never let happen again.

I grabbed a variety of rubbers from the lead crystal bowl on my dresser. Two strips of ribbed, three or four Magnums, and a handful of assorted flavors; I hated the cherry ones, but if it was the difference between choking down a Robitussin-flavored cock for a quick three minutes or losing forty bucks, I'd live with the taste of cherry cough syrup. I tossed a half-smoked joint and a handful of airplane mini bottles of tequila in my purse before I snatched my keys from the bookcase, straightened the seams of my miniskirt, and double-checked my bulging cleavage in the full-length mirror behind the front door. There, now it was time to make some money. I strolled past the threshold and didn't look back. No use in turning around when I wouldn't be meandering back this way before four in the morning. I never looked back anyway.

I pulled into the parking lot of an office building a half block down from Preacher's Square, an oxymoron at its best. I always parked my '92 Le Baron far enough away so nobody would see me drive up. It was a car older than dirt and smelled just as bad when I ran the heater. Two years older than me, it'd been around the block as much as a middle-aged hooker.

Preacher's Square was designed to give hardworking people a patch of grass to eat lunch on and bring the kids to play. Instead, it had become nothing more than a cesspool for runaway teens who wanted to get high and hos who needed a place to do their business.

I downed two of the mini tequila bottles and took a couple of hits off the joint before I readied myself for the hunt. It didn't take but two minutes before I got a hit—a businessman looking for an afternoon blow job. He leaned in close enough to be heard but still far enough away so he didn't get caught. Day jobs were more difficult and easier to get arrested. All it took was one cop who wouldn't trade for a tuck-and-pull from any of the girls in the park and we'd all go down. Fortunately, one of the new girls had showed up or the cops were having a shift change, because there wasn't one in sight.

"Hey, sweetheart, what's it cost for you to … you know?" he said as he pointed at the stiffy in his pants.

"That depends on what you want. Lips are forty, a dip is sixty, and if you need both, seventy-five." I sounded like a broken record.

"Well, that little piece of ass over there told me she'd give me both for forty-five." He tossed me a thoughtless smile as he

25

pointed over at a girl who was rockin' her shit back and forth. His eyes were as big as drink coasters.

"You know what, if that ho is willing to bargain basement her coochie for forty-five bucks, I suggest you run your cheap-ass over there and tap it, because I guarantee her prices are already going up as we speak." I stood there waiting for him to respond.

He couldn't, because we both knew he was lying. I knew Patsy, and she wasn't willing to give up her snatch for anything under fifty bucks. Maybe if she was feeling generous she'd blow you for thirty-five bones, but nothing less.

"Pay or get the fuck out of my face," I spat at him.

"I only have thirty-five dollars. Come on, help me out," he whined as he dug pudgy fingers into his suit pants.

"Are you kidding me? You're walking up on me wearing a Giorgio Armani suit worth more than the car I drive, and you're gonna stand here and tell me you can't come up with another five bucks so I'll suck your cock? Get the fuck out of my face, you cheap-ass bastard."

When you sell yourself for money, that's how you have to treat all these cheap-ass motherfuckers. Pull out your toughest trait, own it, and wear it like a glove; let them know you aren't desperate for their money, and always be willing to walk away. If you don't, they're gonna whittle away at your profit, and the next thing you know, you're sucking them off for free.

"Shit," he spat as he dug into his wallet fat with cash. He collected up forty bucks before he twisted it into his fingers and held it up between us. "You better be worth it."

"Put away the money and don't pull it out until I say. What the fuck, you trying to get me pinched?" I growled, staring him down.

He slipped his cash into his front pocket.

"Now, are we doing business in your car or all Adam and Eve style?"

His eyes narrowed. He looked around before he cleared his

throat. I knew by his body language he was about to say something that would make him look like a total douche.

"Just follow me," I mumbled as I began to walk up the grassy knoll.

I should have known he didn't want to use his car. Another perfect example of why I'd rather fuck a dusty old fart hopped up on Viagra in the backseat of his rusty Cadillac than deal with assholes like this, where his briefcase was bigger than his cock and his pinstriped charcoal-gray suit was worth four times anything I owned.

In the far corner of Preacher's Square was a grove of eucalyptus trees surrounded by tall juniper bushes. Behind it, a twelve-foot-tall stucco wall separated the upper-middle class neighborhood from the park. It was secluded enough to be private, but it still gave you a clear view of who was coming over—a perfect place to do our business.

"You don't have to keep looking around. It makes you look guilty of something. Just walk casual. You ever done this before?" I asked.

"Yeah, in a car or a hotel room, but not like this."

"Let me tell you, first, nobody gives a rat's ass about what you and I are about to do. And two, the busy people will still be busy walking down the sidewalks, dogs will still be taking a shit on the edge of the square, and their owners will still be the assholes who leave it there to fuck with my profession, and lastly, as I drop down and give you one of the most ball-tightening blow jobs you'll ever have … we'll have an audience. So when your eyes are rolling into the back of your head and you're about to blow your wad, remember there's always a couple of street rats that sneak back here and jack off to the show. Just make sure you give them one. You ready?" I asked as we slipped behind the sparse juniper bushes.

"I guess so, sure."

His eyes darted toward where we came from. A couple of straggling joggers passed by but never noticed us. He worked to get his cock out. A smirk crept across his face and his eyes gleamed sadistically, as if he had just bought my soul from Satan himself.

"Whoa, slow down there, cowboy, I need the dough before I blow. My policy, payment before any service is provided."

"Of course, forty bucks, right?"

"BJ only, right?"

He answered with a nod.

"Then yeah, *now* you can pay me."

He pushed into his front pocket and pulled out the cash he had tried to give me earlier. And like every prick in a business suit, he slipped it between my tits. *I have hands, asshole.* To make a big deal out of his classless actions would have been just wasted time—it wasn't worth the argument.

I pulled a flavored rubber from my purse and tossed it at him. "I don't do bareback. Cap your cock."

Most of the time I'd put on a show, prop the rubber between my lips and teeth and roll it down as I went to town; but fuck it, not this time. He wanted something like that, at least offer me his car or take me to a hotel room. But behind the juniper bushes? His dick wasn't getting special treatment. He ripped open the package, pulled out the rubber, and started to roll it on. I could smell that motherfucker the minute it hit the air … cough syrup. Cherry flavor, just my luck.

four

"MY FUCKING FEET are killing me!" Sybil moaned as she plopped down on the couch. It was four thirty in the morning, and all I wanted to do was shower, wash off the residue of the night, and go to bed.

"Imagine being on your feet since three thirty in the afternoon. Talk about fucked up. I hate afternoons." I sat next to Sybil, kicked off my heels, and started to rub my toes.

"I don't know why you keep on going to Preacher's Square," she pushed.

"Because I just love being picked up on by snot-nosed, pimply middle school boys, that's why."

Sybil knew Preacher's Square was the best place to catch up when funds were falling short for the month. It was a necessary evil in our profession, but we had to go where the money talked and the bullshit walked, and trust me, everything about selling sex was ripe with bullshit.

"Was the take at the Square any good?"

"Five hundred thirty-five bones. Listen, I am beat. I'm gonna take a shower and hit the sack. We'll talk more tomorrow."

I felt like I had been hit by a truck. Not only did I pull off the nonstop suck-n-fuckfest down at the Square, but then I went straight to my evening pavement. Tonight I upped my prices and pulled in a couple of foreigners; they paid big bucks to watch me masturbate. *Whatever turns you on and pays my bills.* My entire take was fifteen hundred bucks. I had one condom left when I called it a night and it wasn't a Magnum—like I said, hit by a truck.

After my shower, I got ready for bed while I watched the time tumble past five thirty in the morning. It was a quarter to six, and I was wide awake. Sure, my body was exhausted. The tequila and pot were wearing thin in my blood, but my mind wouldn't shut off. This was when childhood memories would come at me with a vengeance; I had no way of containing the dusty clouds of delusion. Keeping my heart on lockdown only produced a selfish, cold-hearted bitch who believed if she didn't invest, she wouldn't lose. Preservation was my only friend. The problem with that was when I was exhausted and the haunting memories boiled to the surface to punish me, there was absolutely nothing I could do to stop them. Like the imprisoned child I was, these were the nights that shattered me.

"You're making me do this, my little Rosalie. You give me this sickness, you see, you keep causin' all of this in my body." He grabs his sickness. His eyes are dark, his fingernails are sharp.

Pain.

Searing pain.

Tears roll down past my temples, tangling in my hair.

Tangles.

I'm cold.

I'm in my bedroom alone. All alone, a moment seared into my soul, another vision, feeling, my body purging my past.

I get out of my bed and pace back and forth across my room.

"I can't keep it in any longer," I yell at myself in the mirror. I've done my best to hold it in for three long years. I never told a soul. I'm being eaten from the inside out.

My stomach twists at the thought of telling anyone. I can't. But I need to.

"Rosalie, you think by holding in your secret for three short years, anyone is going to care? Wake up, girl, nobody cares." The voice in my head pipes up and betrays me.

"My stomach hurts. I can't stop the truth from bubbling out. I have to tell someone," I holler out loud.

I need the voice to understand.

It's me, it's me who needs to find a way to stop feeling so yucky, so dirty for what happened.

"Then what? What do you think anyone's going to do with that information? It's too late to do anything. Keep it in your soul. No matter what. Trust me," the voice in my head snaps.

"I won't. I'm twelve now, and I'm stronger! I have to tell someone. I have to get the poison out of my mind. I can't take it anymore."

"Rosalie, nobody can know about my sickness. You understand? You are the only one who knows. It's our little secret." His words sear across my mind.

"I don't wanna die."

"You won't if you keep this just between you and me."

The traffic in my head is too much. Memories—words—voices—it's all too much.

"Three whole years later? What's going to happen? Nothing, that's what. Get over yourself; people get hurt. You suck it up and move the fuck on, little girl."

Cracking in half, everything draining from my soul.

"Our secret."

Torn ...
Apart ...
In Seconds ...

I rubbed my eyes, hoping if I pressed my fists harder into my sockets, the horrid visions in my head would stop. *Fuck, I don't need this tonight.* It had been six months since my last episode. Six months of freedom from the nightmares. The repulsive feeling curdled my stomach. My heart was in a race it couldn't seem to win, no matter how fast it was beating. My memories created a desert in my throat. They shattered the peace I'd tried to embrace in my adulthood. A hope that a sliver of peace was available to little girls who had found their voices as adults.

I was the little girl who had sweated out the poisonous recollections from her flesh night after night. Tonight, the memories drenched my skin, dampening my clothes. The only physical shift I could manage was rocking back and forth. I pulled my knees to my chest, wrapped my arms around my legs, and surrendered to the fact that the act of one monster, one hour, of one day eleven years ago, destroyed a lifetime I was entitled to have.

Pushing myself, I got up and walked around. I figured if I changed my physical place in the world, maybe it would change my reaction to it. I couldn't pinpoint why my body betrayed me or my mind fucked with me so hard, other than pure exhaustion. I didn't want to be that little broken girl anymore. I didn't want to own the ache that scarred more than my physical body anymore. I just wanted to pick up my life from the point where I'd shackled my heart in iron locks with steel chains. I wanted to pull out the weeds of hate that were rooted deep. Weeds that sprang from the collateral damage of a childhood tainted by a despicable fuck who had chosen to capture my innocence and hold it for ransom my entire life.

"Ro? You okay?" Sybil whispered, shifting to look at me from her bed.

"I just couldn't sleep," I answered.

The problem with sharing a studio apartment with someone

was that our beds were merely steps away from each other, only separated by an open space we conveniently called the living room.

"You having those dreams again?" Sybil propped herself up on her elbow.

"Yeah, but I'll get through them. Nothing I haven't dealt with before."

"Have you thought about going to one of them shrinks? You know those types you go and spill your guts to and they tell you if you're crazy and shit?" she said, wiggling across her bed. She adjusted herself to sit up.

"Naw, I've always found ways to work through the shit clogging my head. The less people know about my business, the easier it is for me to forget about it. I sure as the hell don't need anyone beating *that* fucked-up day into my head over and over again. Besides, I don't have the money to pay some shrink to fuck with my head," I answered truthfully. Every last dime I had saved was for the day I could get the fuck out.

"They say it helps to talk about it to a professional," she snapped.

"Who's *they*?"

"They," she answered.

"Yeah, I heard you say *they*. I just wanna know what *they* you are referring to?" I argued.

"*They*, the fucking shrinks," she spat.

"Right, 'cause, there are plenty of fucking shrinks sick enough to implant fake memories into your dome. Trust me, Sybil, it didn't help me. All it did was teach me how to keep these bastards out of my head. We are manipulated enough, selling our bodies for money. These shrinks are nothing more than a cheap-ass John waiting to take advantage of you."

Okay, so maybe it was my defense mechanism, but I always made someone the bad guy. Let's face it, life wasn't always about finding something beautiful in a heaping pile of shit. I fucked for money; I made guys come because their wives or girlfriends didn't have the gall to do half the kinky shit their men fantasized about. So their boyfriends or husbands found me on the corner of Geary and Taylor and paid a fistful of dead presidents to live out their kinkiest fantasies. There was nothing noble or life-altering in what I did. *I'm a whore.*

"Geesh, Ro, not everyone is out to fuck with you. All I was suggesting was that maybe one of these shrinks can help you. That's all. I wasn't trying to sell you on their shit," she huffed.

"Everyone's out to fuck you. You're the fucking addict who was disowned by her family … did you talk to anyone about that? I don't need you worrying about my problems when you don't even know how to deal with your own."

Sybil let out a gasp before she wiggled back under her covers and faced the wall, away from me.

Oh, man, I fucked up.

Why did I always do that? It made no difference who it was or what they said; I always pushed the other way. If she hated shrinks, I'd find words to argue for them. I was always the devil's advocate, even when I didn't agree with the bastard. I guess it was just my nature to push people away. A nature that had been built upon the disappointments cast on me from the day I was born. A destiny that was seared into my DNA the moment my dickweed father shot his sperm into the snatch of my narcissistic mother. Munching through the barrier of her egg, that fuck's sperm beat the odds, and nine months later, *voila*, there I was, breathing the stagnant air of a life born to a winning combination of alcoholic as well as abusive parents. It was nothing I could have changed and only something I had learned to embrace after night after fucking night of hearing dishes smash against walls, voices spewing hate, skin being slapped, then eventually fists cracking bones.

I'd twisted my emotions into a tight knot and dropped them

into the belly of "who gives a shit" my entire life. Eventually the defense mechanism that had saved my sanity as a little girl became the character flaw that kept me isolated as a woman. I knew I should have said sorry. I should have used the thoughtless word to pacify Sybil, but sorry came at a price I wasn't willing to pay. I couldn't apologize for the sins of others, no matter how much they tried to convince me it was my fault. This time sorry clung to the back of my throat and clogged my ability to find a way to express my remorse.

"Good night," I chimed before I strolled into the kitchenette that filled up less than a quarter of our five hundred square feet. With exaggerated effort, I filled the teakettle with water and plopped it on the stove. When all else failed, tea seemed to help.

There wasn't any reaction from Sybil. I'd pissed her off, and I was going to live with her silent treatment until tomorrow evening when she and I'd go hustle our pavement on Geary and Taylor together. The vicious cycle reared its head in every relationship I had. I never kept lovers, and I had always kept friends an arm's length away. Even though Sybil was one of my only friends, one of two people I considered anything close to family, I couldn't apologize. It was something I just simply couldn't do.

The water in my kettle had begun to boil; I pulled it off the heat, robbing it of its opportunity to announce that it was ready. Marked by the moment I dipped the Sleepytime tea bag into the scorching water, I finally felt the click of my mental clock and the need to go to sleep begin to rule over my need to relive the memory of *that* day over and over again. My eyes became too heavy to keep open, and my mind stopped its endless barrage of torturous bullshit.

"I'm sorry, Sybil," I whispered under my breath … Finally I was able to fall asleep, without taking a sip of my tea.

five

OKAY, SO I was wrong about Sybil forgiving me for being such a bitch to her. I should have known when she took over Bambi's corner for the last couple of nights, down on Jones and O'Farrell, that she wasn't as ready to forgive me as I'd initially thought. Damn, I didn't want to have to work at this. I just wanted to be friends without all the bullshit drama of hurt feelings and guilt-trips. I guessed that was asking way too much.

When I met Sybil a couple years ago, she was twenty-one and just as brash and unemotional as I was. We accepted each other for all the fucked up scars we had. She might not have had the same unhealed childhood wounds that kept oozing on a daily basis, but she had her fair share of demons she fought every day.

Sybil constantly battled the wicked grip of heroin, lured into its ecstasy over five years ago. Three hits later, she was a full-fledged addict. The claws of her sickness dug deep into her flesh, keeping her until she hit rock bottom and was found overdosing on the grimy floor of the AM/PM convenience store bathroom. Black tar heroin stripped her of everything until she was nothing more than a junkie frantically chasing the next hit to function in her daily life and avoid the sickness.

Sybil had been clean for two years now. Every day that she survived staying clean become a huge victory most of us would never understand. She celebrated the basic choices in her life that anyone else wouldn't give two fucks about. Instead of escaping into addiction, she chose to embrace life in all its fucked up glory. She also knew how I felt about it and understood that if she ever fell back into that shit, she'd be the fuck out of luck for a place to live.

Did I care about her? Hell yes, I'd be a heartless bitch if I didn't. When we got into scuffles, we always found a way to work it out. Up until this point, we'd never made it a big deal to apologize to each other. We didn't have to roll that way in our friendship.

But Sybil had deliberately avoided me for two days. Either she was working through something bigger than my bitchy response or she was punishing me. At least I saw her down on the strip last night. Getting a glimpse of her was better than worrying that she was facedown dead in a gutter or falling back into the grips of her demons. Actually, if anyone should be getting pissed, it should be me. We had a pact, an agreement; we were supposed to have each other's backs. Check in with each other every day. She had totally shut me out. She had come home when I wasn't there and spent the night with who the fuck knew.

I couldn't get all caught up in Sybil's shit today. I had to be up and out before noon. I had a dentist appointment at one fifteen. Yes, even though I sold my body, I still visited the dentist. Granted, most hos couldn't afford it or, for whatever reason, chose consciously to write off oral checkups and yearly cleanings. But I'd be damned if I was ever gonna end up looking like some of the older "bitches" in my profession, with their snaggletooth smiles or missing pearly whites.

I was under the gun, running a little late to my dentist appointment. The clothes I had to wear, which didn't scream hooker, seemed to be stuffed in the bottom of my black wicker laundry hamper. I shuffled around the other side of my bed, pulled open my dresser drawers, and looked for anything comfortably normal to wear. I'd pushed longer hours, hustling to make a little more cash from the afternoon seekers and working through the nights I usually took off. No wonder I was scraping the bottom of my drawers for an old pair of holey blue jeans and a tit-hugging white scoop tee. I collected the outfit I'd tossed off last night, with some random pairs of thongs and lacy bras, and shoved the clothes into my laundry sack. I figured after my dentist appointment, I'd take my clothes to the Stop and Wash. I usually went to Soap and Suds, a place that was barely a notch above the one shitty washer and non-drying dryer in my building. Doing my laundry was better than coming back here to silence. Besides, there was a one-in-a-million chance that Crystal's savior, Shane, might be there and, well, why not thank him for saving her.

Flashes of Shane kept marching across my mind when I least expected it. I'd walk into a room, or be flat on my back or down on my knees and making a living, and thoughts of him would pop into my head. Fleeting fantasies where I had played out feisty actions in perfect timing with him. If you named it, I had done it with him in my mind.

Maybe I was fucked up, a little crazy, whatever, but I couldn't seem to stop the laundry man from getting in my head. In the kitchen, stirring tea, I wondered if he drank tea. I'd watch TV; men would be saving damsels in distress, and I'd visualize *his* thick, strong arms pulling me against his strappingly giant body, and he'd save me from my own demise.

What in the hell am I doing?

I was like a little fucking puppy dog willing to piss herself in excitement over the idea of this stranger looking in my direction. *I haven't even talked to the man, for Christ's sake.* And yet I found myself asking, *What's he doing right now? Does he think about me? How will he react when he finds out I fuck for money?*

Physically, I existed as nothing more than an instrument that men used to get off. I could count on one hand the very few tricks who wanted to see me come. Most would shoot their wad, yank off their rubber, and pull up their pants without giving me more than a careless glance. Some tricks were so wrapped up in the guilt of cheating on their wives or girlfriends that they'd act as if I had held a gun to their head and made them fuck me. Guilt was such a shitty emotion. Nothing good ever came of it, and it always ended up in a bad way. The trick would either cry like a baby, pleading to me that this was his first time ever cheating or paying for sex, or his hands would speak for his mouth.

Either way, I'd started to discover what made it bearable for me—besides a joint or alcohol. It was when I saw the glimmer of recklessness in their eyes as I made them come. The shiver that trickled down my spine every time I got them to surrender to me. Sometimes that was worth more than any amount of money they'd give me. Sometimes.

I pulled into a parking space behind the dental office. I wanted to take a couple of deep tokes off a joint before I went in. Numb the scars on the inside before I created more. It was the burn of the first hit as the smoke tore down my throat and into my lungs that reminded me that what I was doing wasn't supposed to be glamorous or celebrated. It was a job—nothing more, nothing less.

I pushed the door open at Brite-N-UR-Smile dental office. The receptionist's desk was vacant like always. I'd never met the woman and only knew what she looked like because of her family pictures that speckled her desk.

My dentist, an older guy wrinkled from the stress from cleaning and pulling teeth all day, was completely about creative financing. A year and a half ago, I'd had a bad tooth and looked him up online. When I saw he accepted all forms of insurance, I booked an appointment and approached him with a perfect way we could square up my financing. We both were in the service business, so I gave him my supreme service and he made sure I'd had the most beautiful smile on Geary Street.

"Hello?" I called out.

The chill of the sterile waiting room used to tremble through my bones when I first started coming. A couple of waxy green plants with huge leaves spilled over the counter that separated clients from hygienists. I looked around the room, recognizing the places I'd reimbursed Danny Carmichael, DDS, for my dental work and cleanings. We had our usual places: his desk, counters, walls, floors, and the couch in the front lobby. Even the dental chair was our little secret. Closed on the third Friday of every month, he reserved that day for personal service. Never emotional, always business, he had a family with a couple of grown daughters, one my age. Pictures of them sat squarely on his desk and hung from his walls.

Was he a sick fuck? Not really, just an older man who needed more than his forty-five-year stagnant marriage gave him.

"Back here," he hollered from his office in the very back. "Would you mind locking the door, please?" he added.

I started toward his office; his door was closed. I gave a light warning knock before I pushed it open. I'd come to learn that Dr. Danny had a kinky side, simple fetishes that ranged from role-playing patient/doctor shit to licking the backs of my knees while he stroked his junk. But this, well, this was a side of him I'd never seen. An edge I'd never let any *date* have with me before. He was dressed in a dominant black leather suit, studs poking from a collar wrapped around his wrist, hands filled with a blindfold, handcuffs, and a flogger hanging from his index finger. A smile built across his aging face, yet he looked like a teenage boy who had just discovered that Cinemax After Dark was laced with porn.

Emotionally, I knew my hardline stopping point, and I couldn't handle giving up so much. Dr. Danny seemed to be challenging the line I'd drawn up with him.

"Hey, oh, wow, is that flogger for you?" I asked.

"Well, Rose, I wanted to try something a little different. Something that maybe I could practice with you and take home to … you know."

Dr. Danny rationalized everything, and I meant everything. From double-charging insurance companies for work his patients had already paid for with cash in full, to the warped excuse he continually chimed in with about how fucking me wasn't technically *cheating* on his wife. Every damn time we finished, him cleaning my teeth and me *teaching* him something new, he'd pipe up with his justification of how I was more like a sex therapist for him. How the angles and ideas he got from our "sessions" made sex with his wife so much better. If that was the case, I should've started charging therapist fees.

I'd let him swat my ass a couple of times and even blindfold me, no big deal, but I stopped at letting him cuff me. Personal rule … my hands must always be free. Pin me against the wall or a waiting room table—hell, I'd even let him restrain my ankles—but when it came to my arms, it was just a no-go, a deal breaker. My arms had to be free. I couldn't handle the thought of not having a way to protect myself if I had to.

"You know, we could use these. How about you let me …" He stopped short of saying it, but his eyes lingered on the shiny silver handcuffs.

"Now, Dr. Danny, we've already gone over this … it isn't ever gonna happen, sweets."

"I know, I just thought … no harm in askin' every once in a while."

"Yeah, well, once in a while or hardly ever, the answer will always and forever be no."

Like clockwork, when the time was up, the routine of Dr. Danny negotiating with himself and justifying his guilt began. He muttered about how much better and more intense sex was gonna be with his wife when he brought home the flogging techniques he'd learned while fucking me from behind. Always talking about coming up with something that was worth taking home to Mrs. Carmichael. He called our encounters his indulgence; I called it our business arrangement. But truthfully, I didn't care what we called it just so long as we both came out benefiting from the time we invested.

"Good evening, ma'am," he played in a drawl as he walked me out.

His lengthened vowel tones rolling between the consonants froze me in my footsteps and created a single shiver that melted down my spine. His tone caused me to think about the strong, tall, gorgeous man I'd seen only a handful of nights ago in a dark, dingy alley.

six

SHANE, THE LAUNDRY man, someone I barely knew and yet seemed to be in my mind more than I cared to admit. The way he'd looked at me that night was different, cryptic, distinctive, like he knew what I was and yet he looked beyond the skin I was cast in. He saw me as something more than a piece of ass he could pay a couple of bills to take. It was the way he'd talked to Crystal that night and the words that seemed to offer freedom from the woman she had to become when selling her body. His warm manner was as foreign to me as having sex to express my love for someone.

I didn't know why I thought searching him out was a good idea. There I was, heading to the laundromat, my dirty clothes in hand and my heart on my sleeve, as I clung to a stupid idea that he was going to be there.

I pulled into the parking garage a block and a half away from the Stop and Wash. Usually there were several open parking spaces, but for some reason, the garage was packed. People poured from their cars and hustled into uppity shops and trendy restaurants. They came here because they were promised happy hour specials and moisturizing treatments with exotic oils; the upper block of Van Ness had always pulsed with a douchy hipster vibe. It was what lurked on the next street over and in the back alleys behind the façade that tainted the veins of the haves with the have-nots. The count of clean and unpolluted souls who found the magic doorway into the impure world of prostitution was endless.

To most people, a full parking garage was an inconvenience, too many people trying to fit into the square footage of an already bulging city block. The only thing I saw was lost opportunity. Maybe that was the problem with hanging out a couple of blocks from where I worked. All I saw was dollar signs strolling across the melting fantasy of possibilities. New *dates*, Johns, clients, tricks meant new energy, new money, and ultimately more referrals.

I pulled my car into a shitty parking spot on the third floor of the garage, grabbed my purse, made sure I had a couple rolls of quarters, and hoisted the laundry sack over my shoulder. By the time I had made it down to the laundromat a block and a half away, my arms felt like they were going to fall off.

I pushed open the glass door with my ass before I tried to muscle the hefty sack of dirty clothes off my shoulder and into a rolling laundry cart. I thought it was going to be a good idea, but when I dropped my bag into the cart, I tripped and fell into it. It wasn't my most glamorous of moments.

The laundry cart went sailing toward the heavy duty washing machines with all of my dirty laundry and me. I just closed my eyes and hoped that I wouldn't break any bones when I collided with the ginormous steel washing machine across the room. When I came to an abrupt stop, I discovered what had become the buffer between my pain and me.

"Whoa, are you okay?" Shane asked. His voice hung with a slight Harry Connick Jr. twang that sent chills down my spine.

All the blood in my body rushed to my cheeks before it drained and collected in splotches across my neck. *What in the hell am I going to say? Holy shit, it's Shane, the man who has carried every moment of escape in my head since I saw him in the alley.*

"Ahh, yeah, me and rogue laundry carts are nothing new."

He chuckled at my stupid answer and the jumbled attempt I made to free myself from the cart.

"Hang on there. Here, let me help you," he said, his voice low and growly. His long, swift fingers tangled in between the metal bars of the cart as he maneuvered around to me. "It isn't every day I get to save a clumsy beautiful woman from rogue laundry carts."

I shot him a hasty smirk before he dragged his big, sturdy hand across my shoulder and down my exposed skin to the bend of my elbow. All the hair that normally lay flat against my flesh pricked to attention. He held the cart steady as I pushed myself out of the basket and stood on my own. His hand hovered close just in case I fell. When I freed myself without incident, his expression broke from lip-biting concern to a relaxed, reassuring smile.

"Well, that was embarrassing. Do you think anyone saw me?"

We both looked around the laundromat and all but a small boy with brown hair seemed to be minding their own business. Owned by their tattered romance paperbacks, or smartphones, most were absorbed in managing their social media.

"Oh, absolutely," he hummed. "See that sweet older lady by the big dryer over there?" He pointed at a silver-haired woman who had to be pushing into her late seventies.

I nodded.

"She videotaped the whole thing on her iPhone. Trust me, you and your rogue laundry cart will be plastered all over YouTube and Facebook before you know it." His hazel eyes bursting with rusty flecks twinkled as they caught up to his smile.

"Oh, it better not! You'll have to confiscate her phone for me," I snapped as I socked him in the arm.

45

"Well, why would I do that? I don't even know your name."

Hooked by the comfort he had established between us, I didn't realize I'd never told him my name. Would it be strange to tell him we'd met before? Sure, it had been nothing more than his acknowledgment of me as a person in the back alley, but still, suddenly the comfort and relationship I'd built in my head seemed more of a whack job's obsession.

"Oh, well, I'm Rose. So there, now you know my name," I answered.

"Well, Rose, I'm Shane, and for some reason, you seem very familiar to me. Have we met before?"

My heart detached and tumbled, crashing into the twisted storm that surged low in my stomach. *Are you fucking kidding me? Really?* Okay, so there was a huge part of me that wanted to tell him who I was and that yes, we'd actually seen each other before and that the prostitute he'd saved was with me. But there was a part of me that wanted to continue on the path we'd established. I wanted to keep our bat-shit-crazy night in the alley exactly where we had left it.

"Um, I don't think so," I answered coldly as I pulled the laundry cart over to the vending machine filled with all different soaps and softeners.

"No, I think we've met before. You seem familiar to me." He followed me over to the vending machine, slowing down at the black Formica counter where a ton of brightly colored suckers were spilling over the edge of a simple, clear plastic bowl.

He pulled a green sucker from the bowl and slipped it into his mouth. I could tell he was rolling through all the images in his head. *Damn, does he even know what he is doing to me with that bright-green sucker?* I was mesmerized by his actions as he dragged the sucker across his tongue … forward and back, forward and back. He broke my trance when he twirled the stick between his fingers and pressed it against his tongue. I watched the stick twist and

46

turn, finally coming to rest in the corner between his firm lips.

"I think I'd remember meeting you," I said.

I struggled to keep from smiling. A pleased grin spread across Shane's face. The stick of his sucker danced in circles, his eyes gleaming with realization. Noticing my answer had come out different than I wanted it to, I tried to pull back the energy swirling between us. And that same ol' voice came out in my head. *"You know, Rose, this can't work."* I took a deep breath and came up with words that would drive the conversation in a different direction.

"Well, maybe you saw me at the grocery store. Do you shop over at the Whole Foods on California?" I answered, looking away as I fed the vending machine flat, crisp dollar bills. *What the hell? Really? Whole Foods, Rose?* I pushed F7 and let a small overpriced box of soap fall off the row it dangled from.

"Sometimes, but that's not it … You ever waitress at Boxing Room?" he asked as he pulled my soap from the space where it had landed.

"The Cajun place on Grove?"

"Yeah, best food in the Hayes," he answered, holding the small box of laundry soap in one hand and his sucker in the other.

"No, I've never waitressed in my life," I answered, grabbing the soap from him and tossing it into my basket. I flattened a collection of bills on the edge of the vending machine and fed it enough dollars to get a small pack of dryer softener sheets too.

"Well, now I hope I didn't offend you with the waitress comment. I know plenty of women who make an honest living as a waitress," he responded, pointing and poking the shrunken sucker in my direction.

Little did he know that my appearance of being annoyed was far from the reasons he perceived. Great, now it would be a matter of minutes before it clicked in his head where he had seen me. It was inevitable—he was going to remember seeing me in the alley and that my type of service wasn't bringing people food.

"Far from offended, Shane."

"That's one good thing I have going for me." His half-tilted smile melted my heart.

"What, that I haven't waitressed before?"

"No, that you don't get offended easily."

Shane caught the sucker between his teeth and bit down on the little part that still clung to the stick. He smiled again, causing my insides to tangle up with his charm. A noticeable pause hung between us, as if we were both waiting for the other to make a move. I liked hanging out with him. He was damn hot and I was attracted to him, but I couldn't pay my rent with flirty conversations and silly crushes. I had to get to my apartment and change into my come-fuck-me-heels and peek-a-boo panties. Unfortunately, I was behind the eight-ball this week. Time was money, and I didn't have any extra minutes to spare. Pressure built in the back of my throat as I knew what I had to do.

"Well, I'd better get to my laundry. It's not going to do itself." The words flew from my mouth as I started to separate my whites from my darks and delicates.

"Yeah, well, I can take a hint, but using the excuse of laundry, really?" he teased with a magnetic smile.

"Hah, very funny, Shane. Thanks for saving me from the industrial washers," I responded in a low tone as I collected my dark clothes from the rolling basket and pushed them into the large washer he was leaning against.

"It was my pleasure saving you, Little Clumsy Rose," he answered as he caught one of my socks that tried to escape.

"Hey, now! Well, I guess I earned that name today."

He handed me my sock. *Thank God it wasn't a pair of my crotchless panties.* I scooped up a pile of ten quarters I'd stacked in preparation of washing my clothes.

"Yeah, you sure did."

"Little Clumsy Rose, huh?" I asked, filling the laundry detergent compartment and feeding the quarters into the machine.

"Yeah, and I think you should come back on Thursday."

"Thursday?"

"We'll see if the name sticks. From what I understand, this laundromat is world-renowned for its suckers." He pulled a yellow sucker from his back pocket. "I'll see you this Thursday, let's say around five thirty? Don't be late, or a stranger." He smiled and emphasized each word by pointing the sucker at me.

I grabbed the candy. He lowered his eyes to the floor before he pushed up from leaning against the washer, buried his hands in his front pockets, and wandered to the back door. His manly swagger automatically caught my eye and caused my entire body to tingle and crave his weight. He pushed open the back door, gave me a short, intentional smile, then left.

Little Clumsy Rose, huh? We'll see. I unwrapped the sucker and pushed it into my mouth.

That was the first day we actually spoke and he learned my name. Sure, I'd say he was super charming and I was totally giddy, but I didn't see him again until I showed up with the same sack of clean clothes three days later, on Thursday, at six o'clock at night. Maybe he'd add fashionably late to my new title, Little Clumsy Rose.

seven

I JUST HAD the three longest nights in the history of my six squares of sidewalk ever! Dealing with cheap-ass pricks and stingy fucks who tried to get a push and pull for half price truly exhausted me. Not even the act of taking on a trick had used the amount of energy I spent haggling with those cheap-ass dickweeds. And let me just say, language barriers didn't count when the foreign fucks were trying to purchase my pussy. They had no problem communicating what the hell they wanted from me with universal hand gestures. And to top off my mood, my feet were killing me from the piece-of-shit snake-skin stilettos I'd bought from the tiny consignment shop around the corner from my apartment.

Hell, if there was one thing I should've known, it was to never wear an untested pair of heels while on the prowl. Lesson learned—stick with the shoes your feet know. The best excuse I could come up with was the full moon last night and the fact that suddenly I'd wanted the last three nights to go by faster than usual. Normally I didn't have very much to look forward to, but knowing that I was going to walk into the Stop and Wash with the same huge laundry sack filled with the same clothes, that were still clean and folded, only to shove them back into another washing machine made me antsy.

I woke up super late and starving. I ate some key lime yogurt sprinkled with granola before I showered and got dressed in my ass-hugging black capris and rack-highlighting sheer V-neck chocolate-brown T-shirt. I pushed on a pair of glossy black Chelsea heels—they were more comfortable to me than sneakers—and rushed out of the door with my sack of already laundered clothes.

Even though the laundry sack was lighter this time, it still caused my hands to go numb as I carried it to the Stop and Wash. I pulled the front door open and didn't expect the music blaring from a couple of little speakers up in the corners of the room.

Only a handful of people turned their heads to watch me enter the laundromat. I guessed the Black Keys' song Fever over a muted reality show of little girls painted by makeup and throwing tantrums was more interesting than me carrying in my fake dirty laundry. I noticed some women leaning into washing machines, while others, who weren't into the TV, had their noses buried in their books.

The laundromat was crowded with more people than were there on Monday. So many people in fact, it was difficult to find an unoccupied laundry cart. Who would've thought the Stop and Wash was going to be such a happening place on a Thursday. They say the city never sleeps, and well, everyone has laundry.

I skimmed the place for you-know-who, hoping that the uncomfortable bubble building in the back of my throat would disappear. Out of the corner of my eye, I spotted him coming toward me. A reassured smile spread wide across his gorgeous face. I couldn't help but smile back.

His vivid hazel eyes lit up as he spoke. "Well, look who

showed up! My new friend, Little Clumsy Rose. I guess she decided to come back to the Stop and Wash!"

I noticed he wasn't tending to a washing machine or hanging out by the dryers. "Yeah, well, I have to keep up on my laundry, you know. Can't waitress in filthy clothes. You don't get very many tips when you're stinky." I shoot him a quick wink.

"And here I thought it was the world's best suckers that brought you back."

"Oh, don't get me wrong, Shane, this place's suckers are hard to pass up, but I tend to be a Blow Pop type of girl," I teased.

"Well, then next time I'll make sure you have at least one Blow Pop in every color and flavor." He raised his eyebrows in a curious tic.

"Now you're just tryin' to sweet talk me. How 'bout helping me find a washing machine that's unoccupied?"

"That sounds good. We don't want a repeat of what happened last time," he mused.

"I can't believe how busy this place is."

"Oh, yeah, so give me this." He shot me a quick wink before snatching my laundry sack and flinging it over his shoulder. "Stay close now," his voice rumbled, coming out with more of a growl than I expected.

My heart drummed in my chest as I watched his biceps flex against the sleeves of his T-shirt. I followed him into a back corner of the laundromat, pushing away the feelings swelling in my gut and surging into my chest. I took several deep breaths, thinking about the words I wanted to use to build a wall between us.

"Are you implying that I am clumsy?"

"No, but I'd hate to see you wrestle with a cart in this place now." Shane looked around.

Every machine was running. Every dryer was humming with clothes dancing in the glass windows. As we swiftly passed the back counter, he snatched a handful of suckers. When I glanced back, every counter had a plastic bowl filled with suckers.

"Where are your clothes? Don't tell me you're the one creepy guy who decides to hang out in random laundromats around the city, ripping off cheap suckers?"

"Nope, I only hang out at this one, and I don't steal suckers." He laughed. I didn't laugh. "Talking about stinky waitresses and cheap suckers, we never finished our conversation about Cajun food last time we hung out."

"You mean the only time we hung out," I corrected him.

"It's just semantics. You eat right?"

"Um, last time I checked, it's vital to my existence."

"Well, that's good news, because it just so happens that I must eat to survive too."

"Yeah, well, the last time I checked, suckers don't count as eating."

"By whose definition?" he quipped.

"Mine. Suckers are a lick-and-swallow product. Eating actual food is a much more detailed and necessary activity."

"Well, then why don't I take you to Boxing Room … for some required nourishment?"

"I can't today, but thanks."

"It's vital to both of our survival." He leaned closer to me and continued, "I wasn't thinking about today."

"Oh—"

"I was thinking some … other day?" His expression was pleading.

"Well, I'll be busy."

"Really? You already know you're busy?"

"Yes."

"Six months from now?"

I nodded. I didn't know what I was doing every minute of the day, but I was pretty sure I was too busy to start something with him.

"How can you turn down eating dinner? The very act is essential to our human survival."

"Oh, I survive quite well on my own, thank you."

"Yeah, but why alone? Why not have dinner with someone … like me?"

"Look, Shane, truthfully, I just can't really *see* anyone right now. My life is a little … *complicated.*"

"Complicated? Everyone's life is complicated, Rose."

"Yeah, well, I don't have time to do complicated."

"Complicated Rose. What if *seeing* wasn't what I was thinking? I just thought we could have dinner as friends?" he said, holding out a rainbow of suckers in front of his face. His eyes were saying something so much more than friends.

"Yeah, well, it starts with suckers and ends with heartbreak," I answered as I pulled the green sucker from the cluster of colors.

"You have us heartbroken over suckers, and all I'm trying to do is go eat Cajun food and get to know my new friend, Complicated Rose."

"Damn, you are persistent, Shane, and I can't do dinner, anyway."

"Ah, come on … fine, how about having lunch … just friends … I promise," he said as he crossed his long fingers over his heart.

My body gave a little. It was almost unbearable staying strong when all I wanted to do was throw myself at him and let him take me every which way to Sunday. A slight smirk filled my face.

"Thank you, Persistent Shane, for saving me from blasting headfirst into the washing machine the other day." I pushed my hand out to him.

Please just take it, shake it, and make your way to the front door.

He grabbed my hand, pulled it up to his curvy lips, and pressed. The energy which swirled against my flesh and shot straight between my legs was electrifying. It was like there was a power line that went straight from his lips to my sweet spot.

"Well, it's always nice to save a beautiful woman who somehow agreed to have *lunch* with me tomorrow at Boxing Room. As friends of course, to avoid making it too complicated."

"I, aahhh—"

"I promise it has actual food there and not just suckers."

"Excuse me, you're the manager, right?" a woman's voice interrupted.

I was thrown off when I realized she was asking Shane. I started to say something when he cleared his throat.

"What seems to be the problem?" He looked over at me for a moment, his eyes narrowed, concern threaded through his expression. He dropped his gaze before looking back at the woman.

"Well, I put my money in the slots and pushed ..."

Suddenly her words disappeared and became the background noise to the imagery of that fateful night when Shane barreled out of the laundromat and saved Crystal; hence, becoming the image that saved me from the grind of my business.

"Will you excuse me, Miss Complicated?" Shane's voice danced against my ears as his hand caught my elbow and pulled my thoughts from that night.

"Sure, Mr. Persistent, I ... ahhh, I'll be right here just ... washing my clothes."

I dumped the laundry sack into the rolling cart next to me, separated my colors from my whites, and started thinking about having lunch with him tomorrow. Every couple of items, I'd look over at him and watch him help the lady who had lost her quarters. Her arms swung as she talked to him. His head bobbed up and down as he listened. I wanted to hear his voice, but the sound of the washing machines whizzing on the spin cycle filled the room.

He reached into his pocket, pulled out a handful of quarters, and handed them to her. He cocked his head in a confident nod, smiled, and started for the office. He disappeared behind the walnut-brown door. The quarter lady pulled her clothes out of the machine and put them in the next washer over. She mumbled curse words under her breath—well, at least that's what it looked like as her lips moved. Shane came back out of the tiny office with a small beige canvas tool bag.

His pace was fast, determined, and yet when he looked over at me, he slowed his stride. His eyes widened as big as the smile that grew over his face. I smiled back before I turned to my clothes and realized I was holding up my slinky black see-through camisole. All the blood in my body was captured in my cheeks. I balled up my top and tossed it in the washing machine with my darks, closed the lid, and reached into my purse for my roll of quarters.

Within several minutes, I had two washers rumbling with full loads. It was the perfect time to take full advantage of my view and watch Shane wrench on the coin taker. He pulled back the front of the coin holder. His hands were large and strong. I found myself staring at him and hardly blinking as his muscles tightened. But when he bit his lip with a focused scowl and his long fingers fiddled with the mechanism for the washer, I got all kinds of damp downstairs. It didn't help the situation that during the random silent instances when the washers had the same cycle changes, I could hear him huff and growl while he torqued on the coin return. Nice manly sounds that made me wonder about him being so vocal during sex. I tightened my thighs together.

Nimble with his fingers, he pulled them out of the machine, tainted with grease and inducing a twitch that lingered down low. I noticed the quarter lady also watching him work on the machine. She pulled a couple of dollars out of her pocket and slowly meandered over to the change machine. Any woman who fucked for a living recognized when a skank was on the prowl for a fill. She churned her hips like she was mixing hot chocolate and spread her legs just enough so she looked like she was inviting a fuck. Yeah, the bitch was making her move.

Shane cleared his throat loudly enough to pull me from watching quarter lady play out her scene. When I looked over at him, his eyes were glued on me, staring at me like I was something that he needed to devour. He hadn't taken her bait, and instantly I was ready to be whatever he wanted me to be.

Damn it, I wasn't going to do this … I wasn't gonna let myself become interested in anyone. Not now, not anytime soon. It's my time to work my way out.

I decided a year ago to save up as much money as I could and get the hell out of here. Get as far away from disgusting old men who matched the burnt sidewalks I strolled up and down, looking for a wealthy fuck. With the money I had saved, I was about a month out from having enough funds to get a little place out in the suburbs. No more filthy back alleys and seedy parks. Unfortunately, my life was played out on the streets of San Francisco while I tried to slay my darkest demons with sex. It was the thrill of the chase, of pushing the limits and making hand-over-fist money while fucking arrogant assholes and breaking them while they were buried balls-deep.

I didn't want to invest in someone who was just gonna break my heart. I wasn't ready to make lunch dates with nice guys, and my ability to express any emotion beyond my survival mode became the façade donned for self-preservation. I didn't want to feel any more of that pain. The best way to avoid the heartache … don't go chasing after it. Keep it where it belonged … neatly packed in a suitcase, waiting for anyone but me to pick it up.

Shane lowered his caramel eyes to his hands before he rolled the corner of his bottom lip between his pearly whites. He pulled a rag from his back pocket and focused on rubbing the grease from his fingers. His actions were intentional. His sex appeal was through the roof. Even if this moment moved beyond flirting into something more, how in the hell was I going to make something like this work? *The minute he finds out I'm a prostitute, it's over.*

I might as well save face and move on. Nothing but a fucked up situation destined to end up like every other relationship I'd tried to become invested in. He got exactly what he needed, and all I was left with was a full suitcase of broken dreams and empty wishes. I realized it was an infatuation that would *never* work. Shane was just too good, and I was whatever people were willing to pay for.

I looked away before walking over to a row of chairs that split then curved in an attempt to make waiting in a laundromat pleasing. All seats were filled except for one, so I lowered myself into the chair and pulled a magazine from the defunct little table next to me. Thumbing through the pages, I saw *him.* It made my heart trip across my chest. A double take, my eyes raked the pictures and words. It was Mr. C. The man I'd thought was sent to save me from my life a year ago. He was featured in a two-page spread about his engagement to Ashley Hancock, the only daughter of the family who owns Hancock Vineyards. I dove in, devouring it like a ravenous animal. The laundromat around me dissolved, and I sank deeper into the memory of him. All it took was an article in a magazine to find out why I wasn't his choice. Mr. C, Garrett Theodore Chadwick, a self-made millionaire, was engaged to a beautiful woman, and I was nothing more than a convenient fuck he'd wanted to keep on payroll. Finding this article was a sign, a premonition that I was never meant to fall in love with guys as seemingly perfect as Shane.

I pulled my clothes from the washing machines and pushed them into the dryer. It was a mindless action, done a hundred times before, but in this instance, as my thoughts solidified on the memory of Mr. C, I couldn't stop the need to replay the very first time I met him. Reading about him had totally fucked with my head, and as usual when it came to him, my heart played along as he consumed my mind completely. Mr. C had something over me; it was a dark force that kept me clinging to the belief that I was someone important to him.

I was nineteen when I fell in love for the first time. He found me on the corner of *I need to eat* and *Who wants to pay my water bill*. It was slow going. My total pull for the night before Mr. C was only about three hundred bucks. Rents, even in the shittiest parts of the city, were way the fuck out of hand, and I needed to earn another grand over the next four days so I could pay my rent and stay in my shit-hole for another month.

He drove past me in the most beautiful midnight black Maserati. Low to the ground, those big, chrome-rimmed wheels oozed sex as they rolled to a stop then backed up next to me. I'd never forget—it was sexy as all hell when the dark passenger's side window rolled down and he leaned across to talk to me. His slate-blue eyes met mine, and I knew, at that moment, he wasn't going to ask me for directions.

eight

PAST

"EXCUSE ME, I'M new in town, and I seem to be lost," he says as his eyes leave mine and track down my legs and back up. His smile broadens before he chews the corner of his bottom lip.

"Well, hello, New-In-Town, sorry to hear you're lost. Maybe I can help you. What are you looking for?" I say, leaning down and resting my forearms across the window jamb of his Maserati.

His eyes draw to my heaving tits, and his smile grows broad before he runs his hands around his steering wheel. His Rolex tumbles across his wrist, and the smell of his sexy cologne takes a stroll through my body.

His tongue wets his nice full lips before he takes an exaggerated swallow. "I'm looking for someone who can help me find my way around this beautiful town."

I smile, shifting my hips, causing my tits to bounce, and his eyes pause on my chest. "Well, I'm pretty versed in the points of interest in this town. Seeing that you are new and all, I can even hook you up with a discount on entertainment."

"I guess we should talk about how much you think this

entertainment might set me back?"

I see the desire in his eyes, the animalistic draw he has to my skin. The attraction isn't a problem, and seeing we both want the same thing, I figure upping my regular fee isn't gonna break his bank. Either he'll go for it or haggle me down a couple bucks. One thing I know for sure—I ain't gonna let him get away. Guys like this are rare and don't just show up looking for a good time.

I drag my hands across the edge of the door, tracing the rubber window seal, before I step back and make sure he sees everything I have to offer. "Entertainment around here is two hundred fifty bones every half hour."

He reaches over and pushes the passenger's door open. "Okay, Miss …?"

"Rose," I say as I drop into his Maserati.

"Rose, beautiful. Miss Rose, that sounds perfect. I'm going to really enjoy getting to know this town," he growls as he runs his lengthy fingers across my knee and up to the edge of my daisy dukes. Goose bumps rise on the back of my neck.

"So mister, where would you like me to take you?" I ask as I pull the five-point-harness across my chest.

"My sweet Rose, I know exactly where I'm going to take you," he says as he speeds away from the curb.

My heart flips and falls into my stomach. My body presses into the seat. I'm not scared, even if I'm supposed to be. There is something tranquil and safe about him. I feel as if he's one of my regular *dates*.

"Exactly where am I gonna entertain you?" I question, leaning close to him. I drop my hand against his black suit pants and stretch my fingers across his inner thigh, only close enough to brush across the tension in the huge bulging seam of his zipper.

"In my hotel room."

"Oh, really? What entertainment are you thinking about in your hotel room?" I tease. I know what he wants—we're adults.

and nobody of his stature hangs out on hooker alley for directions.

He looks over at me, his eyes narrow; his golden skin radiates his intention far beyond any words that pour from between his lips. If expressions can tell stories, I can only imagine the tale they'll tell me. Will it include kinky shit, or is he going to be my missionary man?

"Well, that's up for negotiation. How about we just get there?"

I watch him as he pulls the steering wheel and tugs on the stick shift. I keep my hand on his thigh and feel his muscles flex and relax as he drives me to the hotel where he's staying.

He pulls into the Shelby Heights Hotel. Only people who have a shitload of money or families bred to be key players in royalty stay here. This guy isn't fucking around. He must dangle from the purse strings of royalty or suck the tit of his family's old money. Either way, I'm kicking myself that I didn't pin him for a clear grand per half hour for my *entertaining* him.

The valet, dressed in what looks like a jester suit, pulls on my door and holds out his ghostly hand. "Ma'am, may I help you out of your vehicle?"

The only thought thundering in my head as I'm looking around is that Mr. Loaded and I are gonna fuck in style.

"Sure," I answer, giving him my hand.

Gleaming white marble bleeds thin gray veins that scatter through the columns on either side of the rotating glass-and-gold front door. Never in my wildest dreams did I think that my ass would ever walk through these doors.

Mr. Loaded's arm slips across my lower back, his lips close to my ear. His words dance across my hair as he whispers, "I already like your town."

Shivers jet down my spine, a reaction I want but am afraid to acknowledge. He tosses his keys to the court jester valet and firmly pushes me forward, keeping me in his grasp and just far enough in front of him.

"Mr. C." The jester dips his head.

He nods.

Mental note taken, at least Mr. Loaded has a semi-name or at least an initial.

We push through the circular door, spitting us inside one of the most prestigious hotels on the West Coast. I'm pretty sure this will be the first and only time I'll be standing in the lobby of the Shelby. My eyes wide, my mouth agape, I'm taken yet intimidated as all get out at the same time. A mix of excitement as well as shame churns in my gut. I know I don't belong here. I'm comparable to the beggar's daughter who keeps praying Cinderella is even a possibility. Maybe, somewhere in this world, I'll find my moment to take what has been handed to me. Maybe the glass slipper will for once fit my foot.

An older, hefty bald man comes buzzing over to us. His black double-breasted suit is perfectly pressed with a perfect amount of his white cuff showing at his wrists. I notice his shoes are shiny enough to blind you on a bright day, just like the cue ball shine off his head.

"Good evening, Mr. C. Nice to see you back again. We've put you in the room you requested. Thank you again for choosing the Shelby Heights Hotel."

"I don't want to be disturbed. I'll call down if I need anything," Mr. C says to the short balding man.

"Absolutely, sir. Anything else we could do to make your stay with us pleasant?"

"Yes, this is Rose. She wants anything, you get it for her."

"Yes, sir, done," he says as he hands Mr. C a room key.

Holy shit, fuck, who is this Mr. C guy? What has he done to gain so much power? What is his story?

My heart thumps in my chest. Whatever simple belief I have about Mr. C just being wealthy is destroyed beyond any idea of his material power. He demands the respect from the staff of the exclusive Shelby Heights Hotel, and they do it willingly, without question.

"All right, beautiful, right this way," he breathes.

His hand is anchored against my lower spine, guiding me to the elevator. There are two doors, both gleaming in print-less gold with shine so pure I can actually see myself in the door before it pushes open. An elevator operator, dressed almost identically to the valet in his jester outfit, greets us with a peachy smile filled with enough sweetness that I'm sure the guy must have practiced his speech in a mirror.

"Good evening, Mr. C. Nice to see you again, sir."

Mr. C nods in response.

I watch as the elevator jester pushes his key into the lock next to the letter P. The music barely above a whisper becomes louder as I see myself on the closing gold doors. I turn and look out the back of the elevator. Three glass walls overlook a huge pond with tropical plants and brightly colored birds flying in the mist.

Mr. C's hands slip around my hips as he presses his cock against my ass. He drops his mouth against the side of my head; his words cling to my hair before slipping into the curve of my ear.

"Are you ready to entertain me?" His words drain straight to between my legs as he thrusts himself against my ass.

"Depends on the package you decide to blow your wad on. What's your budget?" I purr as I sway my ass back against him.

He catches his breath and hums across my cheek. He smells so good, his breath, warm and inviting. I want to feel him exhale against the folds between my legs. Sure, this is business, but who says I can't enjoy the benefits of a *date* who seems to know how to please a woman.

"We already agreed on two hundred fifty dollars every half hour. When did you start the clock?" he asks quietly before thrusting again.

I push back.

"The minute I sat in your car," I whisper.

He chuckles against my cheek, his lips pushing, tasting my flesh.

"All right, Mr. C, here we are, the penthouse suite." The elevator jester stands against the doors that disappear into the wall.

Mr. C reaches into his pocket and gives the guy a healthy stack of cash and whispers something in his ear. The man nods before he disappears behind the closing doors.

When we get up to the common area of the penthouse, there's a gigantic black-and-gray-speckled rock table and a huge bouquet of flowers that takes up the entire center of it. White lilies and orchids with green leaves fill the vase.

"Should we discuss terms of this entertainment first?" I ask, leaning against the stone table.

He drags my hair away from my neck and pushes his lips against my collarbone.

"Absolutely," he hums against my skin.

"Well, then before I show you some entertainment, maybe you can show me your sizable deposit for your amusement," I say, struggling to focus on business. But that's exactly what this is. *I'm killing the mood, but I don't want to be evicted from my shitty apartment at the end of the week.*

His eyes narrow, almost irritated as he pulls back from me. "So no entertainment until I pay a deposit?"

"Yeah, you're already into this night five hundred bucks and you haven't even seen me naked yet."

"All right, fine, since you are so wrapped up in the idea that I need to give you a sizable deposit, why don't you tell me what you want for, let's say, the entire night?"

"The entire night?"

"Yeah, let's say five hours of the night? What are your fees?"

"Twelve hundred bucks," I say without flinching.

"What if I wanted you for let's say … two days? How much

will it cost for you to entertain me?" he asks, his eyes wide. His jaw clenches.

"Four grand, and that's a bargain." Again, I say this without flinching.

He laughs out loud. "You are pulling numbers out of the air, you know that, beautiful Rose? Okay, so how about I pull a number out of the air. How about I give you six thousand dollars to entertain me for as long as I am in town? Is that fair?" His steely blue eyes twinkle; a contented expression spreads across his face, and he waits for my quick response this time.

"Well, Mr. C, that depends on how long you're in town," I counter.

He pulls me close, and the edge of his nose traces across my cheek, his lips close to my ear. He pulls and pins my arms behind my back.

"Don't ever call me that," he demands. The heat of his breath tumbles down my neck.

I gasp, my heart thundering in my chest. "What should I call you then? I don't even know your name."

The muscles in my shoulders pull with an ache. I whimper as he tightens his grip. The small injured girl deep within me climbs into the closet, curls up into a ball, and tries to protect herself; but the woman I am, the one I became, the one who sells her body for money and grabs life by the balls, finds this wickedly sexy. Something about him, the wealth he has, the respect he commands, pulls at my gut. Soaking, I don't care what he wants me to call him. I just need him to fuck me.

"Do you like that?" he whispers.

The dusting of his five o'clock shadow drags slowly against my face. His grayish-blue eyes constrict, speaking volumes of who he wants me to be when I'm in his territory. I whimper again and nod slightly.

"Is that a yes?"

"Yes," I huff. Every nerve begs him to caress my skin, touch me like I've never been touched before.

He, the man who doesn't tell me his name, lets go of my arms and pulls my hands up behind my head. I weave my fingers together, and he pushes my hands against the back of my neck. He slowly drags his fingers down across my cheek, pulling them across my mouth until my bottom lip rolls out. The muscles in his neck tighten as he swallows. I roll the tip of my tongue across my lips, tasting the desire I have to consume what he is willing to give me.

"Keep your hands there. Don't move." He inches his fingers between my waist and the top button of my daisy dukes.

Shivers rush down my spine, collecting in the swell of my pussy. He reaches into my pocket, grabs my phone, and tosses it on the table behind me.

"Anything else?" He breathes his words against my flesh as he leans in and presses his plump lips to the pulse slamming against the side of my neck.

"Yeah, eight grand and I will stay with you as long you're in town." I pull in a sharp breath. I go rigid when I feel his fingers unsnap and drag the zipper down on my shorts. His breathing focuses; his hard cock is wedged firmly in his dress pants.

"Eight thousand and you will be mine and only mine? Whatever I want you to do, you'll do? Whatever I need from you, you'll give me? I call bullshit, my beautiful Rose." He slips his fingers across my hip bones, under my shorts, and forces them down into a pile around the sexiest pair of red stilettos I own.

Without flinching, without thrusting my hands down between my legs to cover up, I stand there naked from the waist down, and I watch him take me in inch by slow inch. First my ankles, then my calves, across my knees, his eyes drink in every thirst-quenching cell. He caresses my thigh, and I don't move. I'm determined to win this game. Whether he thinks it's a game or not,

I'm not going to give in. Eight thousand bones is more than a reasonable fee when he's pulling me away from my regular *dates*. Granted, eight grand is something I would make in three very, very good months. But he doesn't need to know that.

His fingers dance across to the inside of my thigh. "Step out of your shorts. Keep the heels on."

I do what he asks, all while my hands are still tucked against the back of my neck. My elbows are getting tight. He kneels down and moves my daisy dukes to the side. His nose is sharp against the inside of my leg. His fingertips skim up the outsides of my thighs, and he stands, twisting his hands in the edges of my wooly sweater and thin black tank top. Our eyes tangle in a silent conversation, one where I think I understand what he's asking before he speaks. I'm standing there for a moment, frozen by his silence. Do I drop my hands to pull off my tank top and sweater, or do I stand here, unmoved until he tells me what to do?

"I want to see every inch of your body react to my touch."

I nod and pull my hands from the worn-out position behind my neck and start to drag my fingers around the thin edges of my black tank top.

"What are you doing? Did I say to move?"

"No, but you want my shirt off right, mister?"

"Just put your hands in the air." He wedges his foot between my ankles and urges me to widen my stance. He pulls off my tank top and sweater in one swift motion.

There I am in nothing more than a black lacy bra and my four-inch stacked red stilettos. The cool air in the room brushes my flesh before his hands caress across my waist and up my spine to the back of my bra. Catching my breath, I stand in front of him, shivers racing across my skin; he leaves goose bumps in the wake of his touch. He takes me in completely. Erasing the space between our bodies, his fingers nimbly unclasp the hooks of my bra, releasing the pressure of my straps across my shoulders. My tits rest in their natural shape, my nipples rock hard. Every nerve in my body either ends between my legs or the points of my tits.

"My gracious, Rose, put your hands down," he breathes.

My nameless lover's eyes bonding to my chest, he removes the loose bra from across my body. He pulls in a ragged breath with a tight smirk as he holds it out in his fingertips before he lets it fall on the pile of my clothes he left on the floor.

He caresses his hands across my shoulders, down past my elbows, before he catches my fingers in his hands. Lifting my arms, he takes a step back from me, naked as the day I was born, developed more than the moment my innocence was stolen. He leans his head to one side and looks me over. For the first time in my life, a man is looking at me like the woman I'm supposed to be and not the object I have become. His focus causes my heart to flounder in my chest. The air in the room tumbles against my vacant flesh; uneasiness finds a home in every cell of my body as I shift in my stance. The ticking of time clocks me in my head as I watch his vision drink from my exposed skin. He inhales another rough breath before he starts saying the words that drench my pussy in pure sexual desire.

"You are the perfect prick of a poisonous thorn, my beautiful blossoming Rose. Cautiously waiting for me to inhale, pluck, and consume you from the bush." His whisper turns into a raw growl.

Every part of my body melts against his words, weak in the knees. A pulse gallops between my legs. In this moment, I need him to take me. I don't care if he gives me a fucking dime; he captures me with his eyes and possesses me with his words. Is this nameless man going to be the one to finally give me the moment of true reprieve that I've been searching for my entire life? Heal me with the words rolling across the tip of his tongue, sewn effortlessly into every fiber of my being. I ache to have him steal my breath and slay my demons.

Melting into any arrangement he'll demand, I'm powerless in

my intention to remain professional. Suddenly, this is personal, very personal. I bend my arms in the attempt to fold into his body, needing to feel his lips consume mine. He takes a step back. My heart, clinging to the edge of my throat, crashes into the pit of my stomach.

"You don't want me?" I ask, standing undressed by his words, feeling stupid because of how easily I let him play me into his game.

"I didn't say that."

"You didn't have to. Your actions said it loud and clear," I say.

Torn apart, I push him away, turning to get my clothes; suddenly his body consumes mine from behind. His lips press against my ear, and his voice is commanding. His chest is heavy against my back, and his arm is firm across my ribs as his hand captures my breast. His other hand becomes lodged between my legs as his long fingers are deep in my pussy.

"Don't ever turn your back to me, Rose. You agreed to be here for me, to do whatever I asked," he argues. His body is still draped over mine. His fingers unyieldingly plunge deeper and deeper into me, his thumb stroking rhythmically at my tingling clit.

"Yes, I agreed—" I breathe my words as I throb, responding to his fingers pushing and pulling.

I rock my hips against his seamless rhythm. His breathing ignites a burn through my body that I've never felt with someone before. Owned. By. His. Touch. Nobody's ever made me want to come so bad. Problem is, I don't wanna come before I get to feel his cock fill me.

"You have no idea what I want. Maybe I need you to ache for me. Maybe I want to watch you twist in your own flawless skin until you can't take it anymore and you beg me to fuck you." He pulls his fingers from inside me, and in that mindless moment when the air licks at the fever surging at my doorway, I turn into a slave to his demands. "I want you to beg me to fuck you."

"Please … mister … please, fuck me." He's got me. Twisted, taken, and ruined.

He turns me around to face him, his fingers digging into my biceps; he pulls me within inches of his lips.

"If you only knew how much I want to fuck you, drag the tip of my tongue across every inch of your body, consuming every ounce of your sweet nectar," he whispers as he drags the tip of his nose across my cheek over to the bend of my neck. He inhales my scent and breathes words that expose my soul. "I want to make you come so hard, you'll never forget who I am and how I ruined your pussy for any other man. Now, get dressed."

Everything I am stops. I don't feel my heart beating in my chest. My lungs empty, and suddenly I can't catch my breath. The surge vibrating through my nipples turn to chills. I soften as he strips my ability to argue. I'm naked and completely vulnerable to him.

"What the fuck? You can't pull me to the edge and leave me like this."

"I just did," he snaps as he picks up my clothes from the floor and holds them out to me. "And after tonight, don't wear this outfit when you are with me." His eyes constrict. His lips pull straight and colorless across his face. The edges of his ears glow with a touch of crimson.

"What do you expect me to wear?" I clip back quickly. I collect my clothes in my all-too-shaky arms.

"Clothes I choose for you." The backs of his fingers graze my cheek before he turns and walks toward the elevator.

Panic fires through my body. The little girl buried deep is afraid to open up to him. But the woman in me, the fighter who shields herself against all who try to enter, she wants what he's offering. I'm hungry to taste him, give him the energy that swirls just below the surface of my skin. I crave him to finish what he has started.

I toss the mismatched outfit onto the table, pulling out my black lacy bra; I hold it up in front of my chest, desperate to stop him from leaving. "So you don't want me wearing ... this?"

He stops, turns back to me. The tip of his tongue slowly creeps along his upper lip as his silvery-blue eyes light up with an excited spark.

"No. No bra." He shakes his head as he pushes the button on the elevator.

"Are you sure about that?"

"My fragrant Rose, I've never been surer about anything in my life. Put on those despicable clothes for the very last time and meet me downstairs," he commands.

My mouth falls open, but not quick enough to rebuke his rudeness. He steps into the empty waiting elevator. Son of a bitch, he rendered me speechless before the elevator doors closed, and now he's gone. *What the fuck was that and what the hell? Nobody talks to me that way.*

I stretch on my bra and pull on my *despicable* clothes for the very last time. He has no idea what he's in for. If that nameless man thinks that I'm gonna let him finger fuck me to the edge of oblivion and leave me aching for relief, he's sorely mistaken. I grab my purse from the huge round granite table in the entry and press the button on the wall. Minutes later, the elevator doors open to greet me. I step into the empty space and push the button with the bright-blue star.

The doors rumble shut behind me with a gut-twisting bang, and in the millisecond it takes me to inhale a heart-settling breath, realization settles heavily in every fiber of my being ... This nameless bastard got me. He owns me, mind and body. He's the only man who has ever gotten me to chase down an orgasm ... one demand at a time.

nine

As MY MEMORY was disrupted by the flurry of busy people and the hum of washing machines, I shoved the magazine into my purse, pulled my clothes from the dryer, and thrust them into my laundry sack. The memory of the first night with Mr. C made my stomach churn. I knew our arrangement. It wasn't built on anything more than the idea that he had bought me for three days.

After eight thousand dollars cash and eight outfits, I was a high-priced fuck, period. Was it worth it? Financially, yes, but emotionally, never. Besides it was over ... Water under the bridge ... A reminder that Prince Charming didn't exist in my world because there was nobody willing to invest anything more than money to fuck me. When I was nineteen, I had been naive enough to want something more—someone who took care of me, made me whole, wrapped their arms around me, and gave me the life I thought I wanted.

I just wanted to get the hell out of this laundromat. The place was still pretty busy with people shifting their clothes from washers to dryers and from dryers to laundry sacks. It was getting late, and there was no way I was going to take the night off. My six squares of sidewalk were open and waiting for my arrival. Not to mention Sybil and I still hadn't worked out our misunderstanding. Hopefully she'd be back on our corner tonight so we could fix whatever the hell was going on between us.

I looked around and didn't see Shane anywhere. Quarter lady was struggling with her clothes as she shoved them into a dryer. The handful of other people were wrapped up in their tattered books and wrinkled magazines. I was thankful that nobody was willing or ready to carry on conversations with a perfect stranger.

I leaned down, readying myself to hoist the sack of clean clothes over my shoulder, when Shane caught my attention by clearing his throat.

"Hey, don't tell me you were gonna sneak out of here. Sorry I got busy. You need help?" He reached out to take my laundry sack.

"No, I think I got it. You didn't tell me you were the manager here." I continued adjusting my grip.

"Well, you never really asked. And just so you know, I'm not really the manager," he said as he dragged his hands across mine and tightened them below my grip. He pulled my clean clothes bag out of my hands and swung it over his shoulder.

"So you just randomly fix broken change machines and hang out in laundromat offices?"

"Yeah, well, something like that. Now where am I taking this, Miss Complicated?"

I wanted to say my apartment, but instead I just smiled and told him my car.

ten

SHANE AND I met at Boxing Room, the Cajun restaurant that he swore by. I didn't want to lead him on, but I figured he wasn't going to take no for an answer. Maybe this would be the perfect place to explain that I wasn't looking for anything right now.

I walked up to the restaurant, expecting it to be some rundown, shabby oyster shack where people didn't have too many manners. To my surprise, Boxing Room wasn't anything like I expected. I peered through the window. It was modern and fresh. The bar curved around in front of the kitchen, while a couple handfuls of tables were scattered throughout the dining area. It was jumping with hungry people who ate with utensils and used their manners. Instantly, my judgment changed as I pulled the door open and soaked up the aroma of spicy garlic.

I scanned the room and noticed Shane was sitting tucked away in the back corner. He was absorbed in the menu, looking so … peaceful, so perfectly delectable. It may have been the restaurant, which complimented his complexion, that made my pulse thrash through my veins, or maybe it was the fact that he'd actually gotten me to meet him for lunch. I had worked so hard to resist him. Either way, he was beginning to weaken my resolve.

I slipped past a couple of tables filled with people chatting and saw that Shane was watching me. His face beamed with desire, his eyes locked on mine. He dropped his menu as he stood up. Playing right into the idea that this was going to be too easy, once I saw him … suddenly, what we were doing wasn't so cut-and-dried.

I took a deep breath, pushed away the wisps of hair that tangled in my eyelashes, and put one foot in front of the other. Chatting with the doubting voice in my head, I was supposed to be strong and definite in my feelings. Bruised hearts, well, they just didn't heal as quickly as most people thought.

Don't let him in, Rose. Stop looking at him!

I'm not.

Yes, you are. Look away. Did you forget you're a hooker?

Maybe he won't care!

Guys like Shane care. They don't want used up broken women.

"You came!" Shane interrupted the shit talk in my head. He came around and planted a sweet, delicate kiss on my cheek before he pulled out my chair.

Damn, and he's attentive.

"Sorry I'm late."

"No problem, I've been keeping busy with these Cajun boiled peanuts and a second pint of Blue Moon." He slipped back into his seat. "I'm so glad you came." He picked up the menu from his chair and handed it to me.

"Oh, you already know what you want?"

"Sure, been here for a little while, so I've already decided on the oysters on the half shell." A smile broadened across his face.

My cheeks flushed from the complete and utter message he was sending. There was nothing lost on me in his choice of food.

We looked at each other, both waiting for a reaction to fill the silent moment between us. Suddenly Shane reached over to the empty chair next to him.

"Oh, and I almost forgot … this is for you." He picked up a beautiful single yellow rose and held it out to me.

I froze. A chill tarnished my flesh as his actions marked and cracked through the rock-hard shell I thought I had built so perfectly around myself. *Fuck, he's already breaking through.*

He pushed the rose toward me, waiting for me to take it. I didn't.

"They say that a single yellow rose represents the beginning of a friendship. I looked it up online," he said in a choppy defensive tone.

I sat silently, shocked that he'd actually taken the time to be so thoughtful. Nobody I knew ever did such a thing.

I still didn't take it. I was afraid if I held it, my whole defense would collapse in his favor.

"Well, if it's too cliché, giving Rose a rose, then let's just get rid of it right now." He pulled it back and acted as if he was going to toss it over his shoulder.

"Hey, now!" I snapped, hoping that he wasn't going to let go. So many times, people have let go. "I just got that from my new friend," I whispered.

Lost in the moment of his kindness, I plucked the rose cautiously from between his fingers. I closed my eyes and inhaled, filling my lungs with the scent of a single beautiful rose and my head with visions of him loving me for who I was.

"Thank you," I whispered.

"You're welcome," he answered.

Again a thick silence rolled between us. I desperately searched my mind for words to shatter the connection that began to smolder. Dishes crashing in the kitchen, a quick breeze that caught my attention, I needed anything that kept me from falling deeply for him. I even twirled the stem between my fingers, hoping the movement of the bud would divert his attention away from my eyes. It didn't work.

"You come here often?" I asked before I focused my attention on my rose. The petals were wrapped tightly yet delicately around one another. Protection, warmth, and beauty, words that described what I longed for and wanted in my life.

This is just a lunch between friends, I kept chanting in my head. *A perfect opportunity to remind him we are only going to be friends ... that's all.*

"Is this your attempt to hit on me?" He laughed. "Yeah, I've been here a couple of times."

"No, I was asking because maybe you'd know what to order and what I should avoid." I placed my rose on the table, abandoned, and pulled the menu up in front of my face.

He caught the edge of the menu with his fingers and pushed it down. Stretching his hand across one side of the menu, he pointed at the jambalaya. "This place makes a killer jambalaya with duck and sausage, if you like a little different twist to your food. I'm getting the dozen oysters."

"A dozen? You won't get sick?"

"You can never have too many oysters."

I scrunched up my nose and looked back down at the menu. Shane noticed my reaction, which was the same as anyone's who had never had a plate full of oysters placed in front of them to eat. They were nothing more than slickery-slimy-gag-reflex little bastards. No matter how sexy people claimed they were, they would never be something I'd choose to ever let past my lips on purpose.

"You've never had one before, have you?"

"No, well, okay, so I tried one once when I was a kid. They are very slimy. I don't do slimy."

"You just didn't eat them right. I think you should try them with me. Let me show you how to eat them. You can't let them sit in your mouth. You have to let it slip down your throat; you have to just swallow. I'll let you have one of my oysters." He smiled.

"Only one?" I teased.

"You prove you can handle one, I'll give you another."

"Yeah, ahhh, I think I'll pass. You don't want me hurling all over the restaurant."

He bent forward across the table and motioned for me to lean in toward him. "I will teach you how to eat them so you won't hurl. Now, what do you think you want in addition to one of my oysters?"

"The little gem wedge salad."

"You've never eaten Cajun before, have you?"

"No," I breathed.

He leaned back from the table. A pleased grin filled his face, and his eyes narrowed. "Don't worry, I'll order for you. I know exactly what to do for first-timers. I'll convert you into my Cajun Queen in no time, Miss Complicated Rose."

I watched his chest rise with his breath; his self-assurance filled the room, and the speeding beat of my heart filled my ears. There was a little twitch owning one corner of his mouth as he pulled it into a smile. Our eyes locked just long enough to make my stomach flip and my breath get caught down in my chest.

"Don't make it too spicy. I usually don't eat spicy food." I folded the menu and slipped it to the edge of the table.

Within a few minutes, a waitress walked over to our table to take our order. She was strikingly beautiful. Her uncontrollable shiny black hair stood straight up in tight curls behind a thick black headband, and her dark skin was as flawless as the women in magazines. Philomena filled her entire name tag pinned to her long white button-up shirt. Her genuine smile carried all the way up to her light emerald eyes, and her Jamaican accent mingled with the chatter of tables around us.

"Ey, Shane, how was de peanuts? Bit of kick, ey?" she said, pointing at the bowl with a couple peanuts left.

"I liked them. Yeah, they were pretty spicy, spicier than I remember."

"Oh yeh, BJ is bein' a bit heavy-handed on de cayenne pepper today."

"Philomena, this is Rose, the lovely lady who kept me waiting and the reason I had to order the peanuts." He winked at her.

"Nice ta meet yah." Philomena nodded. "Welcome to da Boxin' Room. I be servin' yah today. Wha' might me get Eye' and Eye' to fill 'um bellies?"

Shane and I looked at her, mesmerized by her beauty and Jamaican timbre. Shane glanced over at me before he cleared his throat and, with his boyish charm, wrapped the waitress right around his finger, one word at a time.

"Well, Philomena, you have such a beautiful smile."

"Tanks," she answered shyly.

"You see, it's Rose's first time eating Cajun. My goal is to get her to like the food here so she'll agree to come back and have lunch with me again. Can we make that happen, Philomena?"

If he only knew he's wrapping me around his finger too.

"Ey, so, I'd suggest for de girlfriend Rose, de Louisian' blue crab cakes or de fried chicken po'boy. De spice can be adjusted, hot o' mild. Yah see?"

"I do. That sounds good, so let's order my girl*friend* the Louisiana crab cakes, the po'boy, and a little gem wedge salad ... and for me, I'd like the dozen oysters. Also, two drafts of Blue Moon please. Oh, and Philomena, Rose here isn't quite *there* yet. It's our first lunch together." Shane closed the menu and handed it back to her.

"Whoa, that's—" I tried to say something.

"Forward?" Shane quipped.

"No, I was going to say—"

"You don't like Blue Moon?" he interrupted again.

"No, I mean, I like Blue Moon. But I think I'll have an iced tea instead," I muttered. The last thing I needed was to be carded in front of Shane.

Philomena smiled as she jotted down my drink order, before she collected up our menus and hustled off toward the kitchen.

"So what do you think?" Shane asked, contagious in his excitement, causing me to smile.

"I think you just let Philomena believe you're taking me on a lunch date, and you ordered *way* too much food."

"I know. That tends to happens when trying to impress a girl—I mean, a friend who happens to be a girl."

"Oh, so now you're telling me you've done this with other girls before?"

"Well, not necessarily at this restaurant, or the particular food I ordered. But I've been known to order more than I can eat. I suffer from *The Big Eye Syndrome*."

"Big Eye Syndrome?"

"You know, my eyes are bigger than my stomach. I order a ton of food, then I can't eat it all. Besides, they don't really have a sampler, so it only made sense to order all the things I want you to try."

"Well, you better not have that eye thingy going on today. You're gonna help me eat all that food."

"Oh, don't worry, I'm all about sharing. Whatever we don't finish, I'll have Philomena wrap up and you can take it home," he said through a persuading grin.

I liked how he was so smooth with changing the subject too. I guess the other girls he'd tried to impress was a topic better left untapped.

Just as he was about to say something, Philomena came over with his Blue Moon beer with a wedge of orange stuffed in the mouth of the bottle, a chilled mug, an iced tea, and a tall thin vase half filled with water. She lodged the tray against her hip and the table, pulling everything off, and announced its arrival.

"Aright, one iced tea, and a Blu' Moon with a chilled mug." Philomena placed a vase next to the napkin holder. She boldly picked up the yellow rose and dropped it into the vase. "There we go, a pint for de pretty lady's flower."

"Thanks," Shane said before he pushed his orange slice into the bottle of Blue Moon. Ignoring the chilled mug, he tipped the beer against his mouth. His rounded lips were the gatekeepers to letting it roll down his throat as his modest Adam's apple danced up and down his throat in waves.

"And by the way, I am paying for my half of the bill," I snapped before I dropped my straw into the iced tea and pulled it up to my lips.

Call it one of my unbreakable rules—never indebt yourself to anyone.

"But only my half the bill. Those Blue Moons are on you, buddy," I teased in a serious tone.

"Deal. Now if you'll excuse me, I have to go to the restroom."

"Must be those flaming peanut things you ate."

"Or the couple of beers I had earlier."

Shane stood up and folded his napkin, placing it on the table before he smiled and tapped his fingers on the back of his chair. He dragged his hand across the table, intentionally making sure his fingertips brushed against my skin.

"Be right back. Don't go off with some guy who appears to be better-looking than me," he teased.

"Well, we both know looks can be deceiving," I answered back immediately.

"And I know a woman as beautiful as you, at a table alone, is a wide-open invitation."

"Well, thanks for the flattery, but trust me, that's highly unlikely." I snickered as I looked down at my napkin and twirled it between my fingers.

Shane pushed his hand under my chin, pulling my face to look at him. "Never underestimate your beauty, Rose. I guarantee you every guy in this restaurant hasn't." His eyes twinkled with that look.

I knew the look that every guy carried in his eyes when he thought he was seeing an expectation that just wasn't supposed to be there between friends. "Don't worry, I'll tell him that I am on my very first date with my *guy friend*. And that it just isn't in the stars for us."

"Yeah, guys hate that shit. Make sure he knows I'm coming right back too. Maybe I'm getting somewhere with this *friends* concept. I'll be right back." Shane gave me a lopsided grin before his blazing hazel eyes hid behind a lengthened blink.

I gave him a partial smile before I waved him off to the bathroom. "Yeah, you'd better hurry. The whites of your eyes are turning yellow."

He laughed as he walked away. Looking at the wall across from me, instantly the room got a lot bigger. I guessed my personal space just didn't seem so big when he was around.

When I scanned the room, I noticed this one guy with piercing blue eyes who kept staring right at me. He was with a short pudgy guy, whispering back and forth. He looked familiar, but when you were in the industry of fucking for money, everyone started to look familiar. It was bugging me that I couldn't place him. The way he was staring at me, I could tell he was trying to place me too. I was usually pretty spot-on at remembering my good-paying customers.

Then, as if ice water was poured down my back, a chill forced itself right against the ripcord of my soul. A lightbulb clicked between the guy's ears, and the look on his face switched from puzzled to familiar. Shit, he must have realized where he'd seen me. He must've been one of my *dates*; it was written all over his face. He was probably a guy who only came to me once, for a blow job or a quick ball-bustin' dip.

I looked away. *Break the eye contact. Please, don't come over and make this any more awkward than it already is. Great, this is why I don't like to hang out in the city. Fuck, he's coming over.*

His shoulders were back, chest puffed, and he walked as if his cock was too big to fit between his legs. I pulled my single yellow rose over in front of me, trying to give the guy a hint that I wasn't alone. I glanced over my shoulder toward the bathroom. *What the hell am I gonna do?* The last thing I wanted was to have Shane come back with this prick standing here as he tried to figure out if I was the whore he'd paid to fuck a couple or three months ago. The guy stopped next to me, obviously not the sharpest tool in the box, then he stood there in his stupid fucking manner and actually waited for me to acknowledge his presence.

I looked up at the man and smiled. He winked at me just to make sure I was the woman he'd bought down in the Tenderloin.

"I'm sorry if I am being too forward, but you look really familiar to me. Do you have a sister?"

"No, I don't." *The fucking balls on this son of a bitch.*

"You sure?"

"Yeah, I'm pretty sure if I had a sister, I'd know." *This guy must have ironclad ones.*

"A sister named Twyla? I mean, you look identical to her, except she has straight blond hair down to her shoulders." His words were dripping with sarcasm.

The muscles in my back tightened. This motherfucker was calling me out, right here in this restaurant. Sure, I had different names for different situations. When I wasn't too sure about the stability of the John, the ones who seemed creepy, or cheap, or maybe could become violent, I gave them Twyla when they asked my name. This ass-clown was trying to work an angle on me.

"Well, if she has blond hair, then we aren't really identical are we?" I whispered in a slow, precise tone. "Sorry, I'm not who you think I am. Now, I am here with a friend, so I would appreciate it if you'd go back to your table and sit down."

"Yeah, well, heck, I figured it was worth a try, seeing as you look so much like her," he said, staring right at me.

"Sorry, I can't help you," I said through gritted teeth as I stared him down. I wasn't going to look away first. Power was determined when you didn't give in to assholes.

He leaned down close to my ear, inhaling a deep, almost wet breath; he pushed close to my ear. His lips caught my hair, and the words he growled filled my head. "I know who you are. How could I ever forget going balls-deep in a whore as beautiful as you, Twyla? You can take the hooker out of the Tenderloin, wine her, dine her, take her places, and buy her expensive things, but at the end of the day, she's still nothing more than a whore."

My blood was boiling. I stood up and faced him, my body vibrating, ready to slap him for saying what he was saying. He thought he could pull up in my face and disrespect me like that? I was all ready to let him have it and just weaken what little manhood he had left.

"Obviously, a prick like you can only think with your cock, so let me help you understand this in your language," I growled.

I was so determined to chew this prick a new asshole, so fucking wrapped up in the situation with this dickweed, that I didn't notice Shane had come back.

"Rose, sweetheart, you okay?" Shane slipped his fingers around the curve of my waist and caught my hip.

My heart walloped in my chest before it clogged my throat.

"Yeah. Mistaken identity," I whispered, staring into the guy's eyes before I rolled into Shane's chest and wrapped my arms around his neck. Sure, I was playing into a whole lie of being with Shane, but if it kept him from finding out exactly who I was when I wasn't with him, then I'd gladly pay for the repercussions later.

The douchebag took a step back, noticing I wasn't going to

give him the opportunity to fuck up what I had or didn't have with Shane. "My bad. From across the restaurant, she looked like someone I met before." He turned and shuffled back to his table where the short pudgy guy waited for details.

Milliseconds weren't wasted before Shane used the opportunity to pull me toward him and drop his mouth against my ear.

"What was that about? Not that I'm complaining," he whispered.

The warmth of his breath across my ear caused shivers to roll down my spine and settle between my legs. His hands slipped down and rested on the rise of my ass. God, he felt so good. Our curves met so perfectly, each filled flawlessly by the shape of our bodies. I couldn't say it didn't feel good, right, or perfect. But I had to be realistic. I pushed my nose against the bend of his neck and inhaled.

"You want me to say you were right? Okay, so I underestimated the room," I said, intentionally brushing my lips against his skin as I spoke. "Just promise me you'll never leave me alone next time we have lunch."

I tightened my embrace before I pulled back and took in his expression. Goose bumps rose across his exposed skin as a smile broached his lips.

"What? Why are you smiling?" I asked.

"Nothing," he mumbled.

"Come on, what's up?" I playfully banged my fists against his hard, thick chest as I stepped back out of our embrace.

"Just happy that you agreed to go to lunch with me again," he mumbled as he cocked his head and smiled.

Vulnerability drenched his boyish charm, soaking restlessly through his speckled hazel eyes. I wrestled every nerve in my body into submission, hoping the vibe my body was putting off wasn't showing him the real desire that was stirring between my thighs.

Do whatever it takes to keep cool, Rose. Keep it together, for fuck's sake.

I went to say something, opened my mouth to clear up the emotions swirling frantically around us, but thanks to the big guy upstairs, I was interrupted by Philomena bringing Shane his plate full of oysters and me my salad. Shane smiled as the waitress set his cluster of aphrodisiacs down on the table. We both sat down across from one another, hoping that the space between us would defuse the energy, but when our eyes met and he winked at me … The only thought running through my head … *I better avoid eating any oysters*. Whether it was a reality or a myth, at this point, I thought adding any more lead to his pencil would only have me volunteering to be his paper.

eleven

DOING MY LAUNDRY with Shane on Thursdays had become the moments I looked forward to most lately. Every other day of the week had become nothing more than an irritating pebble in the shoe I called my life. Thank God for Sybil; we got back to our normal relationship and she forgave me for being an asshole. She was the one person who wouldn't allow me to push her away. We may have lashed out at one another, but only because that was what you did with the person you were closest to and she was my person. Sybil cautioned me about spending too much time with Shane, that I was setting myself up for a big hurt. But being with Shane, just hanging out with him and doing laundry, had been the most satisfying part of my entire life.

It was pretty sad that my happiest moments were measured by the amount of dirty clothes I brought to a laundromat to be washed and dried. It was the simplest way Shane and I could remain friends in this awkward type of friendship. We'd fostered this kind of connection, but neither of us really knew what to call it. I wasn't fucking him for money or anything else, and he wasn't paying my way.

I wasn't kidding myself. Even though I knew Shane wanted more than I was willing to give, he and I were finding a middle ground. A stage of some sort, a fucked up place that kept us trudging across the sun-beaten earth in the hope of finding a place where we could drink from the fountain of trust and actually name what we were to one another. Until then, Shane and I were simply known as laundry buddies. Laundry buddies who kept certain information off-limits. It could have been the way I chose to answer him when he asked me what I did for a living or why I scurried off before dark. I think he was convinced I was a vampire of some sort.

Shane had somehow persuaded me into having lunch together on Mondays at different Cajun restaurants. He said he wanted me to compare Boxing Room with other restaurants around the city. I knew he used it as an excuse to keep bringing me yellow roses. I agreed to it, but only on one condition—we chose places far enough away from the Tenderloin. The farther away, the better. The last thing I needed was another confrontation with a crazy fuck.

It was our fourth laundry day together, and as usual, we were sitting on the washing machines. Not that I was really counting how many Thursdays we hung out ... Okay, so maybe I was, but I had to. Shane was so sentimental that I didn't want him to think I wasn't aware of how many days we had been friends or the fact that this next Monday marked the fourth yellow rose he was gonna give me. Each rose was saved and pressed between the thin pages of a back-breakingly huge Bible my friend's parents gave me right before they kicked me out of their house. It was the perfect use for a book I had only cracked open once—to come up with a name for the streets. I never ended up finding a name from the Bible though. Not one I wanted to use while making a living. I ended up with the name Twyla after reading about a female warden at some prison somewhere who always carried the Bible under her arm.

The washing machines vibrated and whistled a loud tune on the spin cycle. It was my favorite moment with Shane, a moment where we just sat silently, nothing said, no cautious words. I didn't have to watch what spewed from between my lips because he couldn't hear me anyway. It was the moment when I thought about telling him what I did and I visualized him accepting me for who I was and not what I had to do to make a living.

"Hey, I was thinking—"

"Well, there's your problem right there. What are you doing thinking?" I interrupted, teasing him as I nudged my elbow into the side of his gut.

"Hah, hah, hah, very funny. No, seriously, I want to take you somewhere special tomorrow," Shane said proudly.

"Special?" I asked.

"Yeah, I was thinking, we've been friends for over a month, and I have never taken you over to my favorite place to just hang out." His eyes dropped to my hands in my lap as I scraped the dark-red polish from my thumbnail.

"Shane, you know I don't do surprises. Not like that."

"Well, come on, just this one time let me surprise my friend Complicated Rose with something unexpected. I've followed your lead, kept your rules—let me just have this one little thing. Let me take you some place that is very special to me."

He hopped off the washing machine, shuffled in front of me, and wedged himself between my knees. His hands burned hot through my jeans as his fingers curled around my waist. It wasn't uncommon for him to find ways to touch me that told me he wanted more.

I pushed him back and pulled my legs up crisscross, resting my elbows on my knees. I looked down at my fingernails; they looked so naked without polish. "I don't know. Where is it? What time would we be back? It's a Friday, and well, what am I going to tell Sybil? I ... I ... I just don't know if that's such a good idea." I pulled my thumb up to my mouth and started chewing on my cuticle.

I knew I looked crazy to him, but he'd never get it. I couldn't do a relationship. I couldn't even kinda go there. We'd already spent way too much time together as friends. Now he wanted to take me somewhere special to him without me knowing where it was? Hell no, that wasn't gonna work for me. Not for the prostitute who couldn't throw a rock in the Tenderloin without hitting one of her tricks ... okay, that was a little dramatic, but still.

"Rose, I'm not going to steal you away for the weekend. God knows the crazy hours you keep doing whatever it is that you do. I just wanted to take you over to the East Bay so we can go hiking, that's all." He groaned.

"Hiking? Do I look like a girl who hikes?" I said, trying to lighten the mood and change the energy that ramped up between us.

"Yeah, I think you do! You look like a girl who should say yes to hiking with her best guy-friend. Especially since he promises to have her back before her carriage turns into a pumpkin." His eyelids closed halfway in a lazy blink before his mouth broke into a sexy smile as he crossed his heart with his fingers pressed against his black T-shirt.

If he only knew. If I'd let him into my head ... he'd see the struggle I have had with having him as a *friend*.

"Fine, I can't believe I'm going to agree to this ... I'll go hiking with you tomorrow. Where do you want to meet?"

"I was thinking I'd pick you up at your place."

"Shaaaane," I moaned.

"Rooooose," he replied.

"Why are you being so ... persistent?"

"Why are you being so … complicated?"

"Because my life is complicated, and we already established that the first time we met."

"And you know I like to get my way. We've already established that. So instead of being so complicated, why don't you compromise and let me pick you up? I'll tell you what, let's make a deal. Let's say … I won't even get out of the car. I will honk three times, keep the motor running, and wait for you to get in. I won't even open the car door for you. Now, if that isn't compromising, I don't know what is."

"It's you being persistent, that's what it is."

"So is that a yes?" he asked, lowering his head to meet my eyes.

I glanced at him, popped him in the chest before I nodded. Damn, agreeing to this opens a whole different can of worms. Before this moment, Shane and I really just kept all the life drama outside of the laundromat pretty much on the down low. Minimal information about our childhood, work, and where we lived was the best way to manage my lie. An unspoken rule I enforced, that seemed to work for both of us … well, for me at least, up until now.

A couple of Thursdays ago, Shane asked me what I did for a living. I guessed the cloudy, unclear, broad answers I'd brushed across the piece-of-shit canvas just weren't cutting it for him anymore. I knew it was a matter of time before he'd push back at me to know why I couldn't ever hang out with him after five o'clock at night. My whole life, I had to lie. My. Whole. Life … I had to do what I had to do to make it in the world. Who I was, what I was doing and how I liked to be treated were all made up scenarios. Lying had become second nature to me; I did it so much that I started to believe it wasn't a lie if they ate the shit up. So, when the subject of what I did for a living came up between Shane and me, I lied. I told him that I took online classes two nights a week, and the other five nights, I took care of people in their homes. It was the perfect excuse to justify my crazy hours. What person in their right mind who met me outside of paying me for a fuck would accept what I did for a living?

Was it fair? Not really, but what part of life was fair? Honestly, it ate away at the back of my mind, lying to Shane, but I had to keep my reality in that place where I didn't let anyone see it, the one place that held my deepest secrets. No matter how much I prepared myself for his reaction, I had no doubt in my mind that he'd never want to see me again. When I thought of him finding out that I was a prostitute … well, I just had to prepare myself so when it did happen, it wouldn't hurt so badly. Unfortunately, even the deepest sting of abandonment still didn't stop me from wanting to be near him, and if I had to lie to have a sliver of him, so be it.

Forty-five minutes, the time it took to dry my clothes, that was how long he babbled about Joaquin Miller Park. He was like a teenage boy who had finally kissed the girl of his dreams. His eyes had a spark, a gleam that ignited his whole demeanor. His arms and hands spastically flew as he talked about the beautiful trails with their bay views. The more he talked about it, the more my stomach twisted into knots. I wanted to be excited about hanging out with him tomorrow, but there was dread brewing in my gut.

"What time are you planning on picking me up?" I asked when I could get a word in edgewise.

"I was thinking about nine thirty?"

"A.m.? Like, in the morning?" I spat.

"If we get over there in about forty-five minutes, that will give us most of the day. I'd like to take you to a couple of different places that have great views, and I have this little dive of a place where we can have the best Mexican food before I have to bring you back to the rat race. Damn, I wanted to surprise you."

"Oh, yeah, don't worry, I think this whole adventure is going to be very surprising," I teased as I pulled a cart next to the dryer and emptied my clothes.

"You know you're like the master wrecker of surprises," he said as he leaned into my shoulder and bumped me.

"Yeah, well, you're not the first person to tell me that."

"But I'm the first to do something about it," he retorted as he pulled a couple of Blow Pops from the bowl next to him and held them up between us. "Purple or red?" he asked.

"Purple … I hate red … cherry sucks," I moped.

"What? Cherry's my favorite."

"No, it's not. You told me last week that grape was your favorite, and the week before that, it was lemon, then it was orange the Thursday before that."

"So maybe they all are my favorite," he teased as he pulled off the wrapper and shoved the Blow Pop in his mouth.

"Maybe it's the fact that you don't complain about what you're left with," I whispered.

"Why would I complain when I get to be here with you and this … *disgusting* cherry-flavored—how can you like these Blow Pops?" he asked before he stuck out his tongue, painted red.

"I don't like that particular flavor, but in general Blow Pops are good because you get a two-fer, more bang for your buck. You get to suck and then blow. I'll do any flavor except cherry."

He didn't miss the innuendos in my statement, his expression painted on like any thirteen-year-old boy with his libido on overdrive. He gave me a slight smirk before he pointed the Blow Pop at my nose.

"You're right, cherry sucks!" he said as he tossed it down onto the counter.

I guessed I should've given him props for purposely grazing over my comment. I watched as the glistening red lollipop cracked and busted into a heart shape as it left a trail of broken pieces in its wake.

"I guess I'll be calling you the cherry wrecker from now on," I teased without giving my response a second thought.

Shane's eyes grew large, and a sinful smile spread across his face. It seemed like forever crammed between us before he had a smart-ass remark that clung to the thick air between us.

"I've been known to wreck my fair share of cherries in my life." He smirked before he intentionally glimpsed down at my feet and shoved his hands in his front pockets.

"Oh. My. God, you called me a surprise wrecker. I only thought it was fair I'd call you … All right, okay, score one for Shane, the cherry wrecker." I pushed my fingers in air quotes as I spoke about his new nickname.

Fuck, Rose, why not just put your foot in your mouth now? Cherry wrecker, really?

"Hey, I wasn't the one who came up with the name," Shane teased as he pulled open the dryer next to me. "I'm just willing to own it, that's all." He collected his clothes in one huge bundle wedged between his arms and chin.

"Oh, okay, now let's not get too confident and start talking about conquests of virgins and shit." I tangled my fingers into a pile of my panties and thrust them into the bottom of my laundry bag. I knew the minute I said it, it was a mistake.

"Who mentioned virgins? What type of cherries are you exactly talking about, Complicated Rose? Because if it is *that* type you are referring to … let me clear the air now—curiosity never really killed the cat. It just took one of its nine lives." Wisps of his brown hair brushed across his bedroom eyes. He flashed his bright pearly whites, teasing me into instantly turning bright crimson.

What the hell are you doing? Keep this boy at a distance. It is for his good as much as yours … You're nothing but a two-bit whore.

My inner voice filled my head, the one thing that kept my heart protected. Resistance flooded every cell in my body, changing my demeanor. When the walls of my life began to crumble and my heart started to beat at a different speed, my intuition blared the warning sirens when I was getting too tangled up, too close to feeling something I wasn't supposed to feel.

I snatched up handfuls of my clothes, unfolded and jumbled, and shoved them into my bag. I glanced over my shoulder and noticed he had dropped his bundle of clothes on the folding counter. Listening to my intuition, I turned back and tied up my laundry sack. I needed to get out of here before I get twisted into a situation I couldn't get out of, a road I wasn't ready to travel with him.

"You know, I better get going," I deadpanned as I lifted my laundry sack and rolled it over my shoulder.

My words didn't go over well with Shane. I tried to leave but couldn't. The pull of my muscles across my shoulders was strong before I shifted my weight and stumbled back. I turned around and saw that Shane had grabbed my laundry bag and held onto it.

"I'll walk you out. Come on, let me carry this for you," Shane insisted as he pulled again on my clothes bag.

"I have it. You know, I can do it on my own. I'm very capable. I've been very capable my whole life. I don't need any help," I argued as I adjusted the bag over my shoulder.

"I know you're capable, Rose. Besides, it has become somewhat of a routine for me to carry out your laundry for you," Shane said as he muscled the bag away from me and flung it over his shoulder.

"So now I'm Capable Rose. Make up your mind, Shane. Am I complicated or capable?" I fumed.

"Whoa, where the heck is this coming from? I just want to help you out."

"Well, maybe I don't need your help." I dug out the rage that I'd buried deep within the seared crevices of my soul and plastered it across the space between us, trying with everything I had to rebuild that wall he was tearing down.

"I never assumed you needed my help. I carry your bag for you because that's what friends do ... I never thought you weren't capable."

I turned and headed for the door. I wasn't going to fight him. I'd let him carry my bag and walk out to my car. Hiking with him tomorrow was a huge mistake. I felt it in my bones.

He shuffled behind me, up through the first flight of stairs of the parking garage. I was so determined that I didn't slow down even when my calves felt like they were on fire. When I got to my car, I thrust the key into the lock of my trunk and pulled it open.

"Thanks," I barked as he dropped my clothes into the back.

Shane stood staring at me. Silence stormed around us, his eyes not leaving mine. After waiting for something to stumble from his mouth, I just couldn't stand there any longer and wait to hear anything he was going to tell me. I slammed my trunk, turned, and walked to the driver's side of my car.

"So this is it?"

"Yep."

"You're going to go because I teased you?" Shane snapped as he followed me.

"I just need to go, that's it. I'll text you about tomorrow." I didn't turn around.

Instead I started to get into my car, then his enormous hand crashed against the edge of the car door, slamming it shut. He grabbed my arm, spun me around, and pushed me back against the car. His eyes were filled with all the pain I was causing, all the confusion my mind-fuck was playing on him ... it was the only thing I knew how to do when expectations were changing. It was time to shut him out.

"I call bullshit, Rose. I think you're scared of me." The space between us vanished as he inched closer.

"Scared? Scared of what, Shane? Scared to hear about the type of girls you've slept with? Please, that's the least about you that scares me. I just need to go, get ready for work."

He pushed his face within inches of mine. Pinning me against the car, he continued. "What is it then? I want to know … what it is about *me* that scares *you*?"

He caressed the backs of his hands across my flaming cheeks. His eyes filled with storming tension, the same eyes I saw when I was with the only other man I'd let have my heart. My pulse thumped across my neck, keeping time with his.

"This," I said as I thrust my fists against his chest, attempting to push him back. "Expectations … your expectations … you have expectations of me … you expect me to be someone I'm not. I can't be that *someone* you want me to be. I'm not that girl; I'll never be that girl for you, Shane."

I turned away from him and fumbled with the door handle. His hands closed over mine, his body pushed against my back, his face pressed into the curve of my neck, and his breath steamed against my hair as his nose glided against the base of my head. The pressure sent me reeling.

"Then I won't ask you to be *that girl*. I won't push you for something you're not ready to give."

"Don't you see, Shane? I will never be ready. I can't give you what you want."

"Who said it had to be anything more than friends, Rose?"

"I can feel it. I know you'll need more, take more, ask for more … and I just don't have any more to give."

"Rose, all I want is to spend time with you. If it's only as friends, then I guess I'll have to be okay with that. But god, I just wish you'd trust me. Let me in … for just a moment, let me know what you're feeling."

My heart thrummed at his words. I began to curl within myself as everything I thought I was nosedived into the pit of my stomach. Shane pulled my hands, subdued in his grip, from the door handle; he took my arms and tangled them around my stomach. His body swallowed mine in his embrace. His body felt so warm, so good, and so right.

I was totally fucked up. Like the pendulum in my head was swinging full force back and forth, hammering against each side of my fucked up brain. On the one side, I wanted him to take me and pull me around and kiss me so hard that I would forget who I was. I ached for him to keep pushing, fighting to peel back the façade that it had taken me years to build, and yet on the other side, I hated how vulnerable I felt when I was with him. Everything he did while we were together would send sparks barreling through my body. I resented how he made me feel excited again and gave me something to look forward to, convinced all the while that his expectations would only give me more heartbreak.

My lungs ached with a burn equal to inhaling black smoke—choked to death—while I breathed in his scent. *Damn, I want to stay like this forever.*

"I can't, Shane … I just can't," I whispered as I bucked, working to shed his body from mine.

I pulled open my car door and got in. There was no way I was going hiking with him tomorrow. I just couldn't. I shoved the keys into the ignition, and I didn't look over at him. I didn't want to give him a chance to stop me from driving away. I just needed to go. I was good at shutting off to the rest of the world while I gave my body over to some slimy fuck who didn't give a rat's ass about my feelings or how I was falling in love with Shane.

Truthfully, Shane had just moved way too fast for me. I felt him and how he got under my skin when he looked at me or even how he acted around me, the way he'd find ways to touch me. It wasn't just at the laundromat but anytime we talked on the phone or met at restaurants. He had become too comfortable for me, a habit I ached for. I knew that would lead me to nothing but pain.

I couldn't let whatever it was, this thing we had built between us, take any more of my attention. It had become familiar flashes of Mr. C all over again. There was no way I could deal with another heartbreak like that. Everything with Shane was gonna come crashing down, I felt it in every cell of my body. I just knew it—call it a premonition, or whatever—but I just couldn't be in the middle of it. I was better off alone.

Another "gift" had come today from Garrett Chadwick, aka Mr. C. Like clockwork, every three weeks he sent me a package, and I knew it was his twisted way of staying under my skin. Like a drug, or a high that had me hating myself every time I went back for more, I struggled to stay clean from his influence.

Painstakingly, Mr. C had built a strong case for hope. He knew it would be the best way he could control me and the driving force that destroyed me. Three days, that was all it took him to make me believe I was more than what I saw in the mirror, and it was all defeated within seconds. He'd created so much doubt in my memories of having someone who had taught me to feel loved beyond my shitty expectations. Memories that I'd thought I had buried away with my broken heart. All it took was Shane pushing for more and another package from Mr. C to hurl me into a downward spiral that weakened the grip I had on my past.

I slid the package under my bed with my foot, giving it a place among the cluster of other unopened packages he had mailed me. Memories of us together twisted across my thoughts and how he had torn me open and made me believe maybe I wasn't the piece of shit I had always thought I was.

twelve

PAST

THE MORNING SUN blazes fiery against my closed eyes. My hair tickles my shoulders as the forced air blows chilling cold waves across my chest. The thin, soft bedsheet, twisted down across my stomach, does nothing to warm my body. Mr. C, a name he demands I don't call him, has set up the expected behaviors and rules for our time together.

He didn't touch me last night. Instead, he made me strip naked and he told me that when I'm in the hotel room, and he's with me, I'm expected to be completely nude. I admit, it was a little uncomfortable at first, walking around in stilettos and nothing else. Sure, I've had *dates* who liked to watch me undress and even watch me masturbate, but they never just paid me to walk around their hotel room buck naked. But Mr. C, he's different; so, after a couple of hours of being completely nude around him, it wasn't so bad. His eyes drag across my body, but he never reaches out to grope me when I walk by. It's so foreign to me, it seems almost strange, but to each their own.

Harmless in his demands, this morning, he makes my task clear by his actions. I'll be rewarded if I make him hard ... without touching him. So, I make it a game—games are easy and they always have rules. Most of the time, those rules only apply to me, but nevertheless, they are rules. I already know what he's packing in his pants and what he did to me with his fingers that first time in his suite, so I know he has skills most of my *dates* didn't have. My reward, besides the money, is his touch and my pleasure ... at least that's what he keeps telling me.

Mr. C shuffles over and sits next to me on the bed, already dressed in a pair of black dress pants and a white T-shirt. Pulling the sheet down my body, I push up off the bed. I need to go to the bathroom and brush my teeth. His eyes follow my body as I walk across the room, my hips swaying against the sunlight falling between the curtains. He drags his arms up behind his head, curling the tip of his tongue up against his lips and dampening them to a glisten.

"I'll be right back, I'm just gonna freshen up."

"Take your time. And Rose?"

"Yeah?" I quip.

His eyes grow large. "Answer me properly."

"Huh?" I ask.

His eyes instinctually scorch my skin, his lips press into a tight line—he's lighting me up. Springing from the bed, he grabs my wrist and pulls me around into his chest. My ass against his erection, his mouth presses tight against the curve of my face. His warm, earthy aroma is subtle as it lingers around me. He holds me tight across my chest, his other arm pressing across my stomach and tightening his hold he turns me toward the full-length mirror at the end of the bed.

"Beautiful women speak eloquently, and using words like *gonna*, *yeah*, and *huh* will not sustain your beauty. Rose, look at how beautiful you are." His breaths are brief and quick.

Shivers fall down my spine in waves. I close my eyes, unable to look at what he sees in the mirror. I thrust my ass back against him. Beautiful isn't a word I use to describe myself. I want him to prove it to me.

"Open your eyes, Rosebud, and look at what I see."

"I don't want to," I whisper as I lower my head. My hair falls in front of my face, the perfect barrier so I don't have to look.

"I wasn't asking you. Open your eyes and look." He drags his hand from my chest and clears the hair out of my face. "I need you to open your eyes."

I do.

I open my eyes and look in the mirror, painfully seeing every last mental scar people have left. People who were supposed to love and protect me. I see the fear of a nine-year-old who grew into a woman, I see the searing pain of a teenager rejected by her parents, and I see the shame of a woman who longs to find someone who wants to love her in spite of all the mistakes she has made.

His hands caress across my every body part as he describes them. "Now look at the flawless curve of your hips, the marvelous swell of your breasts. Look at the unsullied bend of your neck and the arch of your creamy, smooth thighs. My Rosebud, keep your words as beautiful as you are," he whispers across my flesh.

Dropping his fingers down below my navel, he tickles his fingertips across the outside of my pussy.

"Mmmm," I breathe as I push my hips into his touch. I ache—no, yearn—for him to heal the scars I carry around with me every day of my life.

"Find your stilettos and put them on before you go to the bathroom," he says as he pushes my body out of his embrace.

The chill of the room rolls from my shoulder blades down to my ankles.

"And, Rose, leave the bathroom door open." He gives me an impish smile.

I find my heels and put them on, making sure I don't look at myself in the mirror at the end of the bed. My darkest demons, better left unnoticed, come alive in mirrors. I leave the door to the bathroom open, and he watches me pee and wash my hands. I find the extra toothbrush and toothpaste he left out for me on the counter. Never taking his eyes off me, he sits on the bed and watches me. I steal a deep breath and make a decision to keep my past experiences buried deep for the next several days.

"Well, are you just into staring?" I ask in a low, breathy tone. I push my ass out and spread my legs just enough to invite him over. "Or did you want to come get what you paid for?" I tease over my shoulder, caressing my hands up to my ass.

"Ahhh, my fragrant Rosebud. Yes, I want you, but this isn't about me ... right now, this is about you."

"About me?"

"Yes, right now, this moment ... is about you." he says as he pats the bed next to him.

Anyone else does that to me, I'll tell them to fuck off, but Mr. C? Well, he's paid for it. I come over and sit next to him. He slips the back of his fingers across my bare shoulder, sweeping my hair off before he pushes his lips onto my chilled skin.

"Why do you think I pulled up to you? Out of all those women, I could have had any one of them ... why do you think I stopped in front of you?" He withdraws his lips from my skin.

His steamy blue eyes invite me to push my lips to his. God, I want to kiss him. No other *date*, no other man deserves the pleasure of that privilege, but his words, his actions, they mesmerize me.

"I don't know." I swallow hard, my tongue buzzing to tangle with his.

"I chose you because of the way you carried yourself. Unrefined and raw, certainly, but you have something those other women don't. You have a spark, an allure that pulls at my deep-rooted need to … take care of you," he whispers against my flesh.

My heart falls into my stomach, and my skin runs cold. *I can't believe what he just said to me.*

"Great, I've become your charity case? Thanks, but this weekend isn't about your charity. It's about me taking care of your needs. That's all." I push off the bed and head for the bar.

"Stop!" he demands.

I keep walking.

"I said stop!" he commands louder.

"I'm thirsty, I need something to drink," I rebut. I keep walking, totally naked, utterly pissed and completely ready to give back his money so I can leave. "You, mister, you're asking for something I can never give. I'm not your charity case."

He gets up off the bed and comes charging over. He clutches my biceps and drags me away from the bar. "I never called you a charity case."

"No, you just treated me like one. And for your information, I don't need your money. I got plenty of my own. You wanna know why I got into your car? I got into your car 'cause I felt sorry for you. That's right; you looked so lonely with those sad, puppy dog eyes." I walk in circles, scanning the room for my clothes. I'm done, I'm the fuck out, but not before I finish telling him off. "That's why I got into your car. You didn't choose me … I chose you! Yep, um-hum, that's why I got into your car."

He remains at the bar, watching as I frantically search the room.

"It's *want to*, *because*, and *yes*, not wanna, 'cause and um-hum."

"What?"

"When you are speaking to me, I expect you to speak properly."

A bullet of a whole-hearted-fuck-you-mister shoots from the barrel of my mouth, and how-fucking-dare-you is the finger pulling the trigger.

"Are you fucking kidding me? You gotta be kiddin' me? I'm trying to leave, and you're all bent out of shape about my goddamn grammar?" I explode.

"When you decide to stop acting so irrational, I will expect you out on the terrace."

"The fuck I am. I am not your—"

Before I can even finish my words, he wraps me up from behind. One hand on my mouth and the other around my ribcage, he thrusts me against the wall. My face pressed up against the cold cream-colored plaster; my body sandwiched between him and the wall. His breathing is fierce as a deep growl grows in his throat. His hands pulse down my torso, catching my nipple in one, pushing the other between my thighs.

Fear thrashes through my body. Suddenly I'm that lost little girl, the one who's so scared.

His hands are hot. The tips of his fingers scratch my waist when he pulls my pink shorts and flowery panties down and off my legs.

"Is this what you want, Rose? A man who will just take from you and leave you with nothing?" His voice echoes down into my gut.

"You's making me do this, my little Rosalie. You give me this sickness . . . you keep causin' all of this in my body and you're gonna help me with it."

"No," I whisper as I squeeze my eyes closed, trying to clear my mind.

"Shhh, Rosalie, don't cry, you's gonna fix me up. Make me all better. You's about ripe for the pickin', girl."

A single tear collects in the corner of my eye before it breaks free and rolls down my cheek. An instant of resolve shoots through my body as he traces the tip of his nose across my cheek.

His breath is hot against my skin as he continues. "You think I don't know who you are and how I make you feel inside?" He pushes his fingers deep inside me. My legs sway and my muscles clench as he pushes deeper and draws a long pull back, before he thrusts again. "I will never be that guy for you, my Rosebud. I will never take what I didn't pay for; I will never take what isn't mine."

His other hand catches the side of my neck as he pulls my head toward his. Still holding me from behind, he strokes his ever-ready cock across the bend of my ass.

"Let me take care of you," he whispers against my cheek.

The guard I carry, holding men at a distance, crumbles as he spins me around and dips his tongue between my lips. I push against him. Our tongues tangle forcefully as colors burst from my desire to feel something more than the brokenness that taints my heart. For the very first time in the couple of years of selling my body, I let a *date* kiss me. He kisses me, and I am his …

thirteen

THE THICK FOG of emotion, coupled with the vivid images of being lost and betrayed by Mr. C, weighed heavily on my mind. This time, it wasn't butterflies that had swirled in my stomach when I thought about Mr. C, but the sick burn of betrayal as I thought about Shane and how much I wanted to see him.

It was the garbage truck's squeaky brakes that plucked me from my dream and thrust me smack-dab in the middle of my reality. Today was garbage day, and that also meant it was Thursday, the same day that I would spend with Shane doing our laundry. It had been six days since I heard from him. I'd be lying if I said it wasn't fucking killing me, and I hated it. But after I bailed on our hike, I had asked him to give me some space.

I resented the fact that Monday rolled around and I craved his conversation and the spice of his favorite Cajun food. I couldn't stand the fact that instead of being with him, I had spent the afternoon in my shitty apartment, eating a bologna sandwich as I watched some fucked up Spanish soap opera. I missed his random texts of dorky jokes and one-way conversations that made me laugh. It wasn't fair that a lifetime of fucked up situations kept me going in the same circle over and over again.

Sure, Shane and I had only hung out for a cluster of Thursday afternoons to do laundry and a handful of Mondays for lunch. It shouldn't have been that big of a deal ... but it was. I'd gotten used to it, goddammit—gotten used to him and his crazy texts on the days we didn't see each other. He had become my comfortable, sharing my Thursdays and filling my Mondays with conversation.

Pulling my phone from my purse, I did everything short of crossing my fingers and toes in the hope that Shane had texted me. Needing any type of confirmation that he was okay or surviving without me and our lunch day. I looked at my phone. He still hadn't texted me ... not once in six days. Maybe he was done with me. If I had to guess, I was just too complicated for him.

It was probably better that Shane had never called me. That made it a little easier to move on from our friendship. Obviously he didn't have a problem letting go of whatever we'd had. Yeah, it was better. Besides, I really didn't need to deal with the extra pressure.

Several conferences had come to San Francisco over the weekend. When I had to pull extra tricks on my six squares, knowing Shane didn't want anything to do with me made it an easier pill to swallow, so to speak.

Sybil and I had worked it systematically and raked in some good money with a handful of extra suck-and-plucks from the Chinese Plastics and Paints Conference on Friday and Saturday and the politicians from the Clean Energy Summit on Sunday and Monday. We'd had four busy nights, and it gave us a nice little stack of cash we hid under our mattresses.

Okay, so what if I had used the fact that Shane didn't call me as motivation to make as much money as possible? I just took all my feelings for him and stuffed them into the emotional vault I had buried deep in my body. It was the same space where I hid every other fucked up situation that shaped who I was. I'd been trained by circumstances to be the girl who looked like she didn't give a fuck. I'd been down that road so many times ... I knew where every crack, bump, and pothole was and the damage each one did when I didn't steer clear.

The problem was, even though I threw myself into my work over the weekend, it really didn't help as much as I thought it would have. *Like they say, appearances can be deceiving, and boy did I deceive everyone when it came to Shane, especially myself.*

Ever since Shane and I had begun spending so much time together, doing my job had become harder and harder. I used to take on anyone without a second thought. I'd strip my mind of any emotion and work the *dates* into doing whatever the hell I wanted them to do. I could fuck and play into their kinky fetishes because I was damn good at turning the whole thing into a game in my mind.

But now the minute those fucks went to town doing their business, my mind collapsed into images of Shane shaking his head. His eyes burned through my skin and left scars of shame for being with men who didn't love me. Guilt flooded my body— yeah, the one emotion I'd always kept an arm's length away. But now, trick after trick, all I could think about was Shane. I wished it was his hands that touched me and his lips which kissed me and his tongue that traced perfectly scrumptious lines on my body.

Without a doubt, love would kill this profession for a girl. The worst thing any prostitute could ever do was fall in love. It didn't matter if you got tons of money for your pussy or pennies on the dollar; love was like a poison that slowly seeped into your veins and hijacked your heart. Eventually, it killed any ability you thought you had to spread your legs for anyone but him.

Thursday, the day Shane and I usually did our laundry together.

Different thoughts rolled through my head. Should I just go into the laundromat and tell him I was sorry I was so complicated? Fuck it … maybe I'd just drop the bomb on him that I was a prostitute. Why not risk losing him for good? At least it would be done and over.

Six days, and he still hadn't called. This routine, the pain that stabbed at my heart and the breaths I wasn't able to catch when I thought about him, was familiar. I hadn't signed up to fall in love with him. Sybil had warned me; she'd told me to walk away. Why hadn't I listened? I just needed to move on.

fourteen

THE PROBLEM WITH trying to move on was the moment you decided to do it … it became the only thing you could focus on. All I'd done was think about Shane. If I wasn't wondering what he was doing, I wanted to know if he missed me and our conversations. Every flower stand I passed made me think of him. Every time I threw my dirty clothes into the hamper … I thought about him. Even brushing my teeth, somehow he'd enter my thoughts. I had lost any handle I had on controlling how much I thought about him, and it had become fucking annoying. It seemed like everything I did came with the thought of Shane.

I pulled at the refrigerator handle. I hadn't had much of an appetite lately, and I wasn't too hungry, but it was a quarter to twelve. If I didn't at least put something in my stomach, I was going to pay for it later. *Cramping hunger pangs on the job suck, bad.* I snagged a hardboiled egg that Sybil had made a couple days ago. She'd been on this weird health kick, starting her mornings with some type of protein and no carbohydrates. Usually eggs just grossed me out, but when I needed the protein and I didn't feel like cooking, it did the trick. Besides, Sybil had been gone since yesterday morning; she'd mentioned that she had a lengthy fuck coming into town.

I took my hardboiled egg and snatched a slice of sourdough bread before I sat down on the couch and wrestled with the idea of just showing up at the Stop and Wash. It wouldn't be too hard to act like nothing had happened between us. I was really good at acting. I'd learned early on that a prostitute couldn't sell her body without the ability to turn on the dramatics. There was something to be said about hooking up every couple of weeks with the same trick and making it seem new. It was my job to make them think that what they did to me was the most mind-blowing sex I'd ever experienced and, well, I was pretty damn good at my job.

I had to be stronger than any simple desire to feel worthy of something beyond numbness. I knew what would happen if I truly let him in—things would get complicated, fast. Shuffling my feelings for Shane around in my mind was as fucked up as being beaten simply because I had been born. Nothing in this world had convinced me that if I slid that thin blade of emotion against my flesh, I'd feel whole again. No love, no desire would ever be worthy of that searing pain.

I pulled my legs up under my ass and curled up on the couch. Tears I hadn't let go of since I'd sold my heart to the loveless fuck who took my soul and crushed it fell fast and swirled from my chin before they soaked into the front of my camisole. I cried. My eyes burned with the sting of every thought about all the mindless, sick fucks who had stolen pieces of my life and never returned them. My controlled aching whimpers turned into uncontrollable belly-deep howls as my entire life busted from the vault in my heart.

I didn't stop crying, not even when my voice was gone and my throat begged me to feel the burn of tequila. And even though I had lived through the horrors of alcoholism with my parents, it didn't keep me from knocking back an entire bottle of that golden poison. I welcomed the warm burn against the back of my throat as the scorching pressure pushed at my lungs and the tequila blazed down into my stomach in waves of gut-rotting satisfaction. Finally I felt something before I had become ragingly numb.

WHEN I WOKE up, I was lost ... lost to what time it was or even where the fuck I was. My phone was blowing up with messages from a couple of my regulars, ones I had arranged *dates* with for Thursday night. I unfolded from the ball of mess I'd created, letting the empty tequila bottle hit with an echoing clunk against the old worn wooden floor. My head was spinning still, and the room was dark except for the faint glow of my phone and the digital clock from across the room.

I took a moment to gain my bearings before I looked at the time. I dreaded the glance I gave my clock. Three thirty Friday morning ... I had drunk myself into an unconscious clusterfuck of missed jobs, a night's take of close to five hundred bucks. It was so fucked up. I might as well have given all my clients to some other ho who had been willing to work through her demons and collect a fee along the way.

The couch wasn't comfortable, not a place where I should have lost my shit. As I sat up, my feet plopped to the floor while my head felt like it was being chopped up in a blender. Steel blades mangled the space between my ears, and the pressure drained down behind my eyes. I was paying the price this morning. I snatched my phone and cleared the texts from the guys

I'd stood up last night. If those horny fucks needed to get off, they'd probably found some other ho who'd give them just enough. Still I hoped to see a text from Shane, but no luck. Probably better that way. I needed to get my head clear.

I stumbled to the kitchen, popped a couple Motrin, and choked down a small glass of water. My stomach hated me, curling and growling at the introduction of drugs and water without food. But the thought of eating something made me want to hurl. I pulled off my clothes and changed into something a little more comfortable than the last bit of clean clothes I had. I dropped my phone on the small rickety table next to my bed. Even though I didn't want to think about the predicament I was in, not having much to wear and the necessity of having to go to the laundromat later today flashed through my mind. My head was still spinning. All I wanted to do was to fall back asleep. Within minutes, my eyes closed, and I welcomed eight hours of pure, unadulterated shut-eye. It cost me more in lost revenue than a sailor who'd pissed away his best bottle of scotch.

I woke up half past noon, glanced over at my phone, and saw that I had a message … it was a text from Shane. I stared at it as the text vibrated my phone and lit up my screen again. I won't lie—I looked at it for a while, wondering if I should even respond or make him wait and wonder. To some people, it might be cruel, selfish, and even evil to make him suffer for not contacting me sooner. I simply called it tit for tat. It was the only way I kept my heart from breaking again. Sure, I physically ached to spend time with him, be friends again, but that wasn't a good enough reason to set myself up for heartbreak again. I held just enough pain against my heart so I'd never forget the gut-wrenching sting of betrayal. I needed Shane to see I wasn't someone who'd come running the minute he realized how much he missed me.

SHANE: Can I say I'm sorry? I hope it's not too late. I know I should have texted you sooner. I was trying to give you space. God, I missed you yesterday! I missed hanging out with my friend. Rose, I'm sorry I upset you. Will you please meet me today at the laundromat?

ME: What time?

SHANE: It doesn't matter. I'll be here until you show up.

But then again, broken girls always ached to be loved, even if it wasn't perfect. I read our texts, drenched in the loss of a week we'd never get back. I craved the same hopeless attention that he did, even when I totally knew it wasn't going to work. Friends and only friends—that was what we had to remain. No matter the feelings he had for me and me for him. That was the only option for us.

I collected my dirty clothes, stuffed them into my laundry bag, and wrestled it into the trunk of my car. I moved fast and with purpose. Suddenly I had a reason to drive down to the Stop and Wash. I knew I had to tell him where I stood with our friendship, but even so, this tiny part of me—the littlest piece—wished I could be with him, claim him as mine and only mine. But no matter what, I knew it wasn't possible. Even the voice in my head never failed to remind me of who I was.

Come on, Rose, you really think he wants more than a free roll in the hay with you? You are nothing more than a dirty fuck for him. He'll always be too good for you. Laundry, huh? Really, you'll be nothing more than his dirty laundry secret. He can't take you home to his parents. Just turn around.

As hard as it was, I kept driving. The voice in my head, my own personal recording from hell, wasn't going to change my mind.

I pulled my car into a spot on the first floor of the parking garage. It seemed like forever since I'd been here. And even though I had begun to claim some type of ownership of this familiar space I'd come to every Thursday for the last month, for some reason, today it felt foreign to me. Maybe because it was a Friday and I had never come to the laundromat on a Friday, or it could've been the out-of-control beating of my heart that thundered in my ears. Either way, I had too many things hinging on seeing Shane that day, one being my soul.

I wrestled the laundry bag from my car and down the street to the Stop and Wash. I pushed open the door, fighting to keep my laundry bag from falling off my shoulder. I plopped it on the floor in front of me and scanned the place for Shane. On my second pass, I noticed Shane talking to this really beautiful blonde. Her tits were so round and perfect, they bounced behind her skin-tight tank top as she laughed. Jealousy rushed through my body as she smiled and dragged her hand down his forearm.

I hadn't expected to see Shane giving his attention to this perky little thing. I thought he'd be waiting by the door for me, hoping he caught me as I came in. She turned and danced her hips back and forth before she shuffled away from Shane, showing him her perfect ass peeking out from her daisy dukes. *What was I thinking coming here? I shouldn't have come.*

Just as she pulled him to an open washing machine, he looked over at me. His eyes slowly burned through my soul. His smile pulled at every string connected to my heart. It was crazy how images could become distorted in our minds, and we'd just never quite remember the little details of someone or how their expressions affected us to the core of who we were. Oh, fuck, I was so off on my recollection of Shane when I had thought about him while I earned a living. Every vision of him was wrong, so very wrong. I had forgotten about the slight wrinkle that showed up next to his eyes when he smiled, or the way his Adam's apple bounced in his throat when he swallowed. I'd failed to recall the way his arms flexed as he dragged his hands across his jeans when he was nervous. I never visualized his swagger as he walked over to me, or the clean, citrusy smell of his cologne.

"Hi," he said as he buried his hands in his pockets.

God, how I wish he had leaned over and kissed my cheek, a small gesture of chivalry I've missed from him.

"Hi," I answered, twisting the top of my bag.

"Here, let me take that for you." He reached down and grabbed my laundry and pulled it up, hoisting it over his shoulder. "I have a couple of machines over by my office."

"Oh, okay." I followed him through the laundromat.

The girl Shane was with when I showed up gave me a dirty look. I smiled back, grateful for the fact he wanted nothing to do with her.

"I'm glad you came," he said over his shoulder as he continued toward the washing machines with "Broken" tags hanging from them.

I watched the muscles in his shoulders flex and the edge of his shirt as it danced across his ass as he walked. The slight glisten off his bare arms ruled my tongue as it slid across my lips. *What I wouldn't give to skate my fingers across his skin.*

"You were so desperate with that text," I clipped, hoping to stop my mind from raging for him.

"Desperate? You're really calling my text desperate?" he quipped, dropping my laundry bag in a rolling cart before pulling off the "Broken" tags from the two washing machines.

"Really? You put a fake 'Broken' tag on them?"

"Just for you." He gave me a quick smile.

I pulled the drawstrings on my bag and started to collect and sort my casual *non-working* clothes before I tossed them into the belly of the first washing machine.

"If your text wasn't desperate, then what would you call it?" I knew my words were sharp. They could've even been

118

interpreted as painful.

"Apologetic, remorseful—I'd even say miserable. I've missed you, Rose. I like—" He broke off as he leaned back against the dryer across from me. "I like doing laundry with you." He pushed his hands through his hair.

"I guess being pitiful has its advantages."

"If that's what you call being here with me, then I'll take pitiful any day of the week," he said as he crossed his feet. "But let's not forget, you came here to see me." He slipped his hands back into his front pockets.

"I came because I have nothing clean to wear."

"Really? What about all the laundromats between your apartment and here?"

"They're too gross. Besides, it's a habit … coming to this place. I've been conditioned; blame it on those damn Blow Pops. I really missed all the different flavors." My voice broke off as I busied myself with the laundry soap for the washing machine.

"Yeah, well, so did everyone else. I stopped putting them out—figured I didn't need any Blow Pops if you weren't here."

"You only put them out because of me?" A smile crept over my face.

"Well, I had to impress you in some way. You weren't very excited about my cheap suckers, so I figured what's better than bubble gum wrapped in crystallized sugar on a stick? It's a Blow Pop, a two-fer, for Christ's sake," he answered as he pulled quarters from his pocket, dropped them into the coin feeder, and pushed them into the machine.

"Hey, I can pay for my own laundry."

"I know, but you struggle with choosing the right temperature," he teased, pointing at the machine as the water started to fill the tub.

I clicked the permanent press option and spun back around to him. "Well, now that I'm here, are you going to bring back the Blow Pops?"

"Does my answer hinge on you hanging around?"

"Depends," I huffed as I collected my next load of laundry.

"On what?" he asked as he pulled open the door of the next washing machine.

"The flavor," I answered as I shoved my clothes into the washer.

"The flavor?" he asked, sounding confused, before he shut the door.

"Of the Blow Pops! You know, for someone who claims to be quick-witted … just tell me you kept some stashed away in the bottom drawer of your desk."

"Sure, I do … my emergency stash. You like cherry, right?" His eyes glistened, matching his smartass remark.

"Very funny," I quipped before he turned on his heels. "Where are you going?"

"You said you'd hang out if I bring you lollipops—Blow Pops, to be exact. So, I'm going to go get them."

I gave him a quick smile before turning back and repeating the routine of filling up the machine with a tall stack of quarters. Once I had both washing machines humming, and nothing to occupy my attention, I figured I'd go to the bathroom then see if Shane needed help finding the box of Blow Pops. Sure, I could be pissed off that he hadn't called me or texted me for all that time. But truthfully, being around him again gave me a sense of normalcy, even if it was completely fake. When I was with him, I fell right into being comfortable again. I wasn't a tangled up mess of unexpected or a total wreck filled with all the battle scars of what my life had become.

Shane has a natural talent of making me feel like a plain, ordinary girl, and well, being ordinary made me feel like I was something *special*.

On my way back from the bathroom, I figured I'd stop in on Shane and find out what was taking so long to find my Blow Pops. His office door was partly open, and I saw through the door crack that he was still sitting at his desk. He wasn't rummaging through his drawers; instead he was looking over to the other side of the room, talking to someone.

"You know how hard it is to find you?" a female voice teased him.

I froze in my tracks.

"Well, I haven't been hiding," he answered lightheartedly.

"Maybe not, but I just thought you'd reconsider my offer to thank you properly for your kindness," she replied.

My heart throbbed in my chest. I inched closer to Shane's office to see who in the hell he was talking to. I saw that she had on a long black trench coat and matching spiked stilettos. Jealousy stabbed at my gut.

"Oh, I appreciate that, but—" Shane's voice echoed against the flimsy walls.

"Well, I just want to return the favor, even if it's paid back in a little different way. You know, this offer does expire. A girl can only be turned down so many times before she stops offering."

The woman spun his chair around and wedged her stiletto between his legs. I craned my neck to see what the hell this woman was going to do to my man.

Shane had let out a nervous chuckle before he answered. "Well, Crystal, you are a *very* beautiful woman, and like I've said before, if I was ever interested in your *type* of service, you'd definitely be the first woman I'd call. But right now I'm pretty satisfied in that department of my life, and truthfully, I don't think my girl would like this very much." Shane volleyed his hands back and forth. "But, hey, just knowing you're okay is enough for me. No disrespect, I've just *never* been into … *this*." He slipped his hand down between his legs and removed her foot.

My heart thrashed in my chest before crashing incessantly against my bones. My ears filled with a slight buzz. All those shitty feelings of unworthiness I'd buried deep began to boil to the surface of my skin. I was burning, aching for the possibility that Shane would see me as something more than a fucking whore. But his words to Crystal were clear—he could never be with someone who sold her body to other men. The voice in my head took the opportunity to twist and stab his words into my already battered heart.

You will never be anything more to him than a dirty whore. Just turn around and leave.

Damaged goods.

I pushed off the wall, hurried back to the washers, and yanked out all of my damp clothes. That was it; I would listen to the advice from the voice in my head. Shane had rejected me. Unknowingly or not, even if his words were aimed at Crystal, he'd basically told me that he could never be with me. She and I were prostitutes, whores, women who laid down with men for money. Adrenaline coursed through my veins, feeding the urgency to leave. I couldn't breathe anymore. I stuffed my laundry sack with my clothes and swung it over my shoulder before I hightailed it outta there. Questions poured through my mind, and my inner voice was happy to answer.

What the hell was Crystal doing there anyway?

Well, Ro, you're a whore. You know what she was doing!

I never saw her come in. When did she come in?

She came in expecting to fuck Shane, and he turned her down, just like he'll turn you down. Told you to fucking cut him loose.

My back ached, barking at the pain of carrying what felt like a body flung over my shoulder. I didn't stop until I was at my piece-of-shit '92 Le Baron. I tossed the laundry sack into my trunk, squeezed in past the door, and drove home. Broken by the evidence that he'd never accept what I was, my head was filled

with the words he'd spoken. *If I was interested in your type of service …
I'm pretty satisfied in that department.*

I wasn't supposed to let him in. I should have never come; I
didn't need to hear him say he had someone. Words began to
saturate my mind, the same voice that always tried to bury me in
my nightmares and attempted to lock me in the darkened closet
where I'd always thrown the most vulnerable part of myself.

*Come on, Rose, you were the one all ready to leave him. Keep him wanting
you, remember? You should have known he wouldn't want your kind even
before you came upon his conversation with that whore. Pull your shit together;
be grateful it wasn't more than a flirty moment in a crappy laundromat. Cut
your losses.*

Major mental fucking note … *avoid laundromats and dark alleys.*

fifteen

ENERGY WAS SWIRLING rapidly through my body. So many thoughts fired off in my head, I had to keep myself busy. I pulled my clothes out of the laundry sack and searched for enough hangers to hang up the couple of outfits I planned on wearing to work for the next couple of nights. Black lacy top, tight shimmering black skirt, and my black smooth bra, all hung to dry. I pulled out the thin-strapped black see-through camisole, and instantly my mind swirled to Shane's face when he saw it. Damp to the touch, warm from being nestled between my cotton V-neck tops, I wrapped it around my hands and pushed it to my nose. Inhaling, I wanted to go back and tell him I was worth anything he'd be willing to accept. The woman in me wanted to prove I was worth everything I had to offer, and yet the little girl in me was scared he'd reject me because of choices I was forced to make. Food or starve, a warm bed to sleep in or the cold, dark sidewalks hugged by wrinkled asphalt. Selling my body for money wasn't a choice; it was survival.

I was pulling on my black stretch skirt when Sybil came

busting into our apartment. Her face flushed crimson, matching her bristle-red hair, as she scurried across to the kitchen sink and thrust her hands into the stream of water. Her breathing was jagged with huffs and growls. Her clothes were pulled and tattered, the neckline of her shirt stretched and ripped.

"You scared the shit out of me. Where have you been? What the fu—are you okay?" I asked as my problems vanished at the sight of her.

Sybil looked like she had been run over by a bus. Her normally clear tawny eyes were dark and bloodshot. I could see dark arcs under her eyes. Full moons of deep purple and black bruises circled both of her eye sockets.

"Ro, I just spent the last twenty-four hours fighting for my life. I don't wanna get into it with you right now, okay?" she blasted as she rubbed her hands under the clear water streaming from the faucet.

I watched as the water drained a light Kool-Aid red. "Is that blood? What the fuck is going on?"

I pushed the handle on the kitchen sink and clutched her by her biceps. Sybil and I were prostitutes without a pimp— renegades, that's what they call us. But being renegades, we had to watch our backs constantly. She whimpered and winced at my grip.

Seeing Sybil fucked up stirred within me the same fear and helplessness that had pummeled me every time my mom flew off the handle and beat me. Feelings I'd buried and ran away from my whole life.

"It's nothin', Ro, I took care of it." She pulled her arms out of my grip and spun to her bed, taking off her tattered shirt before she tossed it to the floor.

"Holy shit. Sybil, who the fuck did this to you?" I asked as I carefully dragged my hands down her bony spine and across her hip.

Clusters of fist-sized red-and-purple-splotched bruises coated her back. Lengthy scratches, too many to count, in the shape of fingernails webbed around her ribcage on either side of her backbone, draining down behind the waistband of her skirt. Sybil flinched as I pulled down her skirt and panties, exposing just the top of her ass. The scratches continued, dragged down across a handful of more bruises.

"I can't tell you, Ro. Please don't make me say," she mumbled in a shaky voice. Frozen from the pain or embarrassment, Sybil pulled her skirt and panties back up over her ass before she wrapped her hands across her bruised and broken body.

I grabbed one of the damp V-neck T-shirts from my bed and gently pulled it over her. When she held up her hands, I saw she had just as many bruises across her chest and stomach. I watched her face as she helped me pull the shirt down. Grimacing at the pain, her puffy eyes were almost swollen shut now and filled with tears. Her lips, cracked and dry, bruised and inflamed, quivered as she tried to hold back her cry.

She knew I was going to find out who did this to her. It was a matter of time before I'd figure out what miserable fuck had beaten the shit out of her. Beyond all the bullshit, the stupid fight, the miscommunication, and all the other crap, seeing Sybil like this bled deep in my heart. There was no way I was going to let any miserable fuck get away with what they had done to her.

"Carl, right? It was that cocksucker Carl. He's been after you for months—"

"No," she whispered.

"Was it that asshole, Trey?"

Sybil shook her head. "No, it wasn't Trey either." She took a shaky breath, trying to collect what little energy she had left.

"Dax, right?"

Like a tire with a hole, her breath hissed as she began to deflate.

"It was! It was that piece-of-shit wannabe pimp who did this to you, wasn't it?"

Sybil's nostrils flared as her breathing increased and her body started to shake. "Ro, don't do anything. It's over," she whispered through chattering teeth.

"That motherfucking, snot-nosed bastard," I growled.

I was so pissed that if someone handed me a gun, I'd wedge the barrel between that motherfucker's shitty gold-capped teeth and pull the trigger. He was nothing more than a piece of shit taking up air and space in this world.

Sybil's body began to quake uncontrollably. "Please, Ro, just let it rest ... nothing can come of it."

"Nothing? Are you fucking kidding me, Sybil? This motherfucker's gonna pay."

"I-I-I can't stop shaking," she whimpered before her body jerked.

Her muscles surged rock hard as she lurched forward and uncontrollably yakked all over the floor. I ran to the dish drainer and grabbed a huge plastic bowl. Everything she had in her stomach had come up.

"Shhhh, settle down. I'm sorry, you're safe now. Don't worry," I whispered as I wrapped the thin throw blanket from the end of my bed around her. "Sit down here. Come on now."

I pulled the phone from my purse and started dialing the only person I knew who could help her.

"Who are y-y-you c-c-c-calling?" Sybil pushed between dry heaving.

"Briggs."

"Stop, don't call him. I'll be okay."

"This isn't normal, Sybil. You need to be seen, and I'm not taking no for an answer."

"I'll be fine. I just want to lie down." She pulled the blanket tight over her chest.

"Sybil, you are not dying on my bed."

"Ro, I don't have the money to pay him. Please, I just need to lie down and close my eyes."

What am I supposed to do? She looks like fucking hell. I can't let her stay like this.

"Don't worry about the money," I said as the phone was ringing against my ear.

"Aye, Rosie, this betta be an emergency," Briggs barked fast, his Irish accent just thick enough to tell you he wasn't born in America.

"Yeah, it's Sybil. She's pretty fucked up."

"Wha' happen?"

I stood silent for an uncomfortable moment.

"Rose? Wha' happen?"

"She won't tell me, but she's all beaten, throwing up, shaking, and shit."

"How long she been down like that?"

"She'd been home about a half hour when she just started yakking and shaking."

"Bleedin'? Is she been t'rowin' up blood?"

"Aww, fuck, Briggs, I can't do this shit." I leaned over and looked in the bowl. My stomach swirled, and the back of my throat watered. "No blood." I gagged.

"Sounds like she'd be goin' into shock. You have yourself a blanket? Just wrap her up. I'm on m' way."

"Yeah, I wrapped her all up. Thanks, Briggs," I whispered.

"Rosie?"

"Yeah?"

"Leave the front door unlocked this time."

"I will," I answered as the line went dead.

Kean "Key" Briggs was one big-ass twisted motherfucker. He was a six-foot-tall black man from Ireland with arms as thick as my waist, covered in tribal tats and tinted ink that told stories more horrific than anyone could ever imagine. Painful chapters he must have burned into the secret corners of his mind after two tours in Iraq. His body had become the visual diary of his life as a war veteran.

Briggs had driven an ambulance in the Tenderloin for over five years before he retired and started making house calls for us hos. He found a need and made hand-over-fist money privatizing his services. Just seven calls a week from suffering prostitutes beaten at the hands of their pimps or clients, and cha-ching, he was rolling in more money than he'd ever made in a month of driving an ambulance. I knew I was going to pay through the nose for his services, but I had to. Hospitals were out of the question, and I didn't think clinics had the capacity to handle this situation. I didn't know who else to call.

I looked over at Sybil; her uncontrollable shakes had turned into barely noticeable shivers. Her jaw was still chattering. Maybe some tea would warm her up. I brushed my fingers across her forehead before I pressed my hand to her cheek.

She looked up at me with a tattered expression and whispered, "Ro, you gotta promise me something."

"Anything."

"Promise me you'll get out. Promise me."

"Shhhh, come on, Sybil, don't worry about me."

"Say it. Say, *I promise I'll get out.* Say it!" She clutched my wrist, trying to pull me closer.

I cleared the strands of hair that clung to her dampened face.

"This isn't the life you want, Ro. Please, promise me you'll get out."

"I'll promise, but only if you promise to come with me."

A forced smile crept across her face as she nodded at me, and for a single moment, I thought maybe she didn't really need Briggs. Maybe all she needed was a moment to relax and close her eyes, like she'd said.

I second-guessed my call to Briggs when the door flew open and relief melted down my spine—finally someone other than me would see her—but it was short-lived. The moment of peace turned into instant terror. Dax, the devil himself, stood before me. That fucking piece of shit lunged, pushing through me to get to Sybil. My feet left the floor as my body flew, weightless as a feather swirling through the thick air, before the crown of my head met the edge of the small rickety table. The rest of my body followed, splintering the table into pieces. The room filled with his scary growls, his words sharp with edges that pierced my ears.

"Get the fuck up! I own your cunt now! There ain't no days off for my bitches."

My vision blurry, I focused on the space where Sybil was being swallowed by Dax. His fist floated high above before the hammering hollow thud of bone against her delicate, damaged body.

"Pleeeeassseeee … no, no, no, hel … paaahhhh." Sybil's voice was hoarse, filled with raspy cries for help, tainted by the mixture of Dax's evil demands.

"I'll beat your shit all fucking day, you crazy bitch. Get your skanky … pussy … up … out … of … this … bed."

Each word sandwiched between the echoing sounds of him punching her. I pulled my hands up over my head as my mind twisted and plummeted into the putrid memories of my childhood, terrifying moments filled with the woman who was supposed to love me more than any liquid confidence she and my father poured down their throats.

MY BEDROOM DOOR creaks open before it slams shut. I know it's my mom by the nasty aroma of stale whiskey that saturates the air. Dad punished her

tonight for mixing his mashed potatoes with cream of corn at dinner. God, I never know what's gonna set him off … my father uses any reason to beat my mother. He tears down her self-esteem, keeps her prisoner to his rage, and now she's standing over me.

I sense the silence before the storm, the split second when God may hear my prayers … I let out a short breath, relax just enough to invite hope, then Mom's hand slaps across my cheek. She grabs bundles of my hair at the nape of my neck and pulls my head back.

"Look at me, you piece of shit! You think lying there, acting like you're asleep, is going to erase the fact that you're the reason he hits me? Huh? Do you hear me? You spoiled little brat … see what you make him do? You push us enough and make us drink … you're the reason. It's all your fault, Rosalie!"

"Please, Mom, please, I'm sorry."

I cry as she continues to yell in my face. Her eyes are so dark, empty, as if some evil spirit possesses her soul. Her expression is missing remorse. The alcohol she drinks feeds the monster she's become while my father gives her the perfect excuse to be brutal.

"Too late, the damage's done! One fucking mistake. A constant goddamn reminder of my biggest mistake," she slurs through her rage and blood-tainted tears.

The back of her hand meets my cheek, my head swings back, and pain radiates through my jaw. The blood from biting my tongue rolls down the back of my throat in iron-tinged waves. Her fist comes down against my cheek over and over again. I feel the cracking of my cheekbone, the gush of blood as it swells into my eye socket. My head falls against the pillow. I pull my hands over my face as Mom's breathy criticisms keep tumbling from her mouth.

"I'm sorry, Mom, s-sssooorryyyy," I cry across my palms.

She's relentless and doesn't stop hitting me until she's physically worn out.

"You are pathetic! Do you hear me … you're an ugly, pathetic girl."

My mother's wicked voice bled and morphed into deep, short huffs and grunts. Words she had sharpened and riddled with rage pulled me from the nightmare of when I was sixteen, the very last time my mother had ever hit me. I forced myself to open my eyes, stinging with pain from the chill of the room; suddenly I recognized what the hell was really happening.

Briggs was towering over someone's body. His fist was covered in blood, muscles rock hard, shirt ripped, ink covered in splashes and sprays of blood. His body seemed to have grown since the last time I saw him. I noticed the spastic jolts of Briggs's victim. Dax's arms and legs jerked as Briggs's enormous fist connected over and over again with his face. Blood was everywhere, almost as if Briggs was tearing through Dax's flesh.

"W'at you gotta say now muthafucker? 'uh? Can't answer me? You just a wee bit fuckin' tough when you'd want to sully innocent women," he yelled, his Irish accent thicker as he continued to punch Dax.

I hoisted myself up. Sybil's body was spread across the bed. She wasn't moving—I couldn't tell if she was breathing or even alive. Struggling to find my voice, I knew if I didn't get Briggs to stop, he'd kill Dax.

"Briggs … Briggs … Key … Kean!" I bellowed, finally unhinging him from the aggressive trance he was under.

It was as if he was in a brutal battle, killing his enemy before the fucker attempted to take him out. I knew war had scarred Kean Briggs. The inked stories buried just flesh deep, attempting to cast out his demons, told me everything … I'd just never seen how cruelly war had scarred his mind.

Key's arm froze in the air above his head. Blood saturated his once-milk-chocolate-colored fist, his short black hair damp with sweat. When he looked at me, I saw how toxic he was. His eyes were hollow and his expression filled with so much hate. It was as if he was someone I didn't know. Someone who scared the living shit out of me. I lost my balance and stumbled as I attempted to stand up. Instantly Briggs's demeanor changed, as if a switch had clicked in his head and the man I knew finally showed up. He let go of Dax's lifeless body.

"Rosie," he breathed as he shuffled over to me.

"No, Key, Sybil … Sybil," I huffed as I pointed at her motionless and sprawled across the bed.

I struggled to collect myself while Briggs rushed to her bedside. I watched as he dropped the side of his face against her lips. His large, thick, bloody fingers caught her wrist, feeling for a pulse. His face melted into a fearless expression as urgency flooded his eyes.

"Call 9-1-1. Now!" he spat.

I froze.

His mouth crashed against her blue lips as he initiated CPR. Rhythmic breaths forced down Sybil's throat, her lungs filling enough to make her chest expand before Briggs pulled her onto the floor, placed his large fist just between her breasts, and began compressions in the attempt to jumpstart her heart. Sybil's body was still unresponsive, except for the rebound of his patterned thrusts. I began to pray to the same god who had never answered my prayers before.

"Please, God, oh … please, God, please, God, please save Sybil. She's the only person I have. She can't die. Please don't let her die!" I forced myself to stand, willed myself to be strong for my best friend. I stumbled, and the moment swirled in my head. I pushed my hands up through my hair, holding it back off my face.

"Rose, 9-1-1!" Briggs demanded.

Clarity finally found its strong grip on me, and I reached for my purse.

"Call from you' landline."

I snatched my home phone from the counter and dialed. One ring, then they picked it up.

"Dispatcher 233. 9-1-1, what's your emergency?"

I took a deep breath, and without any thought of who Sybil

and I were or what we did to put food on the table, words began to tumble from my mouth.

"My roommate, she's been hurt," I barked into the phone.

"All right, ma'am. Is she breathing?"

"I don't know." I pulled the phone from my ear. "Briggs, is she breathing?"

"No, tell them I'm doing CPR. Have her pulse back to forty, but still unconscious and not breathing," Briggs said in a stern, controlled voice.

"No, Briggs is doing CPR. She has a forty pulse. She's unconscious. Please just get someone here as fast as you can, please. Oh God, please."

"An ambulance has been dispatched and is en route," the 9-1-1 operator assured me.

"An ambulance is on the way," I parroted.

"Rose, we're going to need two transports," Briggs said between breaths he forced into Sybil's lungs. His eyes darted to Dax, who was in an unconscious, bloody heap.

"We need two ambulances."

"Two?" the 9-1-1 operator questioned

"For the piece of shit who attacked her."

"She was attacked?"

I didn't answer her question. My attention was still on Sybil and Briggs.

"Rose, is that your name?"

"Yes."

"Tell me, was your friend attacked?"

"Yeah, by a pimp named Dax. He beat her unconscious," I answered. I didn't care if he bled out and we had one less wannabe pimp in this world, but the rational part of me knew if Dax died, then Briggs would be fucked.

"Ma'am …? Ma'am …? Rose, your roommate's attacker is there?"

"Yes."

"But he's unconscious?"

"Yes. Yes, he is still here. My friend came in and knocked him the fuck out."

"Okay, I've alerted the authorities and dispatched another ambulance."

I heard a siren build from a faint whine to an ear-piercing holler. I could see the lights reflect in the old, rippled glass of my window. They must have parked in front of my building.

"Rose ... downstairs ... now!" Briggs demanded between giving Sybil mouth-to-mouth.

Within seconds, two massive paramedics dressed in dark-blue uniforms came through the open door. One of the medics was carrying a huge plastic tackle box. The other held a clipboard and a big square canvas bag with the strap pulled across his chest. They saw Sybil and Dax, and within seconds, the one with the clipboard was on his two-way radio. My conversation with the 9-1-1 operator became an afterthought as I watched one of the medics take over for Briggs.

Medical terms were spat as the urgency in their conversations flew from their mouths. I could tell they were words weighted with life-and-death consequences, and I felt helpless in not knowing what any of it meant. I was so fucking scared as I watched them work on Sybil.

"Key," I huffed under my breath, hoping it was just loud enough that he'd hear me.

He looked over at me, his eyes unbearably tragic as he shook his head.

"No? What? No, what? What, Kean, what are you saying?" I shouted. My words scraped my lungs, and every pain I had became a ghostly ache as I rushed toward Sybil.

Briggs stopped me, held me back. His muscles were rock hard as he wrapped me in his arms. "Sssshhhh, com' on, Rosie. It doesn't look good. Let them do wat tey need to do."

My face buried in his chest, I screamed as loud as I could. I screamed for every time my mother had hit me, screamed for the monster who had taken my innocence, screamed because my parents hadn't believed me. I screamed for all the times I'd fucked someone for money. I screamed for the only person who cared about me. I screamed for my voiceless friend Sybil.

"Briggs? You Kean Briggs?" Someone's voice interrupted my breakdown.

"Aye."

"I'd like to ask you a couple of questions."

"Rosie? Listen, sweet'art, I need you to settle down," he said as he pulled me away from his chest.

I didn't want to feel the air. I didn't want to breathe. I just wanted to go numb.

"Rosie, you need to go wit' Sybil. You understan'? Sybil needs you." His voice was stern, thick with his accent and yet soft enough to keep me focused. His eyes narrowed, like he was telling me that I shouldn't be here anymore tonight.

I pulled away in time to see them rolling Sybil out of our apartment on a gurney. I glanced over at another pair of paramedics working on Dax before I nodded at Briggs. He grabbed my sweater off my bed, snatched my purse off the table, and in a gentle sway, he ushered me out of my apartment.

"Go be. I'll lock up. Meet you in the hospital in a wee bit."

In a fog of faded thoughts, clouded ideas floating anywhere but where I was supposed to be, I heard the ambulance door shut behind me and one of the paramedics asking me what I knew about Sybil's family and next of kin. Something she'd hid since the day she came to live with me, and sadly enough, in the two years we'd been roommates, I didn't know any more about her family than I did the day we moved in together. Well, except for the fact that she had an older sister.

sixteen

THE HEART MONITOR held at a steady tempo echoing some form of life, while the oxygen that kept Sybil alive hissed a sickening rhythm that was scorched into my mind. Every once in a while, the lilt of measuring her blood pressure broke the monotony.

Pssshhhh. Click. Pssshhhh. Click.

Beep … beep … beep … beep …

Grrrrrrr … tick … tick … whoosh.

It was like a symphony of unbearable noise that wore raw against my mind. Like a bad song, it tangled itself into my thoughts and became the only sound I craved. Any deviation, pace change, or missed beat, and my heart would fall into my stomach.

Motionless, Sybil lay there in a medically induced coma. The doctors had told me that her brain had swelled and they had to keep her sedated to avoid brain damage. I'd asked the nurses a couple of times if they'd gotten a hold of her parents or her sister. They would just shake their heads and frown. I expected Sybil's family to show up at any minute, and inevitably I would be asked to leave, but no one ever did. Until it happened, I wasn't going to leave her side.

The nurses had explained that the more I talked to her, held her hand, and spent time with her, the better results they have with recovery. So, I sat next to her hospital bed and watched her life on pause ... unable to press Play, listen to her voice, see her smile, or hear her laugh over stupid shit we saw.

"Sybil, it's me, Rose. I'm right here, sweets. I'm not going anywhere."

I looked at her expressionless face—no emotion, nothing. Her flesh was marked with the pain and bruises of our lifestyle. I would be a fool if I didn't realize that it could have easily been me in that bed, fighting for my life. Quite frankly, that scared the living hell out of me.

"They tell me the more I talk to you, the better chance you'll sit up and argue with me." I held her hand. Soft and warm enough, there was no tension, no response. "Come on, Sybil, you can't leave me. You fight, you fucking fight to get better."

I hoped that Sybil, unable to answer me, could sense I was there, that someone was there who cared.

I leaned down next to her ear, tears dampening my cheeks, "Come on, Sybil, we had a deal. You and me, we're getting out together. Don't leave me here alone. Just give me a squeeze with your hand."

Nothing.

So help me God, tonight wasn't going to be spent on the street or in the backseats of filthy cars in darkened, seedy alleys. It was going to be a solitary night of praying for Sybil. I'd never claimed to be a religious person. Praying had never seemed to help me in my life. God never took the time to answer my prayers, but for Sybil, for her sake, maybe he'd see that I wasn't the one playing the hand. Maybe as the holder of all cards in this game, he'd throw something down that would give her something to fight for. I wasn't beyond hoping or praying that she'd come back to our apartment, fully recovered. If God was willing ... even better for Sybil.

Two nights. Three whole fucking days and two nights and not one of Sybil's family members had even cared enough to show up. It was building to a point where I knew I was gonna lose my shit on someone. I was exhausted, I hadn't slept much, hadn't showered, and I hadn't left the hospital except to bail Briggs out of jail.

Trust me, I felt like a total piece of shit about Briggs. If I had never called, he wouldn't have come over and beat Dax within inches of his life. Briggs had been charged with assault and spent the night in jail. His bail was set at five thousand dollars. Needless to say, I got a cashier's check. Briggs kept reassuring me that he would do it over and over again. He didn't blame me and was actually glad I'd called him and he showed up when he did. Sure, Key Briggs made his money off the violence of the streets, but he also had a heart and was more than happy to get at least one douchebag pimp off the streets for now.

Dax, the wannabe pimp, was still in the hospital with a concussion, broken bones, and a ruptured spleen. He was under twenty-four-hour police watch. I had been told that the minute he woke up from surgery and was able to be moved, he'd be held in jail without bail until his court date and charged with attempted murder.

There was no change in Sybil's condition. I had told her so many stories, my voice was hoarse. Nurses hurried around, lights still shone brightly, and unnatural sounds still jumped and beeped her life's story. I'd been sitting with her for too long as I waited for someone to come and claim her, be her next of kin, and nobody ever showed. It was getting difficult. I needed to go back to the apartment and shower and maybe sleep in my own bed.

Depressing moments were filled with different types of prayers in hopes that one of them would bypass the gatekeepers of God's ears. All I asked for, all I wanted was the swelling in her brain to go down because we had made a promise to one another.

I stood up to stretch and felt my phone vibrate in my pocket. Briggs had texted me. His texts were the only ones I was reading. He was the only one who knew what had happened to Sybil. Even all the texts I had received from Shane were left unread. There was no way to explain what had happened to my roommate. I couldn't, so I didn't. As bad as I wanted Shane to be here with me, Sybil needed me more right now.

Briggs was down in the parking lot, waiting to take me to get something to eat. He had to steer clear of that piece of shit, Dax, as part of his bail conditions. He couldn't come within five hundred feet of him, and since Dax was still in the hospital, that kept Key from seeing Sybil.

I guessed Briggs knew I ached to have a conversation about Sybil that wasn't with nurses, and I knew I needed to stop the scenarios that kept playing over and over in my head. Besides, I just couldn't eat hospital food again and spend another night in that fucking chair. I collected my sweater and decided to tell the nurse that I was going to head home tonight and I'd be back first thing in the morning. I always talked myself into believing that guilt was a bullshit emotion, and yet deciding to walk out of my best friend's hospital room filled me with immense guilt.

I texted back that I was on my way before I pushed the door open. Life seemed to be playing out just fine without Sybil in it. I blinked, adjusting to the change in lighting, and I saw a nurse point me out to a tall, thin woman dressed in a navy-blue pantsuit and a white frilly shirt. The woman had a look of horror on her face as she came at me in a quick stride that broke into a jog. One of Sybil's ICU nurses followed her.

"You Rose? I'm Mandy's sister," the woman snapped at me.

"Mandy?" I questioned.

"Yes, my sister, Mandy Cooke!"

"I'm sorry, I don't know anyone by that name. You—"

"Sybil St. James. She was Mandy Cooke until she turned eighteen and legally changed her name," she said in a bitchy tone.

Her face had the same delicate features as Sybil but more refined, like she hadn't lived the same hard life as her sister. With the exception of her wavy blond hair, she was almost a spitting image of her sister. Her hair, dirty enough to call it dark blond, had been pulled back away from her face.

"Well, I'm Sybil's sister, Martie," the woman said hurriedly as she tapped the palm of her hand against her chest just above her cleavage.

I was relieved that Sybil's older sister was finally here. The weight of leaving her tonight lifted off my shoulders. Sybil wouldn't be left alone.

"I've been in New York on business for the last month. I got here as soon as I heard. Sadly, I've been expecting this call for half of our lives."

I could feel the spite in her words.

"Your sister is pretty bad off." My voice was unintentionally louder than normal.

"Rose, my sister has been bad off her entire life," Martie answered defensively.

"Well, what happened to her wasn't her fault. We've all been dealt different cards in life."

"Please, Rose, let's just call a spade a spade with this entire situation; my sister has put herself in this position. The doctors and nurses haven't painted a good picture about her recovery, if she does at all, so before I go in and see her, I need to know what she owes you?"

"What?" I spat in disbelief of the words spewing from this woman's lips.

"When she crashed my party several weeks ago, dressed like—" She sized me up before she continued. "Well, anyway, she

141

mentioned that she lives with you and that you have helped her. I need to know how much it will take to make *this* go away?" she said as she swirled her hands toward me.

"Your sister is in there fighting for her life and all you're worried about is money? What the fuck's wrong with you?" I roared, letting every last drop of breath flow from my lungs.

"Oh, come on, it's all about the next fix, the next high with *your types*."

"What do you mean *your types*?" I snapped. I was tired, done, and ready to unload on this poor excuse of a sister.

"I knew it was a matter of time before she'd end up in the hospital again, overdosing or beaten and raped, because of the life she's chosen."

"You have no idea what that girl's been through. Do you hear me?" I pushed my face up into hers. Standing nose to nose, I was ready to throw this bitch down.

"Ladies, this is a hospital. Please keep your voices down." The nurse pushed between us and pulled me back from Martie.

"Sybil is a drug addict and a whore, and she'll say anything to get her next fix. So don't stand in front of me and tell me just because you've split rent for a room and sold your body in the bowels of San Francisco with my sister for a couple of years, you know her better than me."

I took a deep breath, ready to blast her for being such a heartless bitch, when her body language changed. She looked past me like I had no place in the world.

"Shane," she cried as she looked over my shoulder.

I turned around and saw him standing behind me. The look on his face was stamped with every filthy word she'd said.

"Shane, oh, babe, I am so glad you are here," Martie whimpered as she fell into his arms.

"Rose, what are you doing here?" he asked.

"Shane? You know her?" Martie demanded as she pulled away

from him. Her eyes darted between us.

Bewildered, his hazel eyes locked on me, and he ignored her question.

"Shane!" Martie spat, an annoyed expression sweeping across her face.

At that point, the flood of humiliation drowned me. My heart was viciously plucked from my chest and torn into jagged pieces, completely lost to the painful moments I wish I'd never felt. My breath was robbed by betrayal. There was no mistake; he was involved with her.

He was someone else's everything.

I shattered our connection, dropping my eyes from his as I forced the huge lump down my throat.

"I'm glad Sybil has family here. I gotta go," I choked out as a mumble. Keeping my eyes downward, I hurried past Shane and Martie.

"What the hell is going on? How do you know that hooker?" I heard Martie question Shane.

"I just do, Martha! Rose? Come on, Rose, wait!"

"I called you, remember? You came to be with me, not that whore!" Martie hollered.

"Please, Miss Cooke, this is a hospital," another voice reprimand her for yelling.

"I'm just fine. I want to see my sister … now!" she demanded.

I never looked back. The anxiety of knowing that the man who wanted to take me to lunch and see what unfolded between us was dating my best friend's sister was too much. I hurried down the corridor, past the waiting area, into an alcove that held a couple of elevators crowded and pressed into adjacent walls. My muscles were burning, matching the sting in my eyes and the ache in my heart.

I clicked the call button over and over again.

Tap … Tap … Tap …

I couldn't stop perspiration from flooding my skin as it became the unbearable reminder that broken girls will never get away without scars. It's the emotional ones that run the deepest and create total ruin.

I could hear the motor winding, delivering the elevator to the fifth floor. I needed to get the fuck out of there. I could hear Martie still arguing with the nurse as she kept yelling for Shane. The elevator doors sprang open, and I hurried in, my body ready to flush out the pain of walking away. I pushed the button with the capital L before I repeatedly pushed the button that closed the elevator doors.

"Please, please, please close. Come on, you bastard, please close," I breathed. My heart pounded the same rhythm of my pleas; my finger must have clicked it over a hundred fifty times.

Seconds later, as if the elevator doors knew I wasn't supposed to be there any longer, they began to roll closed. I peered through the shrinking opening, the sliver of reprieve I craved before I met Briggs downstairs. Trying to collect myself, I looked straight ahead and watched as Shane showed up just in time to disappear behind the closing elevator doors, his face colorless, drawn, and filled with regret.

I didn't need his pity. I really didn't need the heartbreak of being left waiting for someone to come along and whisk me away from my menial existence as a prostitute. Been there, done that … I knew how that turns out.

Without stopping, the elevator dropped five floors, letting out a dull, tired chime as it passed each level until it landed with a soft thud at the lobby. I waited, pushing on the doors with my fingertips, hoping that it somehow could tell I just wanted to get out. I waited impatiently for them to separate and give me the freedom to hurry out of the hospital.

I slipped my sweater over my shoulders as I hustled across the lobby and over to the entry of the hospital. I made it to the front

144

doors before I heard Shane holler. I turned back and saw him jogging toward me from the stairs. I pushed on the automatic doors, trying to get them to open faster.

"Rose! Please! Wait!" Shane grabbed my upper arm and tugged me back around. His expression was filled with remorse, drizzled with guilt.

"Why?" I asked, pulling my arm out of his grip.

"Because."

"Because why?"

"Come on, Rose, stop. Let me say something."

"No."

"I like you."

"You like me? Are you kidding? This isn't preschool, Shane. You can't give me a handful of Blow Pops and think it will fix this. You don't even know who the fuck I am."

"Yes, I do."

"No, you really don't."

"Yeah, I fucking do."

"Just go back to your girlfriend, Shane."

"She's not my—"

"I have nothing to offer you. Do you hear me? Martie was right—I'm nothing more than a two-bit whore."

"Rose," he breathed, pushing closer to me. His aroma filled me as his hands tickled down the backs of my arms, collecting at my elbows.

"Shane. Please. Don't." I pushed him away.

"Do we have a wee problem 'ere?" Briggs asked as he appeared from the direction of the parking lot. His arms twitched under his full sleeves of ink.

"No, buddy, no problem here," Shane spat at Briggs as his eyes never left mine.

"Doesn't look like the wee lady feels the same way as you." Briggs's voice was demanding and protective. "Rosie gir', you okay?"

Shane's eyes grew as he looked at Briggs. I saw the wheels turning in Shane's head. He didn't have to say a word—it was written all over his face. He thought Key was my pimp.

"Go back to her, Shane. It's where you belong."

I turned to Briggs. He was ready to pounce if Shane was going to try to get violent.

"Rose ..." Shane whispered.

"Will you please take me home, Key?" I asked.

He nodded before he pulled me into his chest and I was swallowed in his embrace.

I looked back at Shane once, as Briggs put me into his black Lexus SUV. I noticed that Shane was still standing there, watching me. My heart shattered for him—yeah, even though I wanted to be the one who broke his heart before he broke mine.

seventeen

WE RODE BACK to my apartment in silence. Briggs never wasted words on small talk, especially when his clients were hos who reminded him time was money. Besides, I was exhausted and didn't really want to talk. Sounds pushed past us as life continued outside on the streets of the city. The whines of breathless engines, the growls of cars trying to jockey for a spot, the impatient honking their horns were the only conversations filling the thick barren air between us. I knew Briggs was curious about Shane and that he wanted to hear about Sybil's status, but he also knew better than to ask me right now. *Give me a ride home and then we'll see.*

Briggs pulled up to the front of my building. Dark, dingy steps led to a cracked wooden black door with numbers loosely nailed to the thick part. Not a place where you'd find doormen pulling open car doors. I sat, waiting for the awkward moment to pass and hoping that he'd ask me if I wanted to stay with him for a couple days. I had no idea where he lived, if his apartment, house, or studio even had enough space for me, but I didn't want to stay where that prick Dax's blood soaked the hardwood floors. I wasn't ready to see the broken table that was most likely piled up right where it had been before we were whisked away. And I sure in the hell didn't want to face the nosey manager who made it his business to know every little thing that occurred behind the closed doors of our complex.

"You okay, Rosie gir'?" Briggs asked as he turned off the engine.

"Yeah, sure." *What the hell was I going to say, no?*

"That wasn't too convincin'. You wanna talk 'bout it?"

"I don't think so. I'm pretty exhausted. I just want to sleep for, like, three days. But I can't. I gotta get back to work. Rent's not going to pay itself, and I owe you for ... Sybil."

"What? Don't you disrespect me. I'm not goin' to take your money. You go in there, get some rest. You're gonna be just fine."

Tears welled in my eyes before plummeting down my cheeks.

"Oh, come on, Rosie gir'. Now there's no need to cry." He slid the palm of his hand down across my head, catching the back of my neck. The pressure in his fingertips felt good as he rotated and massaged the muscles on either side of my spine. I felt the stress drain from my neck and clear down through my shoulders.

"I'm just exhausted. That's all."

"You need to take care of you'self now, Rosie gir'. You hear me?"

I nodded.

"How 'bout I walk you up? Come on now," Briggs said as his fingers left my neck and he pushed open the driver's door of his SUV.

"Naw, you don't have to, Key. I'll be fine." I pulled off my seat belt. "Besides, you'll get towed if you leave your car here unattended. I'll text you once I'm in my apartment."

"I don't like this one bit. You promise?" he asked as he tucked his thick finger under my chin and made me look up at him.

"I pinkie promise you," I answered, holding out my pinkie finger to him.

Briggs gave me a confused look until I grabbed his hand and twisted my pinkie around his.

"This is a pinkie promise."

"Fin'," he huffed before leaning over and kissing my forehead. "Take care, Rosie gir'. If you need anyt'ing, you call me. Oh, and here." He handed me a wad of money.

"What's this for?"

"My bail. You ain't payin' me way."

"Briggs!"

"No, Rosie, I won't have it."

"Fine," I answered.

There was no use in arguing—he was just as stubborn as I was. I smiled, just enough so he knew I appreciated him, before I slipped out and pushed the car door closed.

He watched me open the building door, and I noticed he was still sitting there after I looked back right before the door shut behind me. I knew he'd sit there until I texted him. That was just how Briggs was. The eyes that kept me safe. Kean Briggs seemed to have my back even when I didn't know about it.

Broken by his past, just like me, we'd connected instantly the first time we met. It didn't matter who we were. Everyone, at one point or another, has been broken, and you could either sweep up the pieces and throw them away, or find some crazy glue. But through our unspoken words—his, the injustice of war, and mine, the hidden marks of abusive parents—we found a safe haven in each other's company. Briggs had never gone into detail about the war or the appalling things he saw; maybe he didn't because he wanted to protect me. Maybe someday he'd open up about it. All I knew at that moment was I couldn't have been happier to have him in my corner.

The common entry of the building looked the same as my eyes

149

scanned the carpet leading to the stairway. I shuffled toward the elevator but then decided to climb the stairs. By the second flight, my heart began to thrash in my chest. I didn't want to go into my apartment alone. Not because I thought someone could be there, but because I didn't want to see all the blood and leftover mess from what had happened just three days ago. I pulled my key out from my purse, slipped it into my lock, and twisted.

It was the longest fifteen seconds in my entire life. Longer than the disgusting fucks I'd taken when I was seventeen years old and had just started selling my body. Longer than the Greyhound bus ride I'd had to take home from Sonora when I was fifteen because my parents got super wasted and kicked me out of our cabin for not eating all of my dinner. When I pushed my apartment door open, it was like cracking the doors to Hell and waiting for the devil himself to invite me in. I squeezed my eyes shut with an extended blink before I opened them and stepped inside my postage-stamp-sized studio apartment.

I peered around the room. No blood on the hardwood floors. The broken table next to my bed was gone and replaced by another table half its size. Both Sybil's and my beds were made and covered with new bedspreads. Any evidence that a crime had been committed here didn't exist. Even the tinge of blood I had smelled days ago was gone.

My phone chimed with a message from Briggs, pulling my attention from the room.

BRIGGS: HEY, U OK? U DIDN'T MESSAGE ME!

ME: Sorry. I'm fine. Hey, did you clean up my apartment?

BRIGGS: MAYBE.

ME: Come on …

BRIGGS: I HAVE MY WAYS. I DIDN'T WANT YOU TO COME HOME TO THAT MESS.

ME: Thanks Briggs. I really appreciate it. Thank you for making me feel safe.

BRIGGS: GLAD YOU'RE SAFE. SLEEP TIGHT, I'LL CALL IN THE MORNING.

ME: Thanks

Briggs wasn't one to message emoticons in texts, but he always used shouty caps. He claimed his phone was stuck on caps lock, but I thought it was the only way he believed he could be heard over the noise in his head. I looked around. Knowing he had come back to my apartment and taken care of everything made me feel like I wasn't so empty or alone in this world.

But even with Briggs making my apartment comfortable again, every time I closed my eyes, some nightmare would take over. If it wasn't Sybil's sister, Martie telling me how she loved Shane and how she'd never lose him to a whore like me, or visions of Dax beating the shit out of Sybil, it was the reality of my life before meeting Shane tainting my mind. It was my fucked up life that I so desperately hated but tightly clung to for refuge. Insecurity once again wrapped its gnarled hand around my thoughts and made sure my sleep wasn't peaceful.

"WELL, I LIKE *the way the mud feels squishing through my fingers," I say as I push my hands back into the cold, wet mud and pull out a glob I roll between my palms.*

"Well, then I'll be the salesman and you be the baking lady," Billy says, looking at the dry mud pies we left out the day before. "Because my momma doesn't want me dirty before church."

I think about the word church, something my parents really never talk about. I wonder if Billy likes going, because every time he talks about it, he scrunches up his freckly nose. I wonder if God lives in his church, but I never ask because I don't want Billy to know we aren't "God people" like he and his family are. It makes me feel lonely, and that makes my tummy ache.

I scoop up a clump of mud before I pat it into a round flat pancake. I guess I'm the only one making the mud pies today. I don't care. I like playing with Billy—he makes me feel special.

"Look at all these pies!" I sing, hoping to erase the God fear in my belly.

"They are so pretty, just like you, Rosalie," Billy answers before he leans over and kisses my cheek.

My tummy does somersaults.

It scares me.

I don't understand why he kisses me.

It confuses me.

I drop the mud pie and run all the way home.

My Mary Janes are caked with dirt. I flip them off at the front porch and hurry into the kitchen. I don't want any reason to make Mom mad, and I hope I catch her before she swallows the devil's poison.

"Mom, Mom, Billy and I were making mud pies and he kissed me right here!" I cry, pointing at my left cheek. Swirly feelings are rumbling around in my belly.

Worrying about boy germs making me sick, I look up at her and notice her blood-red eyes, then see the devil's poison behind her on the counter, half empty ... I'm too late.

"Dirty hands and a dirty face make for a dirty, filthy girl. Didn't I tell you to never play in the mud with that boy? I bet you let him kiss you! Look at your knees, just covered with filth. Little girls that play in the mud like pigs will be treated like pigs," she slurs.

My mom's monster eyes look through me. Her face crinkles up, and her breath smells like the whiskey more than her skin this time. She's tasting the devil's bottle again, already finished it halfway. Even at seven years old, I know what that means … I'm in for a beating. Nothin's gonna stop her. I look up at the old metal clock in the kitchen above the sink. Five o'clock at night—Dad will be home in a half hour, and if she's already beaten me, he won't find a reason to punish her for not keeping me in line.

She grabs my arm, holding it so tightly I feel the pinch of her nails through the ruffle of my sleeve. The devil's in her again. Spit's flying from her lips as she screams at me about ruining my dress.

I didn't mean to ruin my dress, my favorite pink floral dress. She doesn't care. Her hands are so tight, so sharp, as she pulls at the collar of my dress. The same dress I had worn to see my pee-stinky grandma in her hospital bed. I'd wanted Grandma to get up, and take me away from my life. But she didn't. She just brushed her fingertips over the pleat of my dress and smiled. It was the last smile I had gotten from her that meant anything to me. The smile I tucked in my heart, locked away as the only memory of her that held any value.

"You filthy, dirty little shit! Look what you did to your dress. It's ruined, ruined!" my mom screams, tearing me from the memory of my grandma.

Her hands bunch into fists over the rounded collar of my dress, and she yanks, ripping my dress apart. The back of my collar digs into my neck, my knees buckle, and I fall to the floor. The air brushes across my bare chest, and tears splatter across my skin. When I look down, my dress is ripped clear down the front. My favorite dress, the dress I visited my pee-smelly grandma in, her smile dress.

"Little girls that act like pigs will be treated like pigs." My mom takes a wooden spoon from the counter, slams it into the Crock-Pot of chili, and slops a heap of it into the cat's dish. "Go on; eat your dinner like the pig you are. Letting boys kiss you … did you let him reach up under your dress too?"

My voice is hiding, my heart hurts—I hate her. My toes ache from being cold, and my dress flaps around me.

"I hate you." I cry so loud it makes my belly shake and my lungs burn.

"You have no idea what hate is, you conniving little spoiled brat. But *don't worry, when you grow up and you're forced to marry a man you don't love and he makes you kiss him, you'll find out what it feels like to really hate someone. When your father comes home, he'll see what you did," she answers, pointing at the front of my dress. She catches the back of my head and throws me down onto my hands and knees. "Now eat your dinner before you get your punishment for bringing dirt into the kitchen."*

She holds my head down into the cat bowl until the tip of my nose is buried so deep I can't breathe. She makes me stay down on my hands and knees until the chili's all gone, even the old chunks of cat food at the bottom of the bowl. She swats the spoon across my back before I get up and run to my room.

"You better not come out! Do you hear me, Rosalie? If you don't want a whipping, you keep your whoring little ass in your room … Rosalie!"

Sweat pushed across my skin as I tossed and turned in my bed. A sea of raging fear and hate swelled through my body. The vivid memories of my childhood, buried deep, flooded every recess of my mind and turned my heart, causing it to thunder in my chest. Words I hated to hear, memories I kept buried until my mind was weak enough to let them out. I heard my name being called, at the moment between sleep and restlessly becoming conscious.

"Rose, promise me you'll get out."

My eyes flew open and I was frozen in my bed, not knowing where I was. Seconds passed, clearing the way for my mind to catch up, and I realized I wasn't seven years old.

"Sybil!" I hollered before I threw back my covers and stumbled out of bed.

I knew she was still in the hospital and I was in our apartment, alone. I looked at the clock next to my bed. It was ten in the morning. I couldn't believe I'd slept so long. I checked my phone—fifteen text messages, all from Shane, and one voicemail from the hospital. My head was still spinning from the nightmare, and my heart dropped into my stomach as it swirled, causing me to want to throw up. I dragged my finger across the message from the hospital and pushed the phone against my ear.

Please, please let it be she miraculously woke up. Please tell me she's going to be fine. I droned in my head over and over again before the message began to play.

"Hi, Miss Newton, ummm, this is Kate. I'm the early a.m. nurse assigned to Miss. St. James ... ahhh, Sybil. It's policy of the hospital to only call blood relatives about patients, but ... umm, I know you were with Sybil when she was first brought in. There's been a change in her status and, well, I think you oughta come down as soon as possible. Oh, and you never got this call. Please drive safely."

Then there was nothing. No sound, no words, absolutely nothing. No indication of what Sybil's status could be. Whether she was awake and okay or the other way things could go. I didn't waste time calling the hospital back. All I had time to do was throw on a pair of sweats, an old Jimi Hendrix T-shirt Sybil had given me when we first met, and run out the door.

eighteen

FOR NOT BEING a God-fearing person or someone who put much weight into prayer, I got into my car and prayed the entire way to the hospital ... out loud. I begged, bartered, and even made deals with God that I never had before. I even told him that I'd pull Brie and Crystal under my wing and help them find their way to him if he made sure Sybil was going to be okay.

When I pulled into one of the parking spots near the entry of the hospital, I saw Shane. He was standing in front of the sliding doors with his phone pinned against his ear, and everything that happened yesterday flooded over me. Seeing him there busted open the wound I'd bandaged last night when I left with Briggs. It was so much easier when I didn't see him, when I visualized my life being separated from his. My phone continued to ring in my purse. I watched Shane as he paced back and forth. I knew he was calling me.

If I answered my phone, I'd have to listen to his excuses for not telling me about his girlfriend, and if I let it ring, his voice would be saved in my voicemail so I could hear his sorry excuses later. I let it go to voicemail. I wouldn't waste the time I could have with Sybil trying to make him okay with his choices. A deep breath filled my lungs as I grabbed my purse and pushed my way out of the car. Shane was like poison that pearled on my bottom lip, waiting for the moment he could roll into my system and wreak havoc on my heart. I wasn't about to be that girl. I had plans, ideas that didn't involve falling in love. That was right, Shane had tagged my heart, filled it with love and shattered it with lies. He'd made me lose my way and feel things for a man I never gave my body to.

I'm stronger than what appears in front of me, I chanted in my mind. Words I had found solace in when growing up got rough.

"Rose! Please, talk to me. I've been trying to call you," Shane said as he came toward me.

"I know. I have a shitload of missed calls from you."

"Please, I ... ahhh, I wanted to be here for you. Beyond what happened yesterday, I wanted to get to you first, before you went upstairs."

Shane grabbed me, pulling me back away from the sliding doors. I twisted my arm from his grip. I didn't have time for this shit. I needed to get up to Sybil.

"Look, Shane, we're nothing more than friends, and that's all. Nothing more, nothing less. Now if you don't mind, I got a call to come down here for Sybil." I started for the doors.

He caught me around the arm and pulled me in front of him. His words were sharp and clear as they tumbled across my skin. "I know, I was the one who asked the nurse to call you. This isn't about you and me—it's about Sybil. She had a rough night. A very rough night." His eyes pierced mine. His lips quivered as he spoke in the same tone that echoed through all the moments I ached for someone to ask me to forgive them.

"What are you talking about, Shane? What happened to Sybil?"

My heart felt like it was going to crash down into my stomach. My whole life, I'd lived through bad news. I knew the rippling chill that ran across my skin as I processed what he was trying to say. I pushed him back. His eyes narrowed before he looked away to hide his expression breaking.

"I'm sorry, Rose," he said as he shook his head.

"Sorry for what? What the hell are you saying?"

"It's not good."

"Stop it, don't say that. I gotta get up there and talk to her. She's awake, goddammit!" I screamed as I struggled to get past him.

He caught me by my biceps and pulled me against his chest, wrapping his thick arms around my back. He held me to where I could hardly breathe.

"Sybil didn't make it through the night," he whispered.

"Shut up! Shut the fuck up, Shane, don't say that. She's fine. She's up there waiting for me to come up and take her home. Don't say that. Don't fucking lie to me," I cried as I fought to get out of his embrace.

"Shhhh, Rose, I'm so sorry. God, I wish it wasn't true. Sybil's gone."

The harder I fought to get away, the tighter he held onto me. I couldn't believe him. I couldn't breathe, I couldn't think, I couldn't feel. He was wrong. I'd just left her last night.

"You're wrong. She's gonna be fine. She has to come back to me; she promised to always be there for me. She's my best friend. She's the only one I have. She's my best friend. She promised me she wouldn't leave me! Sybil, you fucking promised you'd never leave me!" I screamed against Shane's chest as every part of me broke down.

"I'm so sorry," Shane kept repeating.

Torn

Apart

In seconds …

The world had just fucked me all over again. Life had bent me over the table and stripped me of the one last thing I held onto for any type of solace in my life. God, in his cruel intentions, saw how messed up my DNA was and had pinned me for a life of complete fuckery. What entity would give a baby to my fucked up parents? Did God not see they belonged in the fiery pits of Lucifer's basement?

It was God's fault. My faith had become nestled in the crumpled sidewalks as I sold my body to eat and have a roof over my head. He'd let me become nothing more than a fucking whore who couldn't be loved or find love. God had laughed at me and dangled Shane in my face. Maybe I thought, somewhere buried deep inside me, that Shane could be the one man I could create a future with. Now God's punishing me for selling my body by taking my best friend from me. The only family I had. *You're cruel, God, so fucking violently cruel.*

I couldn't take the words that continued to echo through my mind. *Sybil's gone.* I couldn't believe what Shane had said to me. I'd never had a chance to say good-bye.

The muscles in my arms ached, feeling weightier than if they were cast in cement. I needed to breathe. I needed him to hear me without consoling me. I pushed and struggled until I was out of his embrace.

"Is she still up there? Where's her body? I wanna see her. I wanna say good-bye!" I said with newfound determination.

"Rose, I don't know if that's a good idea. Her family's up with the doctors and nurses, discussing arrangements."

"I don't give a fuck."

Then it hit me like a ton of concrete bricks. It all became

crystal-clear. I didn't have a right to say my last good-byes to the only person who had ever treated me like a sister. Suddenly, without a second's notice, I didn't belong to anyone anymore. In an instant, I wasn't a part of any family, yet again.

"Oh, I see, they planted you down here to stop the fucking whore roommate from goin' up there. Now that Sybil's family's here, I don't deserve a moment of grieving?"

He reached for me. I stumbled back, far enough away so he couldn't grab me.

"No, it's not like that. Rose, I wanted to catch you before you went up there. I wanted to be the one to tell you about Sybil. I wanted to protect you."

"Protect me!"

"Yes."

"Shut up!"

"Rose, I lo—"

"Don't fucking say it! Don't you dare fucking say it, you have no right! You lied to me … you lied!"

"I never lied to you!"

"You never told me you had a girlfriend, Shane! You took my heart, made me fall for you, with your roses and Cajun food, laundry and lollipops. You're the worst, because you made me fall for you even when I never gave you any part of my body, never shared something that anyone else could get for the right amount of money."

"Stop, Rose."

"Don't you see you were something special to me, Shane? You were something different than any other man in my life. I fought so hard, trying not to give you my heart, trying so hard not to open the ironclad lock, because I *knew* I'd get hurt. But you found the key. You found my weakness and exploited it for your own needs. Whether you knew it or not, whether I knew it or not, I gave you my heart. And just like that, like everyone in my life, you broke it, and now you're gonna walk away, never looking back."

"That's not true, Rose. We have a lot to work out, but I won't leave you. We'll find a way to make this work. Can't you see I'm crazy about a woman who likes me for who I am, a woman who just told me that she loves me?"

"I can't ... don't you see? I can't love you. I can't be with you. Look who's in front of you ... I am a whore, Shane."

"No, don't call yourself that!"

"It's what I am, Shane."

"No, stop calling yourself that."

"What? Are you crazy? Do you not hear what I'm telling you? I sell my body to men for money. I let filthy men fuck me for money."

"Stop it. Stop saying that." He pushed toward me.

I backed away. "Well, it's the truth. I'm so fucked up, Shane, too much dirty laundry."

"Well, then we'll be fucked up with each other. Look, I know we have a lot to work out—I have a lot to work out. I'm not saying it's going to be easy, but it's worth a try. I've seen your dirty laundry; it isn't anything I can't handle. Besides, I own a laundromat, remember?"

"Not everything's a joke, Shane. You can't love someone like me. Someone you can't take home to your parents. I'm not Martie."

"My parents would love whoever I'd bring home."

"Well, good, then they probably already love Martie."

"Stop it, Rose! I don't want Martie. I want you. Maybe I'm crazy for wanting to be with you."

He stepped closer, and I stepped back against the building.

"Do you hear what you are saying? I'm not a forever girl, Shane."

"I don't care. I want you, Rose. Only you."

"Well, you shouldn't. I'm no good for you."

"How can you say that, when every time I'm with you, I suddenly feel alive? Like I can take on the world. How can I get you to see that when I'm with you, everything feels right?"

"Because I heard you in your office with Crystal. You told her that you don't want to fuck someone like her … like me, a whore!"

"Rose, you're right, I don't want to fuck Crystal! I don't want to fuck Martie. I want to be with you! Why can't you accept that? Why can't you see what you do to me? What are you so damn afraid of?" he asked as his hands caught my face and pushed me against the hospital building. He had me trapped between my pain and my fear.

My body responded to him, God, I wanted him to take me away. I needed him to bury himself so deep inside me, he'd take away all the pain that was exploding through my body.

He lowered his mouth toward mine, brushing a gentle kiss against the salty tears that caked my lips. His tongue skated against the fault line of my mouth. I wanted to open to him. I wanted to get tangled up in his kiss. I wanted to do the only thing I knew how to, but I couldn't. I pushed him away; my cheeks ran as cold as my lips. Shane planted his hands against the building, just above my shoulders, and leaned in toward me again.

I pushed my hands against his chest, holding him back from trying to kiss me. "I can't do this. I can't handle another wrecked heart. Girls like me don't deserve to be loved by someone like you. It just isn't in my DNA. Please, don't make this any harder than it already has become. Just forget about me. You'll be better off."

I ducked under his arm and hurried away from him. I only looked back once and saw that he wasn't following me. He just watched me walk away.

He had no intention of following me, and I had no intentions of making it harder than it had to be. I just needed to go home alone and grieve the loss of my best friend.

nineteen

I PUSHED THE door open to my apartment. Heavier than before, the door scraped just a little harder against the hardwood floor. The colors seemed different. The sun burned through the rippled glass of the old kitchen window, and it gave the apartment a different energy. Suddenly, everything in the apartment was soaked in the essence of Sybil. The vacuum lines she'd put in the plush area rug in the middle of the room. Even down to the pillows on the couch she'd angle just right to give the illusion we were expecting guests. I remembered her telling me that through her recovery, she found healing in controlling the things she could and letting go of the things she couldn't. Call it OCD, or replacing one addiction for another, but she'd found comfort in keeping the apartment nice and organized.

I pushed my fingers onto the chartreuse pillow she had put on her side of the couch. The embroidered lines across the silky front caught the pads of my fingers. For some reason, they were more defined than ever before. Each stitch represented a day she was clean, or so I pretended. I pulled the pillow to my chest. Her perfume soaked the lining of my nose and down my throat, sweet with a touch of spice. I sat down in her spot on our couch and curled my feet up under my body. Coiled, I held Sybil's pillow against my face, feeling the chill from the silk against my lips and nose. I breathed her in. I felt like I was living between reality and something I had no name for.

I ached to have Sybil walk through the door, argue with me, laugh at me, and get pissed because I'd creased her favorite pillow. God, I just wanted someone to come and take me away. I wasn't comfortable in my own skin, in my thoughts, or in the expired promises we'd made to each other. Sybil wasn't coming back, and I wasn't ready to figure out what I had to do. Where was I going to belong now?

Goddammit, Sybil, we didn't plan for this!

I hadn't planned for this day to come so soon. I wasn't ready to let go. I wasn't ready to never hear her laugh again, or have her get pissed at me for being such a fucking asshole. I'd spent my entire life pushing people away—so much energy wasted on making sure I never gave too much. It was because of this, this exact reason … it was too painful, too much investment if this was the return.

Goddammit, I'm not ready to let go. I don't want to be alone in this life.

Every agonizing brick hovered over me, waiting for the moment I cracked. Those deep, personal feelings I was a master at pushing away, locking up, and keeping at a distance suddenly slammed down across my shoulders. There was nothing I could do to bring Sybil back. She wasn't mad at me. She hadn't left for work. She wasn't visiting her family or pulling an all-nighter. My best friend, the only person who felt like some form of family to me, was gone … forever.

I pressed the heels of my palms into my eyes and pushed so hard my eyes ached from the pressure. I lost my breath and crumbled to the voice in my head.

Well, Rosalie, if you weren't such a fucking idiot, you would have locked the door. Maybe you could have saved her if you didn't pass out after hitting your head. Weak, you're weak, crumbling to the demons you cling to as an excuse. Maybe your friend Sybil would be here right now if you didn't fail at saving the one person who always had your back. Did you have her back when she needed you?

My inner voice was relentless, reminding me that I was the same worthless, broken girl I had been trying to run from my whole life. I took a deep breath and let it out. I didn't want to listen anymore; I didn't want to fall to the memories of who I'd never asked to be.

"Sybil! I'm so sorry I wasn't able to save you. I wasn't able to protect you. I'm so sorry ... Oh. My. Fucking. God ... you're not coming home!"

My voice cracked as I curled up and let every last thing that had ever broken me flood my existence. Every breach of trust, every second of pain scorched into my soul by strangers and people I thought loved me. Every breath I took drowned my lungs. I was buried in wasted moments and nauseating memories as they flashed through my mind. Incidents that created who I was and how I handled moments like this. I couldn't stop the twisted minds and pathetic excuses for people who had ripped my heart to shreds. I thought about giving up Shane, losing a love deeper than any physical connection I'd ever had.

I bawled until my head hurt and my voice was gone. I cried until I had no more tears to give, until every tear I had left was soaked into the cushion of the couch or Sybil's chartreuse pillow. I cried until I was exhausted enough to fall asleep in the puddle of my agony.

I was woken by my phone vibrating next to me. I guess life goes on, even when it was being torn to pieces. There was no consideration for a woman whose life had just been ripped apart all over again. I peered at the clock, blurry through my swollen eyes—seven thirty. The apartment was dreary, and I was exhausted. The sun was down, and I just couldn't bring myself to get up and go out tonight. I tossed the phone on the coffee table. I knew the messages were from horny clients who had called me to hook up or wondered if I'd left the business or even died.

Today made up almost a week where I didn't manage my six squares of sidewalk, a sidewalk where memories of Sybil and me were the filthy runoff that ended up in the gutter after a rainstorm. What the hell was I thinking? I knew my six squares were already claimed by some other ho who thought she'd found gold at the end of her fucked up rainbow. How could I ever go back? I was done living in a broken world filled with crumbling sidewalks and wrecked dreams.

I sat in our apartment, covered in a fog and knowing there were decisions I ultimately had to make. I looked around at all of Sybil's things and the other stuff that happened to belong to me. There was no way I could even consider going back to my squares. I had to be stronger than I'd ever been before. I had to get my shit together and pack up Sybil's stuff. I couldn't let anything of hers get lost or left behind. She wouldn't want that to happen, especially if her family decided to come and collect what was left of her.

We'd never talked about shit like this. Maybe thinking that we would survive beyond our profession was being optimistic. I was so wrong.

I didn't know where to start. My hands tingled at the thought of touching her belongings. I stood in our apartment and looked around, too overwhelmed to begin. Should I start with her clothes or look under her bed for things she'd kept hidden away? I had to remind myself she was gone and there wasn't anyone else who was going to clean up what was left of her.

I stood staring at her closet door. It was the only closet in the apartment. The day we moved into our apartment poured through my mind.

"WOW, SYBIL, GET your ass over here and check out this closet. It's, like, bigger than the whole place!" I bellow, wiping sweat from my brow. We just finished unloading the last box from the back of my car.

"There's enough room for both of us to hang up our shit," she squawks.

"Hell, no, sistah, we're gonna roshambo for it! It's a luxury one of us should take full advantage of," I quip as I square toward her and throw up my fist resting on the palm of my other hand. I know how to rock, paper, scissor my way into any situation. I'm quite good at it ... until today.

"Fine, one, two, three," she counts before slamming her fist down in unison with mine.

She drops the infamous rock, and well, when my two fingers protrude from my fist, my fate is sealed and the first game of three is lost. Sybil wins two out of three roshambos, and in less than two minutes, she claims her closet. To the victor goes the spoils—well, all except for a little section in the front right side, a spot she reserves for me, just in case I have something that doesn't fit in my rickety freestanding armoire. Me being the stubborn shit I am, I never give in to her requests, and eventually she absorbs that space with more clothes she's never gonna wear.

But today is the last time I'll ever play roshambo with anyone. I learn my lesson; Sybil is the best at anticipating people's choices.

I let the awkwardness roll across my skin as I pulled open the closet next to her bed and stared at all of her things. Dresses and tops she'd let me borrow a hundred times, methodically hung from the clothing rods. I thought about the moments when I'd been in this closet before, when she had let me riffle through her clothes because she insisted I wear something of hers. Now I was in her closet, riffling because she didn't have a voice. Sybil would never have the option to tell me it was okay ever again.

There wasn't a square inch of her closet she didn't use. Boxes of high heels were stacked on the shelf above her dual clothes rods, and a shoe organizer hung on the inside of the door. It was organized by outfits and their matching shoes. She had so many dresses, which reminded me of events that marked our lives beyond what we had in common. I pushed her clothes apart, noticing the little black leather dress she had worn when she had an overnighter at the Sir Francis Drake. She had been so excited to find red alligator-skin pumps that looked like they were made for that dress. She looked beautiful with her deep-red bristled hair and shoes to match.

I collected a heavy handful of her clothes from the closet and laid them across her bed, a ritual that tore my heart apart with each step I took back and forth between her closet and her bed. Tears poured down my cheeks as each stack I created became the story of her life, where someone either threw her away or paid for who they wanted her to be. I balanced the last cluster of designer coats and sweaters on the disorganized stack of shirts on the bed when I heard the hollow clank of something tumbling to the hardwood floor and rolling under my bed. Normally I wouldn't care, but today, life was different. My life was slow and heavy and moved at a pace where everything seemed thick and raw, magnified by who was missing in our apartment's silence.

I crumpled to the floor and landed roughly against the shaggy black area rug between our beds. My knees rippled with pain. My face burned hot while cool tears clustered at the edges of my eyes, and I ached to go numb. I just wanted to disappear, to get lost in my pain. I wanted to have one more moment where I had the chance to say good-bye, to tell Sybil that in my own twisted way, I loved her like a sister and she was the only person who made me feel worthy of having a family to love me.

My eyes heavy with loss, they floated closed for a moment longer than I anticipated. When I opened my tear-clouded eyes, I saw the collection of white and brown boxes, covered in a thin layer of undisturbed dust, under my bed. Each package was a proposition from Mr. C. They were reminders I kept hidden of how much he still resided just below my skin, even a year later. He knew the power he had over me, and seeing those boxes conjured an ache that thundered across my soul. He was my breaking point, the one I was convinced I could quit after this one last time.

I stretched my hand out to the closest box and pulled it toward me. In its wake, the box left an unmistakable path along the dusty hardwood floor, more evidence that I was disturbing the demons I struggled to keep dormant. It represented the agonizing moment when I would be at my lowest and seek out those who were the most damaging to my soul. I tossed the first box on the bed and collected another, then another. I didn't stop pulling the packages out until they filled my entire bed. I welcomed Mr. C's bribes like a lost friend, hoping by piling them up, I would see the evidence of what I meant to him. I dropped my head one last time to the shabby hardwood floor and saw a silver cylinder tucked under the edge of a manila bubble mailer. The clank against the hardwood floor and the lopsided roll that had led me to the buried past under my bed replayed in my head. Realization clung to me like an old friend … it was Sybil's lipstick. I grabbed it and collected the last package from Mr. C.

I turned over and sat back against my bed. Chills rippled across my skin as memories shuffled through my head. Memories of Sybil as she dragged her dark-red lipstick across her mouth before she rolled and puckered her lips. How she would constantly go around and kiss all the mirrors in the apartment.

"Sybil, why the fuck do you keep doing that?"
"It's the best way to keep track of my new favorite colors."

"No, all it does is create more work for me. I try to look in the mirror and all I see is your freaking kisses all over it."

"Nobody asked you to clean my lips off the mirrors. Maybe you should look at yourself so my kiss is on your cheek and lighten up a little."

I craned my neck, looked over at the mirror behind the front door, and my heart tumbled into my stomach. Just a couple of days ago, I cleaned all the mirrors in the apartment. I wiped Sybil's colorful kisses from the reflection without a thought of never seeing them again. Something she did that was so irritating, but now I desperately ached to have them back.

All right, Rose, it's time to shut this shit down. Yep, time to pull your ass out of this fucked up moment and callus your heart. The familiar judgmental voice I'd listened to all of my life echoed through my head. *Look at yourself, curled up on the floor! Nobody is coming to save your shit, Rose. There isn't anybody who's willing to shoulder Sybil's life. Her family isn't going to fucking come pick up her shit. You know it, deep down; you have to admit that nobody ever cares about the broken girls buried in shady back alleys or abandoned buildings.*

I was good, better than most my age, at shutting down. I'd lived my entire life filled with the sheer agony of wounds rubbed raw by the people who were supposed to love me. You couldn't offer your body to perfect strangers and expect to not have scars. Take it from me—it was the only way you stay somewhat sane when your heart was trampled and you were numb.

I reached over and picked up the dusty bubble mailer from the floor next to me. It was the first package Garrett, Mr. C, mailed me after I told him I wasn't going to see him anymore. Falling for a *date* and pinning your future on him, hoping he'd save you from all the dirty fucks who never gave a rat's ass beyond just getting off, was the nastiest kind of torture.

I got up, stood there, and stared at all the bribes Mr. C had sent me before I pulled open the edge of the package, tilted the bubble mailer, and watched the contents tumble out.

A soft black cashmere scarf fell into my hands. I caressed my thumb against it before I dragged it across my face. A deep hollow ache returned to my gut, a craving I had for someone to fill the deserted hole left in my heart. But I knew this scarf and every feeling it evoked in my body, every sharp stabbing fear it seared into my soul, all the memories of our three days together knotted into one night when Mr. C had broken me and shredded my heart. Truthfully, a year ago, it was the scarf that had become my only comfort. Today, it pulled me back into a memory that was seductively frightening.

It was all so stupid, because broken girls weren't given hooks to hang their dreams upon. I wasn't given the key to the castle; I was buried below the dim streetlights and darkened skies. I will never be the princess or the queen; I will always be the call girl, a romp in the hay, the whore for hire. At least with Mr. C, I was with someone who gave my pain a purpose. I held the scarf to my nose and inhaled, hoping I'd capture Mr. C's essence. Disappointed, I dropped the scarf on the floor, and it became lost against the black shaggy area rug. I was alone in my apartment, nothing but thoughts and memories thundering through my head.

twenty

PAST

THE MOONLIGHT SHINES bright. My eyelids are too thin to protect me from the glow. Mr. C's fingers crawl down around the front of my stomach and slip between the silky soft sheets and my body. He snakes his fingers down between my legs. I stretch, lifting my hips slightly from the bed, and act as if he woke me up.

His chest grows heavier against my thighs. He's demanding and strong when his fingers finally find me. I'm caught, taken from the moment he drags the tip of his tongue along the seam of my ass. I try to spread my legs, but they're locked under him.

"That's right, my little Rosebud, you like that?" he growls before he bites the edge of my ass.

I buck and clench against his long, talented fingers as he buries them deeper in my dampness. I relish the excitement his fingers create deep where they troll.

"Mmm, you're *gonna* make me come," I hum.

He freezes. The friction his fingers create stops and so do their magical assault. His lips leave a cold absence across my skin. Unexpectedly, he climbs on top of me; I lose my breath as his stone-hard cock slides up between my legs. It presses against the crevice of my ass, and I tense.

"What did you say to me?" he quips against the side of my face.

My skin pricks with his tone. I pulse low with an ache for him to fuck me from behind.

"Ummm … something 'bout coming," I answer in broken, breathless huffs.

"Ahhhh, Rose, you're such a beautiful woman. Why must you speak that way?" His voice is deep, low, dark, and pain-filled. Shifting slightly, the weight of his body rests against the curve of my ass.

"What way?" I ask.

"Untrained. It's our third night together. Don't you remember what would happen if you continued to use those lazy words around me?"

"I don't think you ever said." I settle under him, just enough to make eye contact with him.

"You become poisonous to me." He moves his weight to one hand and with the other swipes the strands of hair from my face.

"Poisonous? What the hell does that mean?" I try to buck him off my back. Playing into his fantasy is one thing, but calling me poisonous is something else entirely altogether. I've lived my whole life believing that I am poisonous to people.

He uses his body weight to pin me down. I'm stuck under him, his prisoner.

"It upsets me when you don't speak properly. Someone so beautiful should have a vocabulary to match."

He gets up off of me and lets me go. *Free.*

"Well, maybe I ain't what you think. This is me. If you don't like whatcha got, maybe you should have picked up someone else."

His eyes constrict while he shakes his head as if he is wickedly disappointed … yet again. "If I wanted someone else, believe me, I would have them. I chose you. I want to take care of you. Teach you how beautiful you are." The tone in his voice is breathy, yet constricted and strong.

His eyes are sexy, dark, thought provoking. His jaw tenses as he stands at the edge of the bed and rolls his hand in the sheet. My eyes swallow every inch I can see, from the top of his head down to the lingering moment I stare at his cock.

"You trust me?" he asks. His eyes pin me. "Well, do you?"

I nod.

I'm caught in Mr. C's enchantment; his eyes penetrate every fear I've ever had. For three days, he's captured me in a whirlwind of incredible and unforgettable. Although it makes me uncomfortable at times, he's gotten under my skin and infected every cell of my body, and I let him.

He pulls a slight smirk across his face before he swipes his tongue across his bottom lip. His eyes constrict. "I need to hear you say you trust me."

He saunters to the foot of the bed, and slides his hands across my calf, tangling the top sheet tight around my ankle.

"Yes," I whisper.

"Yes what?"

"Yes, I trust you."

A wicked smile creeps deliberately across his face, and his eyes fiercely consume every inch of my naked body. He pulls the sheet, dragging my leg to the edge of the bed. He makes sure it's loose enough to be comfortable but tight enough to be invitingly sexy.

"If you become uncomfortable, you need to tell me." He pulls on the sheet as he cracks a shit-eating grin. "Tight enough?"

He drags his tongue along the inside of my calf, and his hands traipse their way up my thigh. His breath steams against my flesh, and I crave him like a full-fledged addict.

"Yes." My voice catches as he flutters his fingers between my legs spread wide for him.

He takes my other ankle and wraps it in the opposite side of the sheet.

I gasp.

He smiles.

His hands caress up my legs. Every muscle in my body constricts, tightens, and clings to the idea that he'll lick me into convulsions. I lay in wait, praying for the chill between my legs to be healed by his damp, hot, thick tongue. I hunger for his long fingers to drop me into mind-blowing-sparks-igniting-brain-breaking oblivion.

Instead, he leaves me tied at my ankles and saunters across the room.

"I have something for you. Something I think you might find … helpful."

He lowers his hand into the top drawer of a black lacquered desk. Time stands still as visions crash through my head. Handcuffs and wrist restraints are things I keep off-limits with all my other *dates*.

"What?" I ask. A mix of fear and curiosity thunders through my chest.

What will you do if he has handcuffs? Rose, just this time, maybe you can let yourself trust, the fucked up voice in my head pops off.

Mr. C knows this isn't part of the deal. I don't do wrist restraints. I'm about to call this whole fuckfest off when he pulls out a long, wide black cashmere scarf.

I let out my breath.

He notices. "What's that for?"

"I could ask the same thing," I quip, pointing at the scarf he has in his hands.

He smirks. "You'll see … or maybe you won't."

Relief consumes me, and he notices.

Lowering the fringe of the scarf to my thighs, he tickles me

175

before he drags it slowly across the aching cusp between my legs. Vibrating it, he trails it up and over the edge of my stomach and swirls it around my hardened nipples.

I moan loudly, pleasure bumps exploding across my skin. I need him to take me, to dive deeper than anyone who has come before him, and tame the beast that keeps tormenting me every day of my life. I hope he'll be the one to heal all the scars that others left on my soul.

He lifts the scarf from my flesh; its vacancy causes me to quiver. Pulling the ends of the scarf tight, he bridges it between our faces.

A moment lingers.

His expression is hidden behind the black scarf before he drops the fabric over my eyes. The delicate cashmere covers my forehead and lies across my nose, tickling the edge of my upper lip.

"Lift your head."

I do what he asks. Wrapping the scarf around my head, he's got me tangled in a cluster of need. I blink, and the little light I cling to disappears.

I'm in the dark. I see nothing.

My hearing is muffled.

He pulls the scarf back from my lips and leans down against my body. His heat steals the chill of the room. My heart's thrashing in my chest, pulsing in time with my desire.

I'm unsure but okay.

I'm confused but turned on.

"Do you trust me still?" he whispers.

I nod even when my mind disagrees. I have no control. I can't see and I can barely hear. I slide my arms across the bed and reach for him ... nothing.

He catches my wrist.

I lose my breath ... again.

"You need to answer me. Do you trust me still?"

I want to say yes. I feel the words as they rise in my throat. Released from my heart, I want to trust him with everything I am, but my mind doesn't want me to.

I betray my thoughts.

I lie.

"Yes, I still trust you."

My body tenses, my skin dampens, and I fight to keep holding on to this moment.

I'm not broken, I'm not broken, I'm not broken.

He pulls my hand up above my head, and a chill rolls across my underarm.

He holds my wrist.

Tight … so very tight.

I panic.

The back of my throat runs dry, thieving my attempt to whimper. I try to twist out of his grasp, but he holds my wrist tighter.

"Don't fight, Rosebud."

"I don't know about this, mister." I reach my free hand across and attempt to loosen his grip.

"Stop!" he barks before he grabs my free wrist.

I jump out of my skin. I'm lost, scared, and unsure of this moment.

Too

many

triggers.

Tears prick at my eyes and dissolve into the scarf. My breathing shallows, clogs my ears. Short breaths in, shaky breaths out, I struggle to let go.

My heart's hammering in my chest. I fight against spiraling down into my past. His breath is so warm against my skin.

"I'm not going to hurt you, beautiful girl."

I don't want to say anything more.

But I do.

"I'm scared."

"You're just vulnerable. Let go."

I try to trust where it never has existed. Everything in my body is fighting what my heart wants. I want to feel pleasure beyond the pain of my childhood. I want to trust and feel worthy. I want to be healed by this man and find my freedom.

"I don't know how to let go. Please, mister, I don't know if I can do this," I whisper.

The cold breeze creeps across my flesh. I'm burning up inside and freezing on the outside. My body gambles against everything my mind remembers. I'm a prisoner, a possession; I'm a captive with no free will.

Mister's energy consumes the room. I rely upon my skin to react to his demands. His breath tangles with my messy black hair.

"You can, and you will, trust me. I'm going to give you everything you've ever wanted tonight. Do you understand me?"

I nod.

He lets out a heavy breath.

"Yes," I answer, knowing he wants words instead of gestures.

"Good, because I'm going to replace every last scar other men have left within you when I'm done."

I break. His words pierce me and take me far beyond the seedy streets of my past, present, and future.

Is he for real? Is it the truth? It's impossible. Not my life, not the demons that swirl in my body. There have been too many men, too much pain.

"I wish it was that easy." The words flying from my mouth are unraveled and without forethought.

"I'm going to make it easy. Let go, Rosebud, let me in."

I'm senseless. Everything I've ever let define me, everything I am cracks at his words.

Is it that easy? Is he the one I've been looking for most of my life?

178

The tension in my back and up through my neck breaks free. Mister answers the tingling in my clit and the ache pulsing in the depths between my legs with his hot, wet tongue and his long, thick fingers. I thrust my head back into the mattress. I'm unable to see, yet I see everything.

"Please, make me forget," I moan.

His hot breath rumbles across the swollen pleats of my clit while his long fingers erase the marks of all the fucks who came before him. I drive my hips against his speeding fingers, aching to feel his hands heal the marks left in my soul.

He catches me between his teeth and sucks so perfectly, as if he just can't get enough of me. I'm vibrating and humming. He releases my clit with a pop at the same time he stops his fingers from fucking me. This beautiful man is leaving me reeling. The blazingly chilly air hijacks my body from the top of my head down to the bottom of my feet.

Time is bending my trust, breaking me before he brushes the backs of his fingers against my lips. His touch startles me at first, but tracing his fingers on the outside curve of my lower lip soothes me.

"What if I can't trust?" I ask in a hushed whisper.

"You can." He drags his fingers along the outline of my jaw and down across my collarbone.

"What if it's not in me?" I'm still blindfolded, my feet tangled in the sheet.

"You have everything you'll ever need right here." The tips of his fingers circle between my breasts.

My heart reaches for his touch as it leaps and crashes against my chest. "You don't understand, mister. I need to have a sense of control."

"Rosebud, control is an illusion. It's a decision to trust a certain outcome. All you have to do is trust me, and you'll have all the control you need."

I want his words to soothe me and his calm, direct voice to caress the strength within me as I cower from letting go of my scars. I want to trust him. I crave to taste the freedom he wants to give me. I want him to save me from a future tucked under cracked sidewalks, cold gutters, and from ever having to fuck another man for a pittance. I try to convince myself that he wants to keep me off the streets.

He drags his thumb up across the crevice of my lips before he slides it into my mouth. I roll my tongue and suck on his thumb as he pushes it deeper into my mouth.

"I know what you want to do to me. I can feel it," he moans under his breath.

He pulls his thumb from my mouth, and instantaneously, I feel desperate and vacant. I need to take him. It's unexplainable, intangible, this desire I have to please him.

"Let me suck your dick, mister. I want to make you come. Please let me finally show you what I can do for you."

My eyes still covered, my legs still bound, and all I get from him is a long, breathy sigh.

The last three days, he's only pleased me. Sure, he came when he fucked me, ate my pussy like a champ, but he still hasn't let me take him.

"I'm starting to take it personally. Why won't you let me give you head? Is this your sick way of controlling me?"

"Is that what you think?" he snaps.

"Well, maybe. Anytime I try, you stop me and pull me back up. Do I disgust you?" My voice breaks to a quiver, and my eyes are still blanketed in darkness. I pull in a deep, shuddering breath while every ounce of confidence drains from my soul. He's succeeded in tangling me up in his game of cat and mouse.

His whereabouts are lost to me for a couple of seconds before he removes the scarf covering my eyes.

He's not gentle.

The air hits my skin. The freedom to see stings. I squeeze my eyes shut and turn away from him.

A long minute waits between us.

"Look at me, Rose," he demands.

I ignore him.

"You need to look at me now," he says, anger dripping from his words.

"No."

"I'm not asking you," he replies as he catches my face and pulls me to look at him. "Haven't the last three days been everything you've ever wanted?"

He waits for me to answer.

I don't.

"Haven't I put your needs and desires before mine? This has been my gift to you, and instead of enjoying it, you are pained by my attention. I don't understand." His expression is narrow, dark at my words. Shards of sadness twinkle in his eyes.

I'm breaking all over again. His words dismantle me. I'm confused, vulnerable, and hurt by his actions.

"Why are you doing this?"

"Because I need to understand. I've never been with a woman who desires to fight me so much."

"Well, welcome to my world."

"I've given you everything you could want."

"You've not given me every part of you. You've held back with me."

"You want to take me that bad?"

"Yeah, that bad. Why don't you understand? It's who I am. All I do is give, give, give—that's all I know how to do. The last three days, all I've done is take, take, take."

"I think it's the only way you can feel in control. You give me head, make me come, and somehow you feel vindicated. I want you to trust me, surrender your need to control this moment."

"Maybe it is about control, maybe it isn't. What does it matter?"

"Why don't you take what I give you without question?"

"I asked first. Why does it matter if I need to be in control?"

"It matters. That's all I'm saying."

"Well, that's not enough for me."

"Well, it's going to have to be!"

His look is intense. I can see he's determined to win, so I stare back in silence. Nothing to say, nothing to give someone who won't lose for me.

He continues, "I need to give to you, and you need to take from me. That's the end of it."

"That can't be the end of it. Please, let me do this."

Our eyes lock, as if if we look away, one of us will lose the battle.

"Don't you see, it's more than giving you a blow job. I've broken every rule with you, and I'm scared that I'm gonna leave here, return to my reality, and never have this with another man, ever. We've done everything. You've given me three days of fear, and confidence, pleasure and pain, ecstasy and confusion. Please, please, mister … I need this."

The result of this weekend pummels me in a matter of seconds. I cling to this experience with all that I am. Finally, a man wants to make me feel validated for who I am, and for the first time in my life, I'm willing. But in my basic need to survive, I have to show him that I'm worth it by doing what I know best. I need to give him the pleasure of letting go into me as I push past the fear of trusting him. He's more than a *date* who's keeping me for a wild fucking three days. I hope once he gives me every part of who he is, he'll see I'm worthy of being with him beyond this moment that burns between us.

Breaking to me, he climbs over and straddles my body. "Oil and water, that's what we are."

"At least we know it," I answer.

His cock is level with my mouth, hard, beautiful, swollen, and aroused by what he sees, or I hope so. Thick, lengthy, and waiting. I reach out to touch him.

"Nope. No hands. I'll let you do this, but you can't grab my cock. Let me have this."

I have no control. None. If he decides to thrust and hit the back of my throat, gag me, push, and pulse until he empties every ounce of seed he has to plant, I won't stop him.

For the first time in my life, I'm deciding to trust a man.

Our eyes meet. He strokes his cock, a couple of drops pulse from his tip, and he catches them with his thumb and rubs over the head of his erection. It excites me. My pussy surging, tingling with the need to be filled, pounded into oblivion. I swipe my tongue across my lips, ready for the moment he gives into me. He smiles, seeing that I'm hungry, he urges his thumb between my lips, and I lick his flavor from his skin.

"That's right taste me, do you like that?"

I hum and grab at his ass.

He lets out a tisk, before he pulls my hands away.

"No hands, Rosebud. Just trust me."

I have to trust.

He leans in and glides the tip of himself into my mouth before he pulls it out. He's teasing me into trying to lean forward. He huffs and answers me with a deep growl in his throat.

Looking into his greedy eyes, another couple of seconds tick away before he slowly slides his cock into my mouth. I take him deep. No hands, no way of controlling the depth of his thrust, his thighs flex, his hips roll, and his right hand brushes across the side of my face while his left is anchored against the wall.

Pushing forward, he huffs his desires out in breathy words. "Oh, fuck, Rosebud, you feel so good, so fucking good. Oh, God."

I suck, release and roll my tongue across the back side of his shaft, opening my mouth just far enough to take in a breath. I let the cool air ripple across his cock. He tangles his hand into my hair, his dick hardens, his skin tightens, his speed quickens, he's about to come. I want to taste him, I suck harder holding my hands on his ass making sure he isn't going to pull out. I look up at him and watch his face twist in ecstasy and release. His body stiffens and he lets out an unrestrained holler that fills the room. Jagged energy ricochets between us as his warm release pulses down my throat, and I swallow every last drop of him. His hips jolt and thrust spastic before he slowly withdraws.

Nothing, no words are wasted before he lowers his body dragging his face across my cheek nudging his lips against mine. He's spastic with his tongue, as he ravages me with his kiss. I have no control, it's lost, my body's howling for him to take me. He's so fucking masterful with my desires.

"Are you going crazy for me, Rosebud?" he asks against my ear.

"Yeah, I can't take it anymore. I need you inside of me."

"Oh, I'm going to make you come. I'm going to fuck you into oblivion." He ties the cashmere scarf around my eyes again.

Fear doesn't own me so deeply this time. Adrenaline races through my body, and I feel geared up for whatever he's going to do.

"Bring it on, mister," I tease.

It's dead silent—nothing except our tangling breaths fill the room. Cool air rips across my skin, and suddenly all I hear is my heartbeat thrashing in my chest.

Mr. C senses my tense reaction. "You still trust me?"

"I do," I answer with hesitancy in my voice.

"We're still keeping the same rules, I'm here to take care of you, Rosebud. You must remember that." His voice is laced with a threaded compassion dangling from a place that could easily tip into the unexpected.

"I will ... try."

His words are slow and visceral as he kisses down my body in between his promises. "You don't have to try. I'm ... going ... to ... take ... care ... of ... you ... like ... you've ... never ... been ... taken ... care ... of ... before."

My body is covered in chills. His lips speak words of truth nobody has ever spoken to me before. I need to believe him, even if I struggle to comprehend his definition of what taking care of me means.

"Why?"

"Why what?" he counters.

"Why do you want to take care of me?"

"Because you deserve to be treated like a queen."

"I want to believe you, but I can't." My heart thunders in my chest, my nerves crashing through every line of my body. Every emotion intensifies because I'm blindfolded and can't see his reaction.

His hair stops tickling my flesh. His tongue swirling across my hip is gone. His weight shifts, and before I have a chance to lose my breath, he's whispering in my ear.

"Have I ever given you a reason not to trust me? Have I hurt you?"

"No, but I need to know—why do you want to take care of me?"

"Stop it, Rosebud."

"What aren't you telling me?"

"There's nothing to tell. I'm a man who desires to take care of a very beautiful woman."

"I want to believe you, to give you what I've never been able to give another man ... but ... this scares me—you scare me."

"Let go, Rose. Let go and let me in."

I start to answer when his mouth slams down on mine. His

185

tongue, strong and determined, swipes and tangles with promises I don't have to question. All he's ever done for the last three days is take care of me. He never asks for more than I'm willing to give. He's given to me in three days what I have longed for my entire life.

I

came

apart.

twenty-one

PAST

MY BODY SURRENDERS to him. I finally let myself trust. He kisses me, takes me in his arms, and tangles me into something I have no idea I could ever become. I open my heart and let him reside where very few have ever been.

"That's right, let me in. Let me take care of you."

I nod—words are too much work.

"You feel that? You did that to me, Rosebud. It's all for you," he says, thrusting his hips back and forth, rubbing his cock against my flesh. He makes me eager to have him fuck me, take me—I dare even say, make love to me.

"Yes," I say breathlessly. "Yes, I feel you." My voice cracks as I shudder.

"You ready for the repercussions of your poisonous words?"

He adjusts himself against me before he rocks his thick, stone-hard cock between my legs, spreading me just enough to where the tip of him strokes and grazes against my clit. He thrusts until his cock stretches and presses against me.

"Yes, take my poisonous words away."

He thrusts his cock one last time in a long, slow stroke against my surging clit, his tongue swirling and lapping at my pebbled nipple. I'm eager to believe he'll be the one to replace the demons holding me captive.

He slips his fingers into my pussy. "Mmm, I feel how wet I make you. Your juices excite me."

I buck against his touch, and he senses my need. With my hips still thrusting at the tips of his fingers, I try to get him to slip his fingers inside me. Instantly, he pushes his fingers deeper and drives his mouth against my waiting mound. He rolls and drags his warm, thick, strong tongue across my clit, lapping at every ounce of flavor he induces in me. It's fucking wild. Instantly I'm invested, more now than ever before in my life. He growls against me and thrusts his fingers deeper, catching the space that drives me wild. I roll my hips, inviting him to go faster.

He slides his fingers out, leaving me aching for more as he lifts his tongue from between my legs. I huff and vault my hips against the air.

"I can feel you want to come. You ready for me?"

He tears open a condom, and for a moment, I only hear the unraveling of my soul. Seconds tick away as anticipation steams through my body. He drags his fingers across my leg, driving me further down into the frenzy rushing my body.

The chill of the room startles me as he unties my ankles. Kneeling between my legs, he spreads me wide with his stiff cock pressed firm against me. I hope—no, pray—for the split second he'll penetrate the defensive wall I've always built every time I've ever consensually had sex with a man.

He rotates his hips, teasing me with the head of his cock, leaving me desperate for his return. I rock my hips. Wordlessly I'm begging him to fill me, fuck me, sink himself so deep into me that we'll both be lost to where his body meets mine.

He collects a sharp breath before he slowly stretches me, opens me up, and splits me apart. He pulls back, faster this time, and thrusts again. I lose my breath, vibrating from my core. Back and forth, inside and out, he's annihilating me, taking me beyond any other moment I can remember. He's so much more than a *date*, more than a demon slayer—he's a savior, someone I believe can cleanse my soul.

He grabs my legs and drapes them up over his shoulders. He pushes deep, thrusts into me until my body breaks into a full-fledged orgasm owning every part of me, from the deepest place nobody has ever seen to the edge of where my skin meets his. My words stolen, I can't tell him I've come. My body language speaks volumes. The motion of every cell in my body gets to experience what sex is supposed to be like between two consenting adults.

He speeds up, driving deeper before he buries his fingers in my clit and massages. My body accepts his offer, rolling stronger than before. I bust apart for a second time as his body stiffens and his hips jerk spastically against me. I'm vibrating harder than ever. I can't see, I can't talk, all I can do is grab him and hold him tight on my body as his cock pulses inside me, pouring into the condom what my womb craves to consume.

He slips the scarf up off my eyes, his body still collapsed against mine. In the glow of the room, my eyes adjust to see his body glistening, his dark hair damp, his skin ravaged with goose bumps.

I am safe.

Finally, someone who makes me believe I'm worth more than a casual fuck. I am worthy of sexual pleasure without fear or guilt.

He looks at me, and a smile creeps across his tawny-tinted face. He reaches up and dries my cheeks. A reprieve sweeps through my body.

"Did I hurt you?" he whispers with a sense of urgency. He delicately caresses my face, his concern apparent as his thumbs swipe away the last tears rolling down my cheeks.

"No."

"Why are you crying then?" He shifts his body off mine, pulling me into his chest simultaneously.

"It's so much deeper than the surface pain," I whisper, barely audible.

He stares at me. We look at each other for a lengthy moment. I know down in my gut it's fucking crazy to think I'll let someone into my heart after a lifetime of so much pain, but the last three days have been like nothing I've ever experienced before. He's like a breath of fresh air in a polluted city.

"I want to take care of you, if you'll let me."

I want to believe him—I crave it as a matter of fact. And for a moment, I let my dreams cloud my reality. Maybe he'll take me wherever he's going. If he starts to love me beyond the label of who I am, I won't have to spend the rest of my life being paid for careless fucks with pricks who shoot their wads and move on. Mister makes me better. I feel like a better person when I'm with him. Shit, even when I fight him, he still makes me feel beautiful, wanted, and desired beyond a simple quick fuck.

"You want to take care of me?" I ask, but I know, in my gut, he's talking about the present and I'm talking about the future.

I'll make sure I answer and question him in broad fucking strokes on a painting of my future. I've spent my entire life shutting myself off to the idea that there's a knight in shining armor coming to save me. Why's my heart flipping the switch on my mind now?

Betrayal, fucking betrayal.

"Yes, let me take care of you." He pulls me into his embrace.

My limbs are listless and heavy. My body's exhausted from giving him everything within me.

"What happens now, mister?" I ask, scared to hear his answer.

"I take care of you, and it's Garrett."

"What's Garrett?" I ask, legitimately confused.

"My name. It's Garrett, Garrett Chadwick."

He's let me in, just as I have let him in. His name's Garrett, the man who's healing the broken girl residing just under the surface of who I am.

"Well, Garrett Chadwick, looks like we both learned how to trust tonight."

"It looks that way, doesn't it?" he answers rhetorically.

We kiss until our bodies are steaming and smoldering. His body responding to my touch, my body ready to go, he pulls me to the edge of the bed, rolls on a rubber, and takes me from behind. This time it's raw, fierce, and primitive. We both have a burning need that must be satisfied. Clutching my waist, he pummels me with his entire length. I thrust back, taking every inch he is giving me.

"Garrett." His name rolls across my tongue so freely, beautifully, breathlessly. I sing it.

"I like the way you say my name while I am fucking you. Say it again."

"Garrett," I repeat.

He moans as his pace quickens. He drags his hand up my back and takes a fistful of my hair, pulling my head back as he buries himself deeper. Our eyes meet, and he watches me in the mirror across the room as he takes me. The way my body moves, and how my tits bounce with every thrust he makes.

"I want to watch your expression when I make you come, be the man who breaks you wide open, Rosebud. I want you to scream my name."

I clench my pussy around his cock, knowing it will throw him over the edge.

"Rosebud, you feel so good." He fucks me with even more determination.

"Garrett," I huff before throaty, bellowing sounds escape me. "Yes, please."

"Rosebud, damn, you're so good, I want to fuck you every day, every night, right here, forever."

Our words to one another, promises in the heat of the moment, become nothing more than primal moans as we both detonate at the same time. Loud, beastly calls hum across my back. Sweat beads trickle down my hairline as my eyes roll up in the back of my head and I scream his name.

He pulls me up into the bed, wrapping us up in each other. I feel safe, needed, wanted, and finally important.

"I want to keep you to myself. Will you let me … keep you?" His words are filled with contentment.

I don't want to say anything. I want to just hum or moan my answer, but I know from before that he likes me to communicate with my words, to use language in a beautiful manner. "That depends."

"Oh really? On what?" he asks as he tangles his fingers in the random loose strands of my hair, clearing them out of my eyes.

"On where you live," I answer as I prop myself up on my elbows and caress my fingers against his chest. I'm safe, comfortable. I see myself getting used to waking up next to him.

"Why would that matter?"

"Because as much as I hate southern California, if you move me there, then I'd have to adjust. But on the other hand, if you move me to New York—"

"Who said you'd leave San Francisco?" He adjusts himself out from under me.

"You did."

"No, I didn't."

"Oh, so wait, you're relocating to the city?"

"No," he snaps.

"Wait, I'm totally confused. If you're asking me to go with you …"

His expression shifts, and at that moment, I realize what

192

he's saying.

He gets up off the bed. "Look, Rose, I really enjoy this. I want to keep this. I want to help you. Get you off the street, keep you safe."

My nerves are exploding and capturing every move, every reaction as he shifts his hands back and forth between us.

"Oh, fuck me. Holy shit. Ohmigod! I'm soooo fucking stupid," I howl.

I spring up, wrapping the loose sheet around my naked body. He doesn't want me. He doesn't want me to be with him. He really wants to just *keep* me.

My mom's voice plays over and over in my head.

"It's your fault your father hits me. You were never wanted. I was forced to keep you. Forced to marry him. It's all your fault, Rosalie. You weren't supposed to be born!"

Shredded.

Torn.

Apart.

In seconds …

"Wait, wait, Rosebud."

"Don't call me that!"

"Hold on, what did you think I meant? I want to get you off the streets, pay for an apartment for you, and give you money so you don't have to—"

"Fuck other men for money? Whore myself out? What is it, Garrett? You'll keep me for yourself, but only as your own personal piece of ass when you're in town?"

"What did you think this was, Rose?"

"Don't worry, I get it. Three days, that's about all I'm worth."

Mister reaches for me. I pull away.

"Rose, stop it. I'm trying to help you."

Frantically I'm looking for clothes so I can get the hell out. I stop at his words; my heart is breaking with every word out of his mouth.

"Please, stop. You don't have to help me. I'm capable. I've lived perfectly fine without you before these last three days. This was my fault. Stupid, thinking that you'd want this." I swing my hand up and down my body.

"I don't want you to go. Not like this. All I wanted to do was keep you safe."

"For what, Mr. C's pleasure? Or for Mister's twisted needs? Oh, no, wait, maybe I was gonna be for Garrett Chadwick? Who the fuck are you? Huh? Who are you? You wanna keep me for a fuck, but not for all the other parts? I'm not good enough to take home and love, be something more than a fucking convenience or entertainment? Fuck you Mister-Garrett-Mr. C-fucking-Chadwick."

My heart's crashing into my chest. The only thing I can think of doing is hitting him, so I pick up the alarm clock next to the bed and chuck it at him. Everything pressing down on me … everything's lost, nothing's safe. My body and mind twist up into a complete knotted mess.

"It didn't have to end this way. I care about you, Rose. But this is your choice, not mine." He walks over to the safe, opens it, and pulls out two rolls of hundred-dollar bills. "Here. It's eight grand. What we agreed on. I wish it didn't have to end this way."

"Yes, it does. See, I'm Rose, the fucking hooker you picked up in the Tenderloin of the city. I did my job, and it's time to move on. There *ain't* enough room for people like me in the lives of all the Garrett Chadwicks of the world. I knew better. Never again."

He pulls on his pants and a white undershirt. His demeanor runs cold, unattached, and distant.

"I'm going to give you some space. Take your time to collect your things. The dresses in the foyer closet are yours. Please take them. When I get back, I'll expect you to be gone," he states as he calmly puts on his socks and shoes.

"That's it? Just like that, you're done! Just because I don't take your deal and you can't keep me, you're gonna wash your hands of me? You're one coldass bastard, you know that?"

"Rose, you're such a beautiful woman, much too beautiful to talk like that. And you're much too smart to be selling your body. You're still young with your whole life ahead of you. Take the money I gave you and make something of yourself, outside of this."

"Fuck you!"

I go to slap him, but he grabs my wrist. His eyes constrict. His cock hardens and presses firmly against my thigh.

Is he getting turned on watching me suffer … lose … hurt?

Sick motherfucker.

He pulls me against his chest, his words just above a whisper. "I like you, Rosebud. I really do, but I'm not going to stand here and tell you what you want to hear."

I crumble from his words. He doesn't want me. I'm not good enough. Torn apart, shredded, and lost. This is all I'm ever going to be to him—*a convenient fuck …*

twenty-two

IT HAD BEEN over a year since Garrett Chadwick, aka Mister, aka Mr. C, aka whoever the fuck I thought he was, left me broken in the penthouse suite of the Shelby Hotel. From that point on, I promised myself I wouldn't give my heart to anyone ever again. And up until Shane, I had kept that promise to myself.

It only took Mister three days to make me open up and fall in love with him, and just one night to completely break me. He destroyed every last drop of trust I had mustered to be with him. Sure, we'd fucked, but it was different with him. Mister peeled back my walls, dug under them, and broke through like nobody before. He made me vulnerable and unprotected, and he methodically collected everything I gave to him. Selfishly, he took the small broken pieces of who I was and molded them into something presentable, something that made me believe I was worthy of a man's loving touch. I never thought he'd have the power to convince me to then turn my own weapon of insecurity on myself and pull the trigger. Garrett Chadwick was the worst kind of devil. He'd contaminated me with the most venomous type of poison—love.

He broke me, destroyed the delicate, and annihilated who I thought I was going to become. He was responsible for the ironclad lock around my heart. Looking back, maybe I had been in love with the idea of him loving me.

It wasn't until three weeks later, when Garrett Chadwick sent me the first of many packages, that I realized just how deep the idea of him resided under my skin. Every three weeks like clockwork, another gift showed up at my front door. At first it obliterated me, and I relived all the pain he'd created. Eventually, his gifts became a strange routine I craved. It woke up those feelings that lingered just under my skin, and for a split second of total confusion, I believed he still wanted me, needed me, and maybe even loved me.

In the exact precision of his character, whether it was clockwork or perfect presentation, nothing would flank the packages but a label, handwritten in black Sharpie pen. FROM: MISTER / TO: ROSEBUD.

When you spent your nights working instead of sleeping, it wasn't too hard to forget the demons that hid under your bed in the dark. But Garrett Chadwick made sure I'd never go too long without thinking about him—just long enough to begin to forget, but always fleeting enough to draw him right back to the surface of my skin.

It had been a year now, and I hadn't opened one, never gave any of the packages a second glance until today … until I was broken enough to accept his invitation to a world of hurt.

Now, I was fighting to keep a handle on my life. My heart was being ripped to shreds by the death of my best friend and the gaping void that was growing every minute. Sybil was the only woman I had ever trusted. The walls were closing in on me. My life was crumbling into nothing more than memories of painful betrayal and the people I'd lost because of it. Even Shane, who claimed he loved me, had become collateral damage.

Shane ... just thinking about him confused me and drove shivers down my spine, straight into the guilt of wishing he was here. What he once meant to me had now become the fuel for letting him go, especially now that he had found out what I was. The friendship we'd created and the unfulfilled desire I had couldn't become anything more than memories of a life I'd once desired. I had to let him go. Let everyone go and move on. Besides, Shane was with Martie. He had a woman who loved him, and no matter how screwed up she was, I'd never be able to compete with her. I just didn't have it in me, not anymore. I was a girl who had nothing to offer him. Nothing that would last longer than a three-minute roll in the sack.

"Good thing you cut him off before you made that mistake."

A wave of relief thundered through my body as the voice in my head interrupted my self-induced fuck-off party.

The truth of my relationships stung deep. It was Garrett Theodore Chadwick who had announced he was engaged to Ashley Hancock. It was Sybil St. James who had died at San Francisco General, leaving me to navigate the streets alone, and it was Shane West who had made me fall in love with him even though he had a girlfriend. They were the only three people who were able to thieve my heart and become the dealers of my missed chances.

I stood on our black shaggy carpet between our beds and looked around the apartment. Sybil's bed was covered in stacks of clothes, mine was covered in boxes from Mr. C, and I realized time was being a damn snitch and curiosity was being a motherfucking killer. I picked up a package from my bed and wondered if I should open it.

For the next couple of days, I grieved everything I had lost. I spent hours staring at the mountain of packages on my bed and packing up all of Sybil's things. When it all became too much, I'd pass out from pure exhaustion and wake up to the same pain I tried to escape. I never once answered my phone or unlocked my door, and only managed to drink every last drop of alcohol in the apartment.

Without hesitancy, over the last two days, I've picked up that fucking mental dagger every second, since I've been alone, and thrust it over and over again into my heart. I tortured myself with wasted moments, unopened packages of empty apologies and unfulfilled promises, and I loaded what equated to Sybil's entire life into eight large black plastic trash bags.

I figured at this point, would the content of Mister's packaged bribes really matter? They represented nothing more than lost intentions. Packages that were better left untouched under my bed. I hated him for the curiosity the boxes and padded envelopes sparked in my gut, and I hated myself even more for deciding to open one of them, let alone the one I was clutching in my hands.

I held the small white padded envelope, flipped it over, and dragged my fingers down the bubbled texture. It was light yet bulky, dusty from the time it had laid in wait for my attention. I gripped the corner and noticed a gap inviting my finger. *Do I really want to open the promise Mr. C made to me in this envelope?* Promises made to me with material things, things I could easily replace if lost or stolen. It was my heart that ached to be opened and cherished, not this shit. I didn't want what was waiting in the clusterfuck of cardboard and plastic envelopes piled on my bed. All I wanted was my heart back from Mister, Sybil, and Shane.

Lost in the thoughts cluttering my head, I was startled by a thunderous knock on my door. It wasn't a delicate, *I know you're in there and suffering* knock, or a *can I come in and help you* knock. It was a *what the fuck are you doing in there* scary knock, a *pounding knuckles upon aged wood that sounds like it could be splintered into a thousand pieces* type of knock.

I took a breath as I tried to steady myself in my crumbling

certainty. I clutched Mr. C's package to my chest, as if it was something that could protect my heart from dissolving. I wasn't gonna open my door to just anyone, especially iron knuckles on the other side. I shivered from the inside out until I heard whose voice belonged to the thunderous knock.

"Aye, Rosie, you in here? It's me, Briggs."

Kean's voice penetrated the door, floated across, and landed in the gaping hole in my chest. I froze as the envelope I was clutching tumbled down onto my bed. I didn't know if I could handle seeing him right now.

"Come on, sweet'art, let me in. I know what happened to Sybil. I want to make sure you' okay."

I heard him jiggle the doorknob, and I felt the same tempo pick up in my heartbeat.

"I'll only stay a wee bit, Rosie gir'. Com' on now."

I crept over to the front door; the floor creaked loudly with every other step I took. I pressed my face against the cold plastered wall for a handful of seconds before I reached out and grasped the door handle.

"That's right, Rosie. It's goin' to be okay, you hear me? I'm go'na be here, Rosie. When you' ready to op'n the door, I'll be waitin' righ' here."

Tears spilled over my eyelids, drenching my cheeks. Briggs *was* here for me. He'd come here just for me. I pulled the chain from the door and unlocked the deadbolt. It was the last thing between us before I was going to let him see me more broken than I'd ever been.

Briggs cautiously pushed the door open. I didn't stand there waiting for him to come in. If I looked at him and our eyes caught, I would break down and lose my shit all over again. I did the best survival-mode action possible—I shuffled over to the kitchen and started fussing with the handful of dishes in the sink.

"It's been two days, Rosie. I'd been tryin' to call." He followed me to the kitchen, his words filled with concern that sharpened to a point and easily pierced my heart.

Every ounce of resolve I held drained painfully from my soul.

"Well, Briggs, I've been here, living it up!" Sarcasm dripped from my words, words I regretted the moment they flew out of my mouth.

"Com' on, sweet'art. Don't do tis. I'm just here, worryin' about me gir'." With a tug of his hand, he pulled me around to look at him.

"Two days too late, Briggs," I spat before I turned back to the sink. I knew it was an asshole answer, a thoughtless way to let him know I was still hurting and too drunk from the bottle of lemon-flavored Smirnoff I had polished off twenty minutes ago. In fact, every last drop of the bottle of vodka still swam fiercely in my veins.

I pushed on the faucet, determined to keep from looking at him. I'd gone from being in a world of hurt to being pissed at the world in a matter of a couple of days, and well, unfortunately for Briggs, he happened to be the first who showed up. The water poured down and cradled in the curve of a soup spoon before it splashed up like a lawn sprinkler, drenching me, the countertops, backsplash, and even Briggs, who was standing behind me.

Briggs's massive hand and beastly inked arm shot over me and shut off the faucet. His determination to get through to me grew as he flung me around to face him. He wasn't delicate, and the expression on his face told me he was done playing a fool. He clutched my arms in his mammoth hands and held me so I couldn't run away. I was soaked from head to waist as the tears that streamed down my face became the exclamation points to my pain.

"Now you listen to me. I'm not here to play games. I kno' you're hurtin', but you gotta get a grip," Briggs huffed as he shook me with each word. He was bound and determined to get me to snap out of it.

In a feeble moment, weakened by the vodka in my system and made more intense by my grief, I ached to have someone tell me life would be all right, that everything I had gone through would lead to a bigger purpose. He let go of my arms and his wide, thick thumbs brushed my cheeks as his long, chunky fingers tangled in my hair. He held my head between his hands as his eyes, cast with demons he wasn't willing to share, blinked slower than I had ever seen before. I felt the pain of who I was begin to dissolve with his touch. It was as if he was willing to sacrifice himself for my greater good. I saw everything he hated about himself, every moment he clung to in the flimsy idea of who he had become, and for a moment, he let me in to see that he had fears planted deeper than I ever thought.

I dragged my hands over Briggs's warm, wet arms drenched in inked stories planted just below his flesh, stories still too raw to talk about. I craved to feel his pain. I wanted to believe he hurt as deeply as I did. I gazed at his full brown lips, and I hungered to savor the sweet to my salty existence. I wanted to taste the all-consuming pain he had carried around his entire life and just as badly needed him to devour whatever happiness I had left. I needed him to take the last piece of hope Shane had given me so I would just stop hurting so badly.

Our eyes met at the crest of my despair, and we both disappeared. Suddenly, he wasn't Kean Briggs and I wasn't Rose Newton. I was a woman in need of medicine, and he was just the man to give it to me. His lips became my antidote, and I wanted him to heal me. To kiss me, to want me, to savor me the way Mister had over a year ago. I wanted him to want me as bad as Shane wanted me. I wanted to be loved as intensely as any prince would love his princess.

I rose on my tiptoes, as if I possessed the grace of a ballerina, locked my fingers together behind his head, and pushed up until my lips were hard against his. I pressed for him to consume our kiss, but he pulled away. The cold chill invited itself between us, and instead of being our kiss, it was just mine. I had misconstrued his pain for passion, his demons for angels, and his empathy for desire.

"Whoa, slow down t'ere, Rosie gir'." Briggs held me away from his body. His cannon-shaped arms were rock solid between us. His words were a sobering splash in my face.

"Oh, fuck, what did I just do? What the fuck did I just do?" I repeated the same words several times under my breath as I turned back to the sink and made busy work for my hands.

My mom used to scream at me about fidgeting with things. She told me that the devil gave bad children busy hands. I was scared to death to fidget in front of her. She'd convinced me the devil himself was coming to take me to the fiery pits of hell ... personally. I was just eight years old, but never a moment's rest for the wicked or fidgety.

Briggs pinned me between the entire length of his body and the sink. His oversized hands swallowed mine, stopping me in my tracks. I succumbed to his massive embrace. He lowered his mouth next to my ear.

"Me gir', you did nothin' wrong. Nothin'. You' hurtin'. You' achin' for sumthin I just can't give ya. I ain't the one you want." His words rumbled in his chest as he whispered.

He caressed his hands up and down my arms, creating a rhythmic pattern that paralyzed me into submission. Loaded with guilt and ashamed of the actions I'd so easily given over to, I was completely mortified that I had compromised our friendship by kissing him.

"I can't be with Shane. He deserves someone better, someone who can differentiate a friend's compassion from a whore's needs," I snapped.

Briggs's hands froze. His grip across my arms became firm as he pulled me back and turned me to look at him. "This isn't about w'at I tink, Rosie. We both know who's got your heart. Shane'd be lucky to have you. Don't cut yourself so short. You're a mighty fine ca'ch." Briggs pushed his finger under my chin and brought my eyes up to meet his. His dark orbs contained a renewed fire, a spark that burned just behind his retinas. "You don't want to piss me off. Aye, Rosie, this isn't w'at I came here for."

Every muscle in my body went lax. It was as if I thought the words he'd been carrying around for the last couple of days could've saved my soul. Like any one of those televangelists who dramatically pushed on the foreheads of the weak, broken, or lost, and suddenly within seconds, they'd fall back into the arms of his planted disciples, healed. I wanted to fall back into the arms of someone who'd say all my sins were forgiven. But then I remembered you gotta believe in God before any televangelist would lay a finger on you.

"Thanks, Briggs ... and ... I'm ... sorry—"

"Rosie, I came to tell ya Sybil's burial is tomorra'. Nine thirdy. I'll be here at nine sharp to pick you up."

"I can't go. I can't watch them lower her in the ground. It just ain't my thing."

"Too bad. I'm takin' you. Be ready, me gir', nine a.m. sharp." He leaned in, brushing his lips across my cheek before pressing them against my ear. "And I ain't takin' no for an answer."

He pulled away and looked at me. Strength twinkled in his eyes before he leaned in and planted one of the most delicate kisses on the corner of my mouth that I'd ever felt in my entire life. An innocent, yet striking kiss that claimed his love for me, deeper than any physical attention would prove.

Mended.

Healed.

"I love you, Rosie. We're family." It was a slight enough acknowledgment of the truth.

Then he turned on his heels and meandered out the front door.

Tomorrow, I was gonna get my chance to say good-bye to the only family I had left. Well, maybe not the only family.

twenty-three

I WOKE UP every hour on the hour until my alarm burped a fucked up song from a clunky eighties band. Between the guilt about kissing Briggs last night and the scenarios that could happen at Sybil's burial today, a storm of images kept flashing through my head. It was already gonna be a tough day. Add sleep deprivation to the list, and I should be sweet as pie to be around.

Violent images of a blow-by-blow full-on fistfight between Martie and me erupted every time I closed my eyes. Martie with a bloody nose, her eyes blackened by me beating the shit out of her. My eyes swollen to slits as the vision of my dreams morphed into a twisted moment where I clung to Briggs to make Shane jealous. Off-the-hook dreams that I knew weren't real, but every time I woke up from them, I was disappointed by the reality that I was still stuck in my apartment, waiting for my alarm to go off.

Today boiled down to the fact that I was destined to watch Sybil lowered into the ground forever, a finality I wasn't really ready to accept. Death had come knocking on the wrong person's door, and there was nothing I could have done to change it. I had to face the fact that Sybil was gone forever, and I knew her family would do everything in their power to keep me away.

I didn't like to be somewhere I wasn't welcome. Hustling my six squares downtown was different—most of the people who didn't want me hanging out there were cops or other hos. But Sybil's burial was a whole different situation. I was going to go walking into an already stirred up beehive with a massive stick and clobber the hive until the queen fell from grace. I just knew I was gonna get stung.

I pulled on a black scoop-neck top. Classic in its cut, it was my go-to shirt when I had to be more conservative than what the rest of my life required. I pulled my hair back into a careless loose bun and refrained from applying makeup the way I normally did. It was the best attempt at conservative that I could muster.

I had run away from closure my entire life. Today there was no way I could run anymore. For the first time in a long time, I was going to face the reality that my life had to change. And even though I wasn't where I wanted to be financially before I stopped strolling the pavement, something had changed inside me. Sybil's death stirred in me a new desire to move on and prove to her that I was going to be okay alone.

I rolled my lips together, evening out my lipstick, when there was a knock at my door. I looked over at the clock. It was eight forty-five, a little earlier than Briggs said he was going to pick me up. Without thinking, I pressed my lips to the mirror—one last kiss for Sybil.

The chill of the mirror against my mouth kick-started the sobering idea of being in a car with Briggs. What the hell was I going to say to him? I'd fucked up bad last night. I couldn't believe I had kissed him and actually had wanted to use him to take away all of my pain. *I will never be able to take that back.* Last night had been so bad, a burning knot twisted down in my stomach. Silence swept the room, swallowing up my ability to open the door and face him. I simply froze.

"Aye, Rosie, it's me, here to pick you up." Briggs broke the silence, and the breath I was holding escaped in a loud gasp. "You okay?"

A million thoughts are drowning me.

"I'm fine," I answered under my breath.

I pulled open the door and stood waiting for him to come in. Briggs's eyes brushed over my body, a slight smile cresting his lips.

"You look ... nice," he said. "I've never seen you wear somethin' so conservative before." His Irish accent thickened.

"What does that mean?"

"Nothin'. You just look nice and put togeth'r . That's all."

"Ha, well, looks can be deceiving." I straightened the seam of my long pencil-cut black skirt.

Briggs narrowed his eyes, answering my smartass remark with his expression. A look from him and a slight pause in his demeanor held more power than any verbal reprimand could ever express.

"Fine, thanks," I responded.

A moment filled with an awkward silence pulsed between us. Maybe I put more emphasis on silence than it deserved, but I didn't want to lose my friendship with Briggs over my stupid mistake of kissing him last night. I needed him now more than ever.

"I wanted to apologize for last night."

"Now, there's no reason for doin' that. You were hurtin' and t'at's t'at." His eyes told me he wasn't going to have any of my apology. He looked over my shoulder. "What you decidin' to do with all those?" His thick, long finger hung in the air as he pointed at the eight large black garbage bags that held all of Sybil's life as I'd known it.

My breath escaped me. I hadn't expected him to ask about them. "I was just going to leave them until someone from her family asked for it."

"And what if they don't?"

"Well, then I'll take them to a thrift store."

"And 'er shoes?"

Sybil had such great taste in heels: some with leopard prints, colors for every skirt she had, a half a dozen black ones, classics that went with just about anything, and some six-inch stilettos that would make any shoe whore jealous.

"I just haven't gotten to those yet."

Briggs was a no-nonsense type of guy. I guessed when you'd lived through the tragedy he had, you built up a wall that would protect your emotions.

"Got anymor' bags?"

"Under the kitchen sink. Why?"

He took a couple of steps from where he was to the kitchen area and returned with a bag. "Let's take care of tis."

"No, that's okay."

"Naw, com' on now. Let's get tis dun."

"Key, don't worry about it. We have to get to the cemetery."

My objection didn't faze him; he snapped open the black garbage bag and held it open, waiting for me to fill it with more of Sybil's belongings.

"It won't take too long." His accent thickened when he was determined.

I pulled the big black garbage bag from his hands and rolled it up before I tossed it into Sybil's closet and shut the door. I turned around and rested my back against the door. "I'm just not ready … to let go."

I slid down the door, squeezed behind my bent knees in an attempt to stop the pain pouring from my gut. Tears rained across my cheeks and landed on my skirt.

Am I really going to be strong enough to walk up to the six-foot deep hole in the earth dug specifically for her?

Truthfully, I didn't want to pack everything of hers away. If I left a part of her out, then maybe I could hold on to her just a little longer. I had the unrealistic idea that maybe if I kept some things of hers out and where they belonged, it wouldn't hurt so badly when I got back today.

Briggs dropped down next to me, draping his arms around me and swallowing me in his embrace. I was safe and felt comfort as he hummed in his Irish accent. He caressed my head, lulling me away from the fear that clung to every breath I took. And in no more than a slight sway, he convinced me that I was strong enough to make it through the day.

"Shhh, I'm here, Rosie, me lovely lady. I know you're hurtin'. Sybil, she'd want you to be strong. She'd want you to go on … not'ing will bring you down here anymore. Come on, sweet'art. Let me see that strong gir' I know."

He pulled back from me, letting me catch a glimpse of myself in his dark eyes. He wouldn't abandon me. Not here, not there, not ever. He stood up, held out his massive hands, and waited, the first move toward my future. Pulling me up, he caught my chin between his calloused thumb and pointer finger.

"We aren't much different me and you. We're fighters, always and for'ver." He swept the loose strands of hair off my forehead before he pressed his lips across the deep worry lines that made their home above my eyebrows.

He was right. We were fighters. We were survivors in our own right, and this, as hard as it was going to be, wouldn't break us.

A glimpse of …

Strength.

I grabbed my purse off my dresser. The crystal bowl which used to hold more condoms than anything else caught my eye, and I saw the cluster of Blow Pops Shane had given me during several of our laundry dates. I grabbed a couple, tossed them into my purse, and avoided the need to add anything else from that crystal

210

bowl. I looked at myself in the full-length mirror behind the door, making double-sure I was just conservative enough.

"Ready, Rosie?"

I nodded as I quickly swept my hands across the front of my skirt and grabbed a lightweight black knit cardigan from the rickety coatrack Sybil had found down the street one night and decided to drag home. A twinge of sadness fluttered across my heart.

Briggs held the apartment door open for me and did the same as we left the building. He was such a gentleman. Everything he did was protective and comforting, from hurrying me across the street with his palm against the small of my back to pulling my car door open, small gestures that most might overlook if not paying attention.

"Thank you, Key."

"For wat?"

"For being here for me."

He gave me a quick smile and a wink before he shut me into his car. All it took was that slight smile and that simple wink to reassure me that we were good. That we were going to make it through today together, as friends and as family.

Trusting …

The drive to the cemetery started out quiet, until a pressure started building inside me. I felt as if a vise was being tightened across my chest, pinning me down in a sticky leather seat and poking me with fiery sharp needles up and down my spine, arms, and legs. My skin flushed hot before sweat began to cool the raging heat thundering through my body. I tried to look out the window, count the people whose lives seemed so much better than mine. I tried to hold the voice in my head at bay, hoping Briggs didn't notice I was starting to have a panic attack.

But the voice in my head knew when to strike. *She* knew when I was at my weakest. *She* was the same voice that dictated my moods when I couldn't handle the stress of trying to be someone everyone else wanted me to be.

Now, here we go again. Rose, when will you ever learn that whores like you ain't worthy of grieving?

"Yes, I am," I answered her in my head.

No, you're not. Do you honestly believe Sybil's family is gonna overlook you being there?

"Maybe. I don't know. I need to be there."

No, you don't. Oh, fuck, come on Rose, can't you see you're the hooker-low-life-roommate who left the door unlocked so Dax could come in and kill her? It's your fault she's dead.

"No, it's not! It's not my fault, and you're not real!" the nine-year-old broken little girl deep inside me screamed back.

Oh, but Rose, I am real, and I'm really in your head. I've been with you forever. I know you best, and now I'm here to help you remember your place. You aren't worthy—never have been, never will be.

I pushed my hands up across my face. My skin and hairline were damp from the perspiration pushing through my pores.

Briggs noticed. "Rosie, you oka'?"

He brushed his fingers across my hands still cupping my face. I didn't look up. This time the fucked up voice in my head was relentless.

Isn't that cute. You almost could have had him. I bet if you'd let him kill Dax, Sybil would be here. You shouldn't have stopped Briggs from killing him. Sybil's death wouldn't have been for nothing. Oh, wait, it was for something—it took one more filthy, dirty whore off the street. You'll always be a dirty broken girl who whores herself to feed the monster inside. No wonder Briggs and Shane don't want you!

"Shut up, shut up, just shut the fuck up," I screamed at the top of my lungs into my hands as I swayed back and forth.

I was trapped where I was. I couldn't escape her. When she'd shown up before, I'd have a place to go, a motion I could do that would cause her to lose the grip she had in my head.

Briggs stopped the car; my body jolted forward.

"Wha' the fuck?" Briggs's voice carried and filled the car. He was demanding, almost like he was coming from a place of fear, a place he'd known for way too long.

I hopped out of the car and paced the dingy sidewalk riddled with yesterday's trash.

"I'm worthy, do you fucking hear me? I'm fucking worthy. You can't break me anymore. I'm not that scared little girl anymore. You will not win! Do you hear me? YOU. WON'T. WIN!" I hollered into the gust of wind that kicked up and swirled around me.

The chill of the wind coming off the bay spread across my face, loosening the grip the voice had in my head as if the wind cleansed my soul of the wicked. Suddenly, the voice in my head was silent. And just like that, I was left on the sidewalk, clinging to the only thing I knew.

When I lowered my eyes back down to Briggs, he was standing there, unmoved by my outburst. The look on his face told me he was familiar with the demon I was battling, as if in some intimate way, the pain in my life was connected to his. He nodded, his body firm, tense, like he was ready to protect me. I blinked slowly and nodded back. In an instant, his arms were around me.

"Shhh, you' safe. I'm here. It's over."

"I ... I ... I—"

"Come on, Rosie gir', get in the car."

Battling the need to be healed, I knew I was safe, packed away in the care of Briggs until he pulled into the Cypress Lawn Cemetery.

twenty-four

As Briggs passed through Daly City, I recovered from the complete unraveling of my mind. The tick of my heart didn't echo through my ears nearly as loudly as it had just thirty minutes earlier, and the knots through my shoulders relaxed once I leaned back on the headrest. Most of the time the badgering voice won, but today, today it just couldn't. I couldn't let her win.

Kean turned into Cypress Lawn Cemetery, prettified by a massive white marble archway and well-kept rolling hills of manicured green lawns. Suddenly I realized Sybil had been born into privilege. For some reason, I'd visualized Sybil being buried in a decrepit, unkempt, unmarked cemetery. Sure, I grew up in San Francisco, and I knew we buried our dead in Colma, a town that had more real estate for the dead than the alive, but the times that I had actually gone into a cemetery were very few and far between. My only points of reference were the ones in scary movies. Besides that, I'd never actually seen someone buried. I hadn't even gone to see my grandma buried.

My skin was hot. The car had become stifling as we drove the narrow roads. I desperately wanted to peel the pain from every cell in my body and bury it in Sybil's grave. Leave the last bit of expectation where it all started—tucked below the surface of who I was. Life would be so much easier if I was numb.

Briggs pulled to the side as he scanned the sprawling lawn cluttered with a small group of people huddled around an open grave. Suddenly, there wasn't a moment to catch my breath or think about how I was going to react. All I had were tiny pieces of my own awareness that I was here, and up there on those rolling hills across the narrow road was Sybil's body, motionless in a casket.

I looked back at Briggs and watched him curl his bottom lip in between his teeth as he seemed to struggle to recognize any of the people dressed in black. My heart exploded into a hyper rhythm as I noticed him narrowing his eyes. I looked back up and saw Martie sitting behind a polished, dark wooden casket. Standing next to her was a minister, the Bible in one hand as he flicked a stick with holy water from the other. Finality flowed through my veins … done and over. It looked like the minister was setting her soul free.

I kept watching Martie's reaction. Call it morbid, but I wanted to see her grieve. Cry as hard as I did when I lost the only person who had accepted me as family. But her reaction was unemotional, nothing, like the whole process of burying Sybil was extremely inconvenient. Hunched over next to her was an older man with a crooked back. He was thin and drawn, like he was too fragile for his old worn bones to carry his body. He held Martie's hand and the hand of an equally frail woman seated on the other side of him. I assumed this was all that was left of Sybil's family. Each of them carried the same stoic expression, as if they were burdened with a daughter and a sister who had lost herself to a lifestyle choice that rattled them to their very core and spiked them through their hearts with ice-cold reserve. I knew that people grieved in their own ways, but those people looked like they were incapable of showing any form of compassion.

I should be standing there grieving for Sybil, not them. Why did death have to be so cold? All death had to do was walk away and leave me to grieve. But death wasn't simple—it was heartless. It gutted you and drained your veins until they were dry.

I looked back over at Martie and watched as her demeanor changed. Her attention shifted to the grove of Cypress trees across the way. A glint caught in her eyes just about the same time a tiny smirk rolled across her face. I looked over, following her gaze straight to the cause of her newfound expression.

What.

The.

Fuck.

As if God hadn't punished me enough, there *he* was—Shane. He had come here for Martie. Every broken piece of who I was shattered all over again. Forget the idea that I was willing or able to show my face now. There was no way I was going to go up there and look like a damn fool in front of them. My good-bye, saved for only Sybil, would have to wait until she was buried six feet under.

"Let's go. Start up the car and head out. I don't want to go over there. This was a big mistake, Key, I shouldn't have come."

"What are you talkin' 'bout? You and aye are goin' up there."

"No, Briggs, really, I think I'll just come back when nobody's here. Less chance of a confrontation."

"Rosie, I ain't leavin'. If you don't want to go up there right now, we'll wait until tey leave. Me and you 're gonna wait."

There was no way Briggs was going to let me win. He was just as stubborn as I was when it came to shit like this. So I just watched in agony as Martie slipped away from Sybil's burial to go be with Shane.

Briggs didn't miss a beat. "Oh, aye, sweet'art, now I know why. Tat's your beau," he said as he tilted his head and thrust his chin out at the scene between Martie and Shane.

"No, he's not mine, and I don't wanna talk about it," I answered.

"Tat's the guy! He's the one that chased you through the hospit'l, aye?"

"Yeah, but—"

"He's the same guy me keeps seein' down in the district, prowlin' around," he added.

His words soaked into my head but didn't register right away. I wanted to argue with him, make him see that nothing made that man mine.

"He manages a laundromat down there; he isn't prowlin' the Tenderloin. Besides, he's got that!" I tossed my hands forward, pointing at Martie, who had successfully wrapped herself around Shane's body.

"I know exactly who that is. Look, that right there isn't the actions of a man who's in love wit' her. I'm tellin' you, when he's down in the belly of the Tenderloin, aye, sweet'art, tat lad is lookin' to find you. He's in love wit' you."

"Now I know you've lost it. I'm completely aware of the feelings that boy has for me, but trust me, it can never happen. Ever."

"Why? Give me one goot reason." Briggs faced me.

His eyes burned into my profile. I kept staring straight ahead, even if it was breaking what was left of me to watch her pull Shane over to Sybil's grave. I took a deep breath, hoping to catch the courage that was seeping from my lungs before I glanced at Briggs.

"Because of who I am, Key. I sell my body to cheap-ass, horny men. As much as I wish he'd be able to see past my scars, he won't. And just like every time before, every moment I get some type of hope, it fucking fails me and I'm crushed all over again. Trust me, it's better this way." My words pricked my skin just like they did the last time I said them. But it was the truth—it was me and I was it.

I looked out over the rolling grassy hills and the scene playing out in front of me between Martie, her family, and Shane.

"We all have scars. You and me, our scars run deeper than most. Us two, we're more alike than you care to admit. We keep pushin' people away 'cause we're scared to let them see our weakness. Tat we actually have a heart and tat it's lonely. I know you well, Rosie. I see me'self in you a lot. And the t'ing is, the only t'ing we're gonna get from pushing people away is tired. I'm tired, Rosie, and I t'ink you are too. You deserve to be happy."

"Yeah, well, that right there, that ain't my happy … that right there's nothing but a broken heart, trust me."

I slipped my hand down the side of the passenger seat and pulled the lever, lowering the back of my seat so I didn't have to watch Shane and Martie pierce what little dignity I had left. Maybe I just wanted to cuddle with the humiliation as I clung to it like a child who carried around a security blanket, that way I wouldn't forget how painful it was to love someone I couldn't have.

"You know somet'ing, Rosie, I've pinned me pain across me chest me 'ole life. Taken the bullets of sufferin' like the best of them. In the middle of a war zone, I watched me brothers sacrifice everyt'ing they were. For w'at? So I could come back and waste me opportunity on being bitter while they be buried six feet under in the cold hard ground, dead for a country they loved? Shane doesn't love that gir' up there. He's too busy fightin' a war with the demons you're not willin' to give up."

Briggs's words sliced me deep. He'd pinned me in a corner I'd been frightened of my whole life. He saw through me as if my skin was nothing but a thin veil I hid behind to stay safe. I was always a fuck 'em and let 'em go type of girl. Only let 'em get enough from me so I didn't have to give. Nothing ventured, nothing gained. It was my best excuse and my worst reason. It was easier to placate my pain than it was to provoke anyone's love.

A pressure pushed hard against my chest. The guilt of giving up so easily robbed my breath. Now Kean Briggs was challenging me to pony up, live raw, be present, and give into my feelings for Shane. A roll of the dice in a gamble I'd always lost.

"I'm not sure I can give up my demons. They've been with me for so long, I don't know who I am anymore without them."

"Ma'be it's time you found out who you really are."

"What if it's too late?"

"And what if it's not? Nothing is guaranteed, Rosie. We could drive outta here and be killed in a he'd-on car crash. And go to Heaven, find me the Pearly Gates, or crash into the fiery pits of Hell." His accent again thickened with his intensity.

"What's your point, Key?"

"Me point bein' you can either be the woman sitting here contemplatin' 'bout how to visit her best friend before they bury her forever, or you can grab your life by the short hairs and claim wat's yours."

"Easy for you to say."

"Damn right it is, sweet'art, but you're the stubborn gir' who needs to swallow her pride and mend t'ings with that boy up there. 'Cause I'm dun watching you throw your life away. I can't stand me dreadful thoughts every time your number comes up on me phone."

"So the truth comes out. You aren't as tough as you look."

"If that's wat you believe, so be it. I'd rather be visitin' you at a house then watch you be buried in a place like this. You're a tough gir', no doubt in me mind, but if you keep doin' what you're doin', you won't be long for this world."

"If you keep telling all your clients to quit the business, you'll be out of a job," I quipped as I forced my seat back upright.

"Well, Rosie, just call it a soft spot in me heart for you. It's the only time I've said this to anyone, but that boy, well, he's your ticket out of this life, me gir'. I think it's high time you cashed it in."

Deep down, I knew he was right. It was obvious he was just trying to protect me, but seeing that I'd had to take care of myself my entire life, I wasn't going to let him think that he knew what was best for me.

I looked out and watched Shane, in his dark charcoal suit, lean down and kiss the old woman on the cheek before he gingerly consoled the old man next to her. Shane rested his palm on the man's shoulder while they shook hands. A familiar gesture that appeared more intimate than the greeting of strangers. I observed Sybil's parents, or who I assumed were Sybil's parents, lift their frail hands while they talked to him, and I watched Shane as he comfortably consoled them. He was so sincere, and even though I couldn't hear what they were saying to one another, I noticed Shane's expression was genuine and filled with compassion.

"Well, I appreciate your concern, Briggs, I do, but this is my life, and what I do with it … well, that's my business. Just tend to your stuff, and I'll tend to mine, and I think it will be better that way."

"Aye, sweet'art. I've said me piece. You can sit here and lose your opportunity, havin' a pity party for one, or you can get your arse out of the car and say a proper good-bye to Sybil. Either way, it's no skin off me teeth. It's your choice," he said as he patted my knee before he opened the driver's side door and got out.

He flung open the back driver's side door, yanked his black dress coat from a hanger, and pulled it on before he looked over at me. His eyes asked if I was going to be an arse or a friend.

"I'm sorry, Key, this wound's pretty deep. I just can't face him right now."

"Suit you'self." He shut the back car door, and I watched him meander up to Sybil's open grave.

I looked over and saw Shane consoling Martie. It was a dagger in my heart. I closed my eyes and wept.

twenty-five

MY EYES WERE still closed as tears drenched my lashes and betrayed me while I tried to stop the ungodly ugly cry from taking over me. I figured I'd wait for Briggs to come back so we could just go, but he took forever. I knew he wouldn't let me get out of here until I'd gone up there and paid my respects to Sybil.

All right, it's time to put on my big girl panties and face the music. Nobody's gonna control me anymore. I have every right to go up there and say good-bye to my best friend.

I waited for the voice in my head to argue back—tell me that I was just a fucked up person, a worthless person, someone who didn't deserve to take up space in this world—but there was no argument, no mean words that fucked with my self-esteem. Relief washed over me when I sat up and saw that Key was the only one at the gravesite. A weight lifted from my shoulders. Finally I was getting my moment alone with my dead best friend safely locked in a dark wooden casket.

I opened my door and regained the confidence to go up and give my last regards when the driver's side door flung open.

A voice startled me.

"Close the door." Shane slipped into the driver's seat, shutting his door behind him, before he stretched his long, thick arm across and grabbed the handle of my door and shut it.

"What the fuck, Sha—"

"Stop. Just don't say anything."

"What? Who the hell do you think you are?"

"I'm the man who loves you. I'm your man."

"No, you're not."

"Oh, sweetheart, yes, I am, you just don't know it yet. But that's all about to change."

His answer caught me off guard. Shane had never talked like that before.

"You can't be my man unless I let you, and as far as I can see, you're still with Martie."

"You can see whatever the hell you want to see, but the truth is, I've tried to come in slow, tried to take off slow. I've tried to take my time, and I've tried to back away and give you time. I'm done trying."

"Good, you should be. I've told you, nothing can come of us. I'm no good for you."

"Yeah, you keep saying that, but you see, I'm not going to try anymore. I'm going to do something about it."

"Oh, yeah, what are you going to do? What are you willing to give up for me?"

"I'm not giving up anything for you. You and I both know that's not what you're asking from me. I know you're scared. I know you look at me and you feel everything that you've had to bury deep your entire life. But that's not the reason you keep pushing me away."

"No? What's the reason? Why? Tell me, 'cause I just can't seem to figure out why you won't just give up on me."

"Because I know what scares you."

Our eyes met. His soul yearned for me. His intentions raged behind his big brown orbs, and I could feel my protective walls being built between us. He pushed open the driver's door and stepped out before he leaned down, and we looked at each other.

"I know you have a lot of things to think about right now, but being afraid to love me back shouldn't be one of them."

He shut the door, and I was closed off again. This time by him. I watched as he got into his car and drove away. I sat there for several surreal moments, trying to process what had just happened, how the power had shifted between us, and how I was left even more broken than before.

My phone chimed with a text from Briggs.

> *BRIGGS: COME ON ROSIE, IT'S TIME. THEY ARE BURYING HER SOON.*

I slipped my phone back into my purse, left it in the car, and headed up the grassy hill to say good-bye to my lifeless roommate, Sybil.

I watched as they lowered the beautiful wooden casket into the ground. I didn't relate to the idea that Sybil's body was in there. Not seeing her lying in the casket gave me the ability to fake like this was just some drama I was watching on TV. But when they hit a snag while lowering Sybil into the six-foot-deep hole, it didn't feel like in the movies anymore. I decided I'd seen enough, I'd cried enough, and I'd paid respect to her. It was enough. I looked over at Briggs and told him I was okay to leave now. We didn't wait around for the gravediggers to shovel from the huge pile of freshly dug up earth. I turned away and never looked back.

Briggs drove me back to my apartment. We barely talked. I didn't tell him what Shane had said to me before I went up to say good-bye to Sybil. I didn't think he really needed to know. Besides, I knew it would just give him the idea that I was going to

GRETCHEN de la O

allow Shane to save me.

"Did you need me to come up for a wee bit, Rosie?"

I thought about his offer. Even though it was only noon, and I was exhausted, I decided I just wanted to hang out in my apartment by myself and face life tomorrow, after I had a clearer head and an idea of what I was going to do.

"Thanks, Key, but I think I'm gonna call it a day. I'm pretty tired, and I have a lot of things I need to take care of."

"Well, you know I can help you."

"I know, and I appreciate your offer."

"You just say, and I'll be there."

He parked in the yellow loading and unloading zone right in front of my building. He helped me out of his SUV. I clung to him, and we hugged like we knew it was going to be the last time we'd see each other for a long time. He comfortably consumed my body in his embrace. I felt so desperate and safe at the same time.

"Well, Rosie gir', I'm so sorry 'bout Sybil. I wish I could have saved her," Kean whispered, breathless across the top of my head.

"Key, you did everything you could." My voice dissolved into his black dress jacket.

"Please, think 'bout what we talked 'bout. I know you have your reasons, but I don't have it in me to lose you."

With those words, I pulled out of our hug and shot him a genuine smile. "Thank you for today."

He smiled, his eyes glassing over, "I'll call you tomorro'," he mumbled before he went around and got back into his car.

I rummaged through my purse before fumbling for the keys to my building. Fifteen seconds and counting after I left Briggs behind, I started to work on what my next move was. Once I got the door to my building open, I turned back and waved him off. I noticed his smile didn't touch his eyes, and it set loose a sad ping deep in my heart.

The door slammed behind me, a noise I never got used. It sent shivers down into my core every time. My phone chimed with a message. I scrolled through all the messages from all the fucks that had been looking for me the last several days. More of the same— Johns I was going to hand over to the girls who fought over my six squares of sidewalk. Winner takes all.

Then my energy changed when I heard someone clear their throat. When I looked up and saw Shane leaning against my apartment door, my knees gave a little. He was still dressed in his clothes from the funeral.

"Shane."

"Rose," he whispered.

"What are you doing here?"

"I couldn't seem to make it home."

"So you show up here? How did you get in? How do you know where I liv—Martie." I brushed past him and thrust my key into the door. "Are you here to collect all of Sybil's things? 'Cause I don't have all her things together. Maybe you can come back in a couple of days."

"Rose, I'm not here for Martie or her family."

"I need time to finish packing—"

He caught me and pulled me up against his chest. Our eyes met, and the storm raged and swirled between our breaths.

"Rose, I'm here because I've done everything I had in my arsenal to get through to you. I'm running out of options. This is the only thing I have left." His eyes twinkled as he spoke.

The slight bounce of his Adam's apple tickled at my heart as he pulled up my chin. I felt gentleness in his touch, but it was the gentle manner in which he leaned down and kissed the corner of my mouth that set me on fire for him. His lips begged for the right to ask for more, and his soft take-off became a raging flight as his hands pulled me into his chest and his mouth devoured me. His kiss was filled with a collection of every time I'd pushed him away, every time I'd sold my body for someone else's pleasure.

Our tongues pierced, swirled, and danced as the pressure of his mouth against mine morphed into the ravenous need to consume me.

God, he felt like home. He owned me, took me entirely with just his kiss. A kiss I hadn't felt before, one that I'd never given to anyone else in my entire life. His kiss was so personal, so intense, so intimate, and so foreign to me. A pressure built in my chest. Fear rolled into my soul, thunder and lightning cracking through every cell of my body, I wasn't ready for what he was offering me. His hands danced across my curves, memorizing what he'd hungered after for so long.

My heart crashed against my lungs, and I couldn't breathe. His kiss cleansed every dirty breath I'd ever taken in my life. I felt his intentions—I knew them as if they were ink pierced in my flesh, experiences I could've etched in my skin until my story took up every last inch of my pale body. I knew if I lived just below the exterior, just below the disguise he saw, then I wouldn't have to ever deal with all the pain that boiled so deeply. All I wanted to do was scratch the surface of who I was. This entire moment was a mistake. A big mistake.

I pushed Shane away from me. His arms scraping across my body left me cold as he and his warmth stumbled back from me. His eyes widen, surprise breaking across his expression.

A gaping moment spread between us before I gave him my excuse. "I'm wrecked, Shane."

"No, you're not."

"Yes, I am, you just can't see it. Did you honestly think that kissing me would fix me? Or if you got a chance to sleep with me or see my deepest wounds, you'd somehow heal me? Did you really think you could take away a lifetime of anguish? Take a number and stand in the long fucking line of all the people who came before you." I turned to go into my apartment. I wasn't willing to wait any longer and pin my hopes on a man who didn't know the first thing about a life as broken as mine.

"That's not—Rose!" He followed me, slamming the door shut behind him. He grabbed me by the forearms and pinned me between the wall and his body. His face close to mine, his breath tickled against my flesh as he continued in a hushed whisper. "Listen, I don't care if you're wrecked. I want to be here for you … I love you."

I pushed back. It was the usual wall I built between people when I knew they had gotten too close. His face grew pale as he shifted his stance closer to me. I could see in his hickory-colored eyes that he knew he was in deeper than he anticipated. So I pushed, like I always did, hoping he'd back away.

"You don't love me, so don't stand here and tell me you do." I slammed my hand against his chest, hoping he'd stop as I continued to verbally assault him. He didn't budge. "Did you honestly think you've got the ability to save me from all the fucked up, uncivilized shit I've lived with every day of my life? There's nobody who can take away the despicable actions of others. The deeds are already done. I have every last wicked scar those repulsive fucks left on me. I'm the woman who will never be able to give enough back to you. I'm the empty veins of that dying tree nobody gives two fucks about."

"That's not true."

"Shane, I'm a girl who whores herself out in the piss-filled dingy alley between the Stop and Wash and the Iron Hog Pub. I keep gasping for a breath nobody has the ability to give. So don't stand here and tell me you love me, or think a kiss will heal me. You will never understand, and don't tell me that you don't care about my past! You'll never know what it feels like to live in my skin or make sense of all the fucked up situations that made me who I am. You'll never understand where I come from or what I have to overcome every fucking day of my life."

"YOU. NEVER. LET. ME. IN. Goddammit, Rose, let me in.

Let me know who you are. I want to understand. I want to try." Shane reached for me; I yanked my arm back away from his massive fingers.

"Do you want to know why I know you'll never understand?"

He didn't respond. He stood silently pleading for my heart.

"Do you?" I snarled.

"Yeah, I want to know why."

"Forget it!" I whipped my arms around, pulling out of his grasp. He caught me, pulled me back, and pinned me again.

"Tell me, Rose. Tell me right now why you think I'll never understand," he said in a low, heartbreaking growl.

A weighty pause, thick and painful, was suspended between us. I looked into his eyes, his beautifully broken eyes, and I saw the sparks of a future that didn't belong to me.

"Because you keep asking me for something that I'll never be able to give to you. I can't give you a clean past. Every time you touch me, you will think about all the men I've been with before you, and every time I make love to you, you'll be questioning if I've done that with someone else. It just won't work. And I don't think I can bear the day you will wake up next to me and find out I wasn't worth it. I can't give you something I'm not."

"I'm not asking you to," he whispered. His eyes cast down. When he looked back up at me, they glistened with a deeper sorrow than I'd ever seen in his eyes before.

Dragging my fingers against his face, I traced the sharp edge of his jawbone, memorizing the texture of his five o'clock shadow. His slight Adam's apple bobbed as he swallowed.

"It doesn't matter. It's a hopeless battle you'll never win. There'll always be a part of me I keep hidden away from you, and you'll always be pushing for more. Please, Shane, you have so much to give to someone who deserves a great guy."

"I don't want someone else, Rose. I want you."

My body gave way to his words, my heart pounding so hard its echo thundered through my veins. I wanted to crash into him, taste the lips of a man who wanted me more than all the reasons he shouldn't.

"That night in the alley, when I first saw you ... I was drawn to you."

My head spun as his words snaked their way into my mind. "What?"

"I know most people don't believe in that love-at-first-sight bullshit—"

"You knew it was me in the alley that night? I was whoring myself out the entire time and you didn't call me out?"

"No, I mean, yes. No, no, no, Rose, I didn't know it was you at first!" He shook his head as the words shot from his mouth.

I recognized the frustration that raged behind his eyes. "What is it, Shane? Either you knew I was a hooker or you didn't."

"Don't say that!"

"What do you want me to say? It's what I am. You can't paint a Pinto Ferrari red and expect it to win the race. It's who I've had to become to make it in this world."

"That's not the person I see standing in front of me."

"Stop it, just stop!"

"No, I can't. You're not the woman from the alley that night. Your eyes, when they met mine, they told me everything I needed to know about you, Rose. The more time we spent together, the more I discovered the woman I was falling in love with. You can't deny it, and even if you try, you know I'm right. Nothing else matters to me when I'm with you. I can't exist in my skin without you."

I stood there, frozen by his words. I knew how he felt. I felt the same way too. But I was afraid, and I hated being afraid. I pulled away and struggled to collect myself. I looked at him, memorizing the man I was going to walk away from forever.

"Please, Rose, you know I'm right."

"I can't. I'll always have a past that'll chase me, and you'll always second-guess when I come home late. What kind of relationship would that be? I'll never stop looking over my shoulder, waiting for the demons to catch up, and you'll always wonder why I keep fighting. I am not your girl, Shane."

He leaned down, and his mouth collided with mine. His lips were desperate and hungry to convince me that we were worth fighting for. Goddammit, what if he decided I wasn't worth the investment? His arms cradled me, protected me, and took the weight of my world as he pressed his warm fingers across my spine.

Is he right?

I almost caved …

I was already saying good-bye, and he didn't know it. One last kiss. One last taste to keep his flavor in my mind before I walked away from him forever. Concerned he would pull away from me too soon, I weaved my fingers into the back of his hair. He pushed harder, urging me to open up to him. I'd never had this, a personal and painful good-bye that lingered a little longer than I anticipated.

His mouth consumed me while he pushed and dragged his hands against my back, desperate to discover if there was something I was willing to leave for him. A strong kiss, a farewell, a hopeless plea to stay. His tongue searched as he tried to unearth my weakness. We tangled our desires for one another with the pain of me saying good-bye. His growl across my lips filled my soul until it forced the ironclad lock around my heart to break open for the woman I wanted to be. His love gave me the ability to see that I could be enough for him someday, but today I needed to be enough for me.

He pulled away to let the chill of the room dance across my lips. "I will never stop fighting for you. Never. You're soaked into the marrow of my bones, and you'll be there until the day I take my last breath." His words tickled across my lips, words that I'd waited my whole life for someone to say to me.

I loved him so much that I knew I had to let him go. It was my first unselfish act as the woman I was trying to become. This wasn't about being a martyr or trying to punish myself for bad choices; this was about finding myself for the first time in my life. I ached to belong to normal, whatever normal could be.

"Shane, I'm so in love with you, I can't think straight. But right now, I have to move forward in my life. Make some changes, learn to become the woman I'm supposed to be. I know it seems selfish—maybe it's wrong, maybe I'll kick myself in the ass for doing this—but I have to be on my own. I need time to find out who I truly am. Without the grind of what I've done, who I am with other people, or who I've become. I don't want to be the woman who let everyone take advantage of her anymore. I need to heal my heart, forgive my past, and be the woman you'll need me to be."

"You are the—"

"Shhhhh." I pushed my fingers to his lips. "It's hard to look at the perfection standing in front of me and walk away. But if I don't do this for me ... for us, we won't have a chance. And I want this. I want us to last. So I'm asking you to give me some time. Don't contact me, follow me, or question me—"

"I can't do that." Pulling my fingers from his lips, he shook his head. "Do you realize what you're asking me to do?"

"Yeah, I'm asking you to give me your love and support."

"You're asking me to remove my heart from my chest. You're asking me to walk away from the woman who makes me complete, leaving her to a world that is cruel and unforgiving. Why are you asking me to do that?"

"Because I've spent my entire life in bad relationships, situations that stole a part of who I was, and I have to find those pieces again. I need to feel that I'm worthy of accepting your love, unconditionally, without fear." I pushed my hands against his face, clearing the fear rolling down his cheeks. "Please, tell me you can understand that I need this. I'll find you, wherever you are, and come hell or high water, if we are meant to be, we'll be."

Eyes damp with so much loss, he pushed his fingers against my face, rubbing, brushing, memorizing what he was having to say good-bye to for as long as I needed him to.

"I'm so goddamn scared that if I walk out of here right now and give you the space you need, someone else will swoop in and take my place, and that would just kill me to lose you."

"When I find my heart, it's yours, I promise you that." I pushed up on my tiptoes and kissed him.

My lips slammed against his, and a yearning sparked so deep, so strong in my soul that my entire body craved him in a way I'd never craved anyone in my life. If that was what love felt like, something I ached for more than my own breath when drowning, then I was willing do whatever it took to make it back to him.

"I love you, Complicated Rose."

"I love you, Persistent Shane."

He let go of me and walked out of my front door. No more words used, no vows, no solutions, or guarantees about what was going to happen to us. He walked out with just a hope that I would find out who I was, and I stood there hoping he'd still want me as badly as I wanted him when we found each other again.

twenty-six

6 MONTHS LATER
PORTLAND, OREGON

"Night, Claire. See you tomorrow," I said as I rubbed my hand across the back of the bent-over waitress serving drinks to her table.

"All right, Rose. Hey, you pulling the lunch shift tomorrow?" Claire asked as she slipped the empty round drink tray under her arm.

"Yeah, Tempest asked me to cover for Steph, so I'm pulling a double," I answered as I straightened the collar on my uniform.

"I'm working lunch too," she said as she collected her two-tone, platinum-and-magenta hair off her shoulders, twisted it into a messy bun, and thrust her pen through it to hold it in place.

"Perfect, just you and me!"

Funny how Shane had teased me about being a waitress and here I was working in a Cajun and Creole restaurant in downtown Portland. It kept me grounded. Angel's Cajun Kitchen was the first place to give me a job with no real service skills, or ones I cared to mention. They had been willing to take a gamble on me.

It could have been that I'd come in all the time for food during the first couple of months after I left San Francisco. The restaurant was the only place that kept me in touch with the feelings I had for Shane.

One day they seemed shorthanded, and I just asked if they needed help. They took a chance on me, and well, it was the best thing that had happened to me since I moved to Oregon.

"Well, see ya tomorrow. I'm off to meet my friend I haven't seen in a while."

"Is this friend a he or a she?"

"He's a he," I quipped.

The manager strolled in from the kitchen.

Claire didn't waste time filling her in on the details of our conversation. "Did you hear that, Tempest? Our girl Rose is having a date with a dude."

"It's not that type of date," I huffed.

"That's great! The people on table four need refills, Claire. And I don't think Rose needs you broadcasting her life to our paying customers. Hustle it up. Rose, have fun, but not too much. Keep those bags out from under your eyes. We'll see you for the lunch shift."

"Thanks, Tempest. See you tomorrow, Claire." I pushed the door open and stepped out into the world.

Another day as Rose Newton, the waitress at Angel's Cajun Kitchen and not the woman who used to sell her body in the Tenderloin. Even though I worked a legitimate job—and waitressing *was* hard work—it was always in the back of my mind that I could make three times more money by selling myself for one night than the meager tips I pulled in in a week. I felt the fear of failing and having to go back to the stroll, but my promise to Sybil was stronger than that fear. Let's face it, Portland had its diamond district where I could easily stroll the track and make a quick couple of dead presidents. But waitressing was the first time

I made an honest living without having to sacrifice my soul in doing it. Sure, I was sore, my feet ached, and my back was killing me, but connecting with people on a level I'd never had before was rewarding.

I wasn't contacted anymore by Garrett Chadwick, aka Mr. C, or any of the other men I'd left behind for that matter. I figured at least Mister was married and happy by now—maybe his wife was enough for him. I hadn't received any more packages from him since leaving San Francisco, and oddly enough, it felt good and, at the same time, bad.

Maybe someday my fear would shrivel up and blow away. Until then, I was taking it one day at a time, in the words of my shrink. *Take each day as it comes.*

I'd found a group for recovering prostitutes. We all had our own fucked up and tainted stories we worked to overcome. We all needed help with self-esteem building and how to manage drug and alcohol dependency, but group therapy was a trip in and of itself. So many broken girls, some with stories more horrific than mine, sat in a circle and waited for their turn to have their actions validated by someone else just as fucked up as they were. Each and every single one of us carried the belief that we weren't like the girl to the left or right of us. But when we had sessions on how to create real relationships with people, we were exactly like the girl next to us. We all struggled with feeling worthy.

I'd lived my whole life creating bullshit stories to fulfill everyone else's fantasies and desires, and I'd never learned how to foster a healthy relationship with myself first and foremost. But as provoking as the meetings were, I never piped up with stories and smartass comebacks. I was a listener; sometimes active and sometimes distracted, but I always listened. Some of the therapists' stuff felt like stupid bullshit, whack-job-nut-case-dome-planting thinking, but some of what they talked about made sense. I went twice a week, so something had to be sinking in. If I could see the worth in those other women, I had to be worthy too. I was getting better at ignoring the fucked up voice in my head. It wasn't perfect, but it worked for me.

It had been five months, three weeks, and six days since I'd talked to or seen Shane. I would go round and round with myself about texting him or calling him just so I could hear his voice and hang up. My self-doubt fucked with me. Not seeing him or talking to him played right into the fear of him not waiting for me to get my shit together. I'd promised him my heart. I had to take care of myself first this time. I had to trust, and as cliché as the saying was, if you loved someone, set them free. If they came back, it was meant to be.

I had to focus on where I was. The air was brisk, and the traffic was too heavy to daydream about Shane. I pulled my thoughts back to the street. It seemed later than what it was—I fucking hated daylight saving. Dark sidewalks did nothing but staple me against a past I was all too ready to let go. I tightened my sweater around my neck and jaywalked across the street, avoiding getting hit, and slipped into the corner coffee shop where I was supposed to meet my platonic date.

"Rosie! There's me gir'."

The sea of people parted as Briggs shuffled through customers waiting in line to order their coffee. He pulled me up against his chest and squeezed me so tight I could hardly breathe. Having his massive arms around me felt so good, a comfort, and a familiarity I had been missing the last six months.

"Oh, I've missed you, me gir'."

"I've missed you too. Oh my God, Key, I can't breathe."

"I'm sorry," he mumbled as he put me down.

The loss of his hug reminded me how much I had truly missed him. He'd come up to Portland to investigate a business venture with an old friend and asked if he could come see me before he had to fly out.

"Let's sit," he said as he pulled me over to a small isolated table in the corner. His accent was a comfortable reminder that someone in this world cared about me. "I hope you don't mind, I ordered you a drink and a lit'le somethin'."

The barista sang out his name across the sea of people waiting.

"I got here a lit'le early. Got a couple mochas and scones."

"That's perfect." I pulled off my sweater and laid it across the back of my chair while he went and got our drinks. Portland wasn't much different from San Francisco—the weather was cold and you always dressed in layers.

"'ere we go. I hope you like whipped cream. I asked for extra." He winked, making me smile.

I'd missed him, especially since we had been almost inseparable during the last days of Sybil's life. "I don't know if I told you how important you were to me when Sybil … you know. Thank you for taking care of her things for me. You were the rock I needed."

Briggs grabbed my hand across the table. His eyes pinned on mine, he gave me a genuine smile. One of those smiles that you could feel all the way down into your toes. Key had saved me from having to deal with the bags of stuff Sybil's family never took and all of the *gifts* Mr. C had sent me.

"You don't have to say it, me gir'. It was nothin' more than makin' a phone call."

I smiled back.

"Now tell me how you're doin', Rosie? Is this going to be home for you now?" He took a guarded sip of his mocha.

"Well, I've been waitressing at a Cajun restaurant, and everyone there is so nice. I'm going to a group that helps those who are trying to mainstream into life after the streets. I don't know if this is home yet." I could tell he wanted more. I shot him a quick smile and pulled my mocha up to my lips.

"Mmmm, this is really goot."

"You know, Kean, I'm doing what I can. I talk to Sybil every morning. It might be crazy, but she gives me the strength to go on breathing. Knowing she will never take another breath, I make sure I continue to breathe for both of us."

He reached over the table again and pulled my hand into his. "I know you miss her. I understan' how you cling to t'at to keep your sanity and her memory alive."

His eyes pierced my soul, and I saw he had more to tell me.

"What's on your mind, Key?"

"That Shane of yours is a nice dude, but the guy keeps findin' me ever' couple o' days, asking me if I seen you aroun'. He hasn't given up, Rosie."

I pulled my hand out of his. "Key, I'm really trying to get my head on straight before I invite someone else into my life. Shane knows what I'm doing. If he waits for me … great. If he doesn't … then I have to live with the choices I had to make. But I can't go there right now. I'm just getting my shit together." I took a drink from my mocha.

"I'm not tryin' to pressure you 'bout him. I know wat you're doin' here. I know, Rosie, I do, but I also know wat will bring you happiness, and I don't want you to lose t'at. All I want is to see you happy, me gir'."

"Who's to say I'm not happy? I'm finally doing what I need to do for me. Just me. What about you, Key? Are you happy doin' what you're doin'?" I knew he could see right through me. I was an open book to Kean Briggs.

"As happy as I can be. Business is about the same, except I miss your smart ass."

I smiled, but it was short-lived as my thoughts were hijacked by the girls I had left behind. "Have you seen Crystal and Brie?"

"Ahhh, yeah, every so often. They're doing what they gotta do to make it, you know?"

"What do you mean?"

"Just t'at they made some choices they though' were best for them. They got themselves a pimp."

I felt my heart break. This was too hard. Maybe I wasn't ready to hear about the life I had left behind. It opened too many memories that I was trying to overcome. "You know what, Key, I shouldn't have asked. I don't think I'm really ready to hear about that."

"I understan', Rosie. I didn't come here to talk about t'at. I came to see you and find out 'bout how your life is goin'."

"Oh, Key, it's been six eye-opening months. It's a struggle every day. I won't say some days aren't worse than others. But every second I talk myself into believing I'm worthy of a better life is a moment I've battled and won. I don't want to ever be that person again."

He slid his hands up across my elbows before he pulled me up into a hug. "I'm real sorry, me gir'. I'd never want you to be t'at person again either."

We stood there wrapped in each other's arms. Peace threaded between us, and freedom swept across every cell of my being. I knew at that moment, I was going to make it. Briggs pushed his lips to the top of my head.

Healing touch.

"I'll nev'r mention you' past ever again. I promise."

My body melted into his, not in a sexual way but in a renewed way. An inner strength kinda way. I was safe.

"Thanks, Key. It'll get easier. It's just something I can't handle right now. It's still kinda raw, ya know?"

Even though I didn't want to hear about my old life, I ached to ask him more about Shane. I wanted to hear about how Shane kept looking for me, but I didn't. I longed to find my strength in Shane's conviction to wait for me, but I couldn't. I had to change because it was something I wanted, needed for myself and not for someone else.

"I know. I'm so happy I got to see you, Rosie."

"Thanks for asking about my life."

He tightened his arms around me before he let go.

"And Key?" I breathed.

"Yeh?"

"Don't ever stop asking to meet me, no matter what my answer may be. Even if there are more days I say no than yes."

"All right, I won't stop." His words caressed my heart.

"Thanks."

Briggs drove me home, a whole four blocks away. I guessed the idea of keeping me safe was still burned into his brain, as it should be. He was still in the thick of protecting and healing the hos in the Tenderloin. Six months off the track and moving to a whole other state didn't stop the conditioned routine I had lived for the last three and a half years of my life. I knew how quickly a turn of circumstances could trump any forward momentum.

Key pulled up to the curb at my apartment complex. It wasn't anything special, nor beautiful. The complex was more industrial-looking, a concrete jungle with the exception of the patch of dirt and grass between the sidewalk and building.

"Well, this is me. Thanks for the lift home and the coffee."

A smile crested his face.

"What's so funny?" I asked.

"Nothin'. Just happy to see you."

I leaned over and hugged him. When I tried to let go, he wasn't going to have it.

His face against the side of my head, he whispered in my ear, as if by whispering, it made him mentioning Shane any more okay. "Don't be mad, *he* asked me to give you this. He hopes you understan'."

He slipped something into my sweater pocket, and I stiffened at his words. Tears spiked at my eyes. Could all the answers to the future I'd been longing for be right here? Should I even read it? *His* words seemed so weighty in my pocket. It would be so much

240

easier to stay with Key, have him take me with him.

"Thanks."

I reluctantly hopped out of his rental car and didn't look back. Briggs tapped his horn a couple of short times before I heard him drive off. I slipped my hand into my sweater pocket and felt the chill of the envelope, the chunk of tape sealing the seam, and the plumpness of the letter inside, filled with Shane's words. My heart slipped and slid through every thunderous beat. I needed to get into my apartment and read what could be the best or the most devastating thing I'd received in the last six months.

twenty-seven

ALONE IN MY apartment—a place that had become my safe haven, where being alone wasn't so lonely—I propped Shane's letter against an old coffee mug on the kitchen island. I stared at it for hours, held it up to the ceiling light, pulled just enough on the edge to see how easy it was to open, then dropped it back on the counter.

I'd spent the last six months working so hard on letting go of who I was. I'd left California and uprooted my life to get as comfortably far away from my past as I could. What if his letter hammered me back into my past? Whether I was crazy for not ripping into it or cynical for being terrified of what it might say, I knew one thing for sure—whatever it said, good or bad, I had to be in the right mindset to read it. Struggling with what to do sounded ludicrous, but it was huge for me. There was no way I could handle his rejection.

"Bite the bullet then, Rose. Pick up the fucking letter, rip it open, and just as if you're tearing off a Band-Aid, deal with the immediate pain. It's easier that way. Deal with it so you can move the fuck on!" I huffed out loud.

I'd rather drown in the moment of truth than spend my life swimming in a lie.

It wasn't lost on me that I didn't have anyone there to rip the letter open for me.

"One … two … three," I mumbled as if the numbers had all the power in the world to change my mind.

Briggs said, "He hopes you understand." What the hell do I need to understand?

I'd waited a half of a year, an eternity to the impatient and a lifetime to a kid. In a blink of an eye, a mere six months and my world could be destroyed by what he had written on these pages. I unfolded the letter as fear pecked at my heart.

~~Complicated~~ Captivating Rose,

I keep writing and rewriting this letter. I know I promised you I'd give you space. I just need to know if you're okay? Not a day goes by where I don't think about you being alone and trying to find yourself. God knows I look for you in the faces of people every day. I keep searching for you in the words I hear, in the memories I have, even the broken sidewalks where you've left your past. I cling to small pieces of you while I walk past the restaurants where we've made memories, hoping to find anything that would bring you back to me, but it never does.

I want you to know that you've ruined my appetite for Cajun food. I can't even go near a Cajun restaurant anymore. I'm not starving myself— I'm just not enjoying the foods that remind me of you.

Anyway, after you left, I went and found Briggs downtown, hoping he might have answers. Every time I asked about you, he'd say he didn't have anything. Five months and Briggs's answers stayed the same. He wouldn't crack. (I think he's getting pissed at me for asking, so I've backed off a little.) Instead of finding him every night, I ask him twice a week; now just once every couple of weeks. He's the only connection I have to you, and if there's the slightest chance he'll be willing to tell me you're okay, I'm going to jump on it. He's the only key I have to you (funny, to find out that you call him key).

Rose, I know I pushed you into a corner that day, and it wasn't fair of me. I let my own past and fear rule over me. I'm sorry if I caused you more problems. It was never my intention. I just felt like I couldn't breathe without knowing you were breathing the same air. I wanted to be that someone who meant the world to you, the one person who broke through the walls you'd put up to protect yourself. It's so damn hard to admit I was scared to lose what little part of you I had.

Now that I've spent some time thinking about it, I can admit you were right. Yes, I struggled with your profession. Every egotistical part of me wrestled with the thought of any other man touching you without concern for your well-being. I guess I was jealous as fuck, because I wanted you. But I knew that if I tried to push you or control you, you'd resist and I'd lose you forever. And I don't want a forever where you aren't in it.

All I've ever wanted to do was protect you, save you from a life that continued to break you, be the one you'd run to when your life was crumbling. I understand now that that's not what you were asking me to be. I've had almost six months to become the type of man I should be for you. I realize how hard it is for you to need someone, to put your trust in a person who has the power to hurt you. But I need you to know I won't hurt you, Rose.

When you told me that day that you loved me, it gave me hope. There's nothing I want more than to be with you, to come find you, and to be the man you deserve. But finding you when you don't want to be found is harder than I thought. So I convinced Briggs to take this letter—God, I hope he gives it to you. I'm not asking you to stop finding yourself for my sake, I would never ask you to do that. I just want to know that I'm still on your radar. That you think about a future with me.

I've left my past in the city. Every single piece of my past, including Martie. She was never going to be a part of my future, even before I met you. I'm sorry she hurt you, that she made you believe she had any part of my heart. She never did. I'm starting new, just like you! Everything I'm doing now is all about our future. I sold the laundromat. I just couldn't keep it knowing that it was attached to a past you're working so hard to get away from. I want a future with you, Rose. I want to be the man you come home to for the rest of your life. I want to hold you when you have those days where you want to give up and celebrate with you on the days you recognize how strong you really are.

I bought a small two-bedroom fixer-upper on the edge of Joaquin Miller Park in the Oakland Hills. The real estate agent said I got a million-dollar view for pennies. The view took a lot of pennies, but I'd spend every last one I had if it meant I'd get to share it with you. I started remodeling. I had to do something to keep myself busy. That way the days don't seem so long without you.

I would really like to hear from you. I hope you've found the peace you're looking for.

So if you decide to make it to my side of the bay, here's my new address.

5222 Crockett Place. Oakland, CA. 94602

If you don't want to see me, I'll respect your wishes.

I really miss you,

Love,
Persistent Shane

I reread his letter over and over again, read it until my eyes blurred with every guilt-riddled tear that splashed against his words. Stunned by everything he'd written, I couldn't believe he had sold his laundromat for me or even left the city. My heart cracked for the steps he'd taken to prove to me that he loved me. Actions I'd never consider anyone ever doing for me in my wildest dreams. It was proof Shane West was the man I was supposed to be with, but I was too torn apart, too tangled in what I said I was supposed to be. I was so close to finally being okay in my own skin. I'd found myself my own way. My brain swirled with his words and my thoughts, how contradictory my heart was to my head, my body to my spirit.

I wanted to go right now and find him. Inconvenient as it was to hop in a car and drive twelve hours or get on a plane, I wanted to be with him, to see him before reality fucked with my head. But, my life was clear in Portland, a life I had committed to live until I was strong enough to bury my past and live in my future.

I held the letter up to my nose inhaled every word he'd written in black ink. Every intention he'd placed before me was clear and to the point, yet uncertainty still drowned me. Buried deep in insecurity, I folded the letter up, slipped it back into the envelope, and put it into my sock drawer. I had to decide if I was going to leave the safety I had in Portland and take a risk for a one-of-a-kind love back in California. Was I strong enough?

twenty-eight

SHANE

IT'S BEEN FOUR weeks since I gave Briggs my letter, and I've heard nothing. No text, no call, no letter, no Rose showing up at my door. Every day I go to my mailbox, hoping that she's written me back. Something, anything to indicate that she's even read my letter ... nothing.

I don't know how much longer I can take waiting. I feel so out of fucking control. I've never been so desperate in my life. Wanting someone so badly, every little shattered part of them, even when I'm not supposed to. But I can't stop thinking about her. I want to wrap myself in her scent, press my lips against her tear-soaked cheeks, hear her voice as she tells me she's okay—*fuck, this isn't good for me.* My mind spins off into the moment in my office when Crystal told me what Rose did every night ...

"Well, Crystal, you are a very beautiful woman, and like I've said before, if I was ever interested in your type of service, you'd definitely be the first woman I'd call. But right now I'm pretty satisfied in that department of my life, and truthfully, I don't think my girl would like this very much." I sway

my hands back and forth between us. "But hey, just knowing you're okay is enough for me. No disrespect, I've just never been into ... this." I slip my hands down between my legs and push her foot out from my crotch.

"You have a girl, huh?" Crystal parrots me.

I smile, knowing my girl, Rose, is just on the other side of my office wall. "Yeah, as a matter of fact, I came in here to grab something for her. So if you'll excuse me." I stand up, reach into the bottom drawer of my desk, and snatch a handful of Blow Pops.

"I love Blow Pops because you get a two-fer. You get to suck and then blow."

Crystal's words play in my head. They are familiar; they're Rose's words.

"Who told you that?" I ask pointedly.

"What?"

"A two-fer, suck and then blow? Why did you say that?"

Crystal looks at me sideways before she answers. "One of my girls on the track. Why?"

"Because you don't hear many people say that."

"Yeah? Well, maybe it's only us girls on the stroll who talk that way."

I try to let go of the fact that Rose says the same thing. Coincidences happen all the time. "Well, I'm sorry to ask you to leave, but my girl is waiting for me and I have to lock up the office."

"Oh, of course, sorry. Thanks again." She gives me a hug.

I pull the door shut behind us, look around, and notice Rose isn't anywhere to be found. I head to the front door, Crystal close behind. Scanning the entire laundromat, I can't believe she just left.

"Where are you, Rose? Where did you go?" I say unconsciously, almost under my breath.

Crystal clears her throat, catching my attention. "Your girl's name is Rose?"

"Yeah."

"Wow, wouldn't that be a trip, if my Rose and your Rose are the same person?" she says in an amused manner.

I'm not amused. "No, it wouldn't be a trip."

I think about Rose and how she couldn't be the same person. It was impossible with what she does for a living and going to school. Doubt is such a motherfucker.

"Well, my Rose hasn't had the easiest life. Fucked up parents, those Newtons."

I do a double take, looking at Crystal. Did I just hear her right? There is no fucking way we're talking about the same Rose.

"What is her last name?" My question comes out harshly.

"Newton. Rose Newton. Why?"

My flesh ripples cold before the air rips and burns across my skin. Heat sears through every cell of my body. I feel sick. The bile in my stomach flicks at my urge to throw up. How long? When did she start? Why would she? A barrage of questions floods my mind.

"I guess by the look on your face, we're talking about the same girl. Long black hair, gorgeous green eyes, warm-toned skin?"

I'm completely devastated and pissed. I don't even give her a response. I push through the front door and hustle out of the laundromat. The only thing I hear is Crystal shouting words I could give two flying fucks about.

"Don't tell her I told you."

My body and mind swirl with the idea that there are other motherfucking men touching her. She's letting them fu—I feel like I've been kicked in the gut, pissing blood and bleeding out. What. The. Fuck?

I push those memories from my mind, work hard to let them go. It's pretty painful to say the least. I collect my tool belt and head out to the front porch. When I get in my head too much, I find work that keeps my hands busy and my mind off of her. Today, I'm struggling to keep my mind busy. I can't stop thinking about those last couple of days, no matter what I do.

I keep trying to call Rose, find out her side of the story. Two days and nothing. I'm not leaving a voicemail, not about this. I need to hear it from her mouth. I need to know the truth. No more fucking lies. I start to call Rose for the umpteenth time when my phone buzzes with a call from Martie.

"Hello?" I answer.

Martie's voice is calm, but I can hear the hurry pushing her words. "Shane! Listen, I don't have much time. I'm on my way to SF General. I guess my sister finally met her fate with her lifestyle and her pimp beat the shit out of her and her piece-of-shit hooker roommate."

"Wait, what?"

"Shane, I just told you I don't have a lot of time. The hospital is asking for my sister's ID, you know, identification. Anyway, I'm almost here and it's too much to backtrack. Since you're probably at the laundromat, and it's literally a couple of blocks from her apartment, would you swing by and get it? I already called the manager and he said he'd let you in. I need you here with me, Shane. Hurry."

I don't hesitate to do it. Even though I already told her a while ago we were done, and we weren't seeing each other anymore, I'm not going to be a prick. She texts me the address, and I recognize that it's only a handful of blocks away from my laundromat.

The manager of the apartment complex is shaken up. He's mumbling about Mandy and her roommate and the trouble this whole ordeal creates for him. He pushes the door open and gives me a couple of minutes in Martie's sister's place.

I step in, and immediately I feel just how tiny the apartment is. Two beds, a kitchen area with a small two-person table, and a small couch in the center of it all make up the place. Looking around, I notice a collage of pictures taped on the mirror mounted on the inside of the front door. Looking at them feels invasive, but I can't help myself. I didn't have the opportunity to meet Mandy.

So looking at the pictures, I'm not prepared to see Rose, my girl, next to Martie's sister. My mind tumbles back to Martie's call. "A pimp beat the shit out of her and her piece-of-shit hooker roommate." My body flushes with a chill as I look back up at the pictures and see one with Rose and me. Suddenly, the idea that she could be seriously hurt matters more than what she does at night. The fear of never seeing her again spikes through my veins,

piercing my heart. I have to get to the hospital. I need to make sure Rose isn't badly hurt. I forget about Mandy's ID, and I hightail it to the hospital.

I pull out my claw hammer and begin to demolish the rotting porch railing. A job I've been doing for the last several weeks, it helps me channel my spastic energy when it has nowhere else to go. It feels good to rip apart something I'll eventually replace. With every swing and every point of contact, I feel myself letting go, even if it's for a fleeting moment.

I get three feet of the railing taken down before the ambush of thoughts I have about Rose keeps coming at me like a freight train. As much as I try to keep myself busy, I can't stop wondering what's she doing. Is she thinking about me just as much as I'm thinking about her? Did she get my letter? I know she can only give me what she has available, and God knows, I want to teach her, tell her, touch her, and bring her to a healing we both can embody.

A familiar relief reaches into my body as I think about that day in the hospital, knowing she was okay and wasn't the one lying in that hospital bed. I would never have wished for Sybil to die, but knowing it wasn't the woman I love gave me a second chance at a life with her. I had a second chance at the possibility of nestling into her breasts, dragging my nose across her skin, inhaling what my heaven smells like. I want to listen to her breathe and whimper at my touch. I want to bathe her in my words. I want to collect her broken pieces scattered between us and create a future with her.

I'm chained to her, I feel it. Being away from her is killing me. I'm struggling to carry the emptiness of not knowing how she's doing. When I think about her, it's as if life is being poured into my soul, but her not being here with me feels as if my life is slipping through my hands.

What if all I've done is create more pressure by sending her the letter? What if she doesn't want the same thing anymore? I know I can't force her, heal her, or save her from her thoughts. I want her, every tiring, twisted, frightening, exciting emotion that makes her who she is. These last six months, I've been determined to get my life ready for Rose. I'm not going to be an empty shell of a person lingering in a purgatory filled with empty promises that nobody wants. One thing I know for sure—I don't want her in anyone's bed but mine.

I'm literally imploding without her.

It's unseasonably hot for fall in the Bay Area, and I drag my arm across my brow, stopping the rolling drips of sweat from getting into my eyes. I take a minute to look around the world I'm creating, hoping that if or when Rose decides to come home to me, it will be what she wants. I think I'm doing the right thing. It feels right.

I pick up a couple of rotting two-by-fours and toss them next to the porch in a semi-organized pile. *Stay physical, Shane. Keep busy, move forward.* Trying to keep my mind from swirling and my heart from thrashing faster in my chest, I head inside the house for a bottle of water. I swig the bottle dry in a couple of gulps. My eyes are burning from the sweat-beads that made it past my brows, and I blink and tear up to stop the pain. A physical pain I'd take any day of the week, compared to the emotional pain of not having Rose with me.

I think about what I wrote to her and how I poured my soul into that letter. I professed my love and told her that I want to work on making a life with her. My mind twists off into visions, and just like anything else, they morph into the reaction I dreaded from her.

"Don't you see you were something special to me, Shane? You were something different than any other man in my life. I fought so hard trying not to give you my heart, tried so hard not to open the ironclad lock, because I knew I'd get hurt. But you found the key. You found my weakness and

exploited it for your own needs. Whether you knew it or not, whether I knew it or not, I gave you my heart. And just like that, like everyone in my life, you broke it, and now you're gonna walk away never looking back."

Doubt attacks my thoughts ... what if she read what I wrote and misinterpreted it? Will I ever be enough for her, or is she going to wait until my words render her numb and she stops listening? Worry flashes through my head, rippling down into my fingertips. Son of a bitch, within seconds, I regret sending it. I don't want anything to inhibit her personal growth, or her finding her way back to me. What if my words threw her over the edge, or she isn't getting back to me because she had to go back to the streets? A pit swirls in my gut. If she'd just respond to the letter, then I'd know and I wouldn't have to live in such fucking limbo.

As if some type of power is answering my biggest fears, I turn to get another bottle of water, and out of the corner of my eye, I catch a glimpse of someone shuffling up my driveway. I freeze mid-gulp, having to push the bottle away from my lips as the water soaks me. I don't care. All I can do is stare, blinking excessively before I recognize who it is. Seven long months, and she's here now. Excitement rapidly thrashes through my body as the most gorgeous woman in the world walks straight to me. She cautiously lifts her hand to block out the sun setting behind me, and her expression throttles me. It's her, my one and only ...

Rose.

Every nerve in my body is firing off, jolting waves of excitement into every atom of my being. Rose got my letter. She's found me and come here to be with me. Every day lost to thinking about her, every moment I ached to be with her, now reality is playing out exactly how I dreamed that it would. She pauses at the edge of the porch, her skin perfect, her eyes emerald, dark, narrow, and damp. I want to open the door, cling to her, hold her, heal her. I want to carry her to my bed so I can just feel her warmth against me. Feel her break for me, break for what I am willing to try to heal. But I can't come at her so strong. She doesn't work that way. She needs me to move slowly, deliberately, and without any expectations.

Suddenly, my skin doesn't exist, and every nerve that covers every muscle in my body is exposed. She's the most beautiful thing I've ever laid eyes on. More beautiful than the first day I saw her and the day she left. A glow is permeating her skin. A glow I want to taste, protect, and be affected by for the rest of my life.

She knocks on my door. A gentle crack against the wood, a subtle knock.

I pull open the door. A slight chill swirls around my soul, tethered under my skin. Our eyes meet, and she pulls her bottom lip between her teeth. Perfection. I notice her pulse thundering across her neck, and all I want to do is bury myself in her, tangle my fingers in her thick black hair, and kiss her mouth. She reaches into her back pocket and pulls out the envelope I gave to Briggs.

"I got your letter," she whispers, holding it up between us.

Her eyes well with so much hope. She silently cries. I don't want her to know I'm scared, so fucking scared. Wordlessly, I reach across and clear her hair from her bare shoulder. I'm dying to brush my fingertips over her exposed skin, but I don't. I know it might be too much for her right now. We are woven into the minds of each other; words are unnecessary.

Yet she clears her throat and begins to explain what she's doing at my door. "I'm sorry I didn't call before I came."

I'm frozen, tangled with her soul. I don't say anything. It's as if all the words I've been practicing for the last seven months have vanished, leaving me speechless.

"It's just, ummm, when I got your letter." She fills the awkward silence with words. "I didn't know if—I shouldn't have come," she blurts before she turns to leave.

I wasn't born yesterday, and I'm sure as hell not losing her again. I reach for her as she turns away. Catching her arm, I pull her back to me.

"No! I mean, yes. Yes … you should have come here," I shuffle through my words.

We cling to the moment our eyes meet. Neither one of us is willing to break the silence, a dance of wills. I choose to lose. I will lose for her. Every day, every hour, every second of the day, I will let her win.

"Please, come in. I'm happy you came. I'm glad you read the letter."

She steps in, and I can feel her pain oozing from her soul, dangerously tainted with such vulnerability. I want to purge every memory from her mind, methodically replacing them with me. Maybe I'm self-indulgent, but could she have come here needing something from me? Just me.

twenty-nine

SHANE

I TRACE MY eyes over her body. The places I want to reside with her. I hunger for her touch, to feel the heat of her fingertips as they traipse over my skin. I want to learn every curve, every bend, every sway of her body. I want to memorize the smallest scars and deepest wounds. I want to fill them with my words, my love, my urge to hear how deeply and madly in love she is with me. God, I've missed her. I just want to forget what we were yesterday, what people think, what the world will make of it. I just want to dissolve in this moment.

She clears her throat. The beautiful sound of her vulnerability twists me in knots.

"My whole life has been a huge fucking mess, and I couldn't ask you to clean it up. I thought if I left where I was just existing, I could find myself, and in some ways I did. God, my throat is so dry," she says, her hands shaking uncontrollably. She doesn't even realize how beautiful she is when she admits her weaknesses.

You don't have to be strong all the time ... let me take care of you.

"Would you like something to drink? Tea, soda, water?"

I ask foolishly.

She shakes her head.

She didn't come here to drink tea. Could she have come here to find what she lost? Could she be looking for what will make her life less complicated and keep her safe?

"Sit?" I ask as she comes in and heads to my sofa.

She takes my hands. Hers are so soft, so delicate, yet filled with stories of a life lived in pain. *Are they willing to explore what she fears? Is she willing to take a chance on discovering I might be the one to calm her raging sea?* A million scenarios skip through my mind. *Has she done this before? Maybe, but not like this.*

She sits on the sofa, pulling me down next to her. She twists, makes her knee a barrier between us. A stance of distance, a fear she doesn't want to face.

"I'm glad you're here."

"I needed to see you. I need to know if you still feel the same way as you did when you wrote the letter to me. I need you to … I guess what I'm trying to say is that I'm scared that I'm … that I'm too late."

She seems like she's not ready for me to comfort her, not completely. I slip my arm around behind her, making sure to rest it on the top of the sofa cushion.

"No, God, no, you're not too late. I'm here. I meant every word, and I'm listening," I answer, trying to harness the electricity surging through every cell of my body.

Her expression is filled with desolation. A tear breaks free and rolls down her porcelain cheek. I want to touch her, brush my thumb across the side of her face and let her tear soak into my skin, but I don't. I see she's trying to find the strength to give me an explanation of how tightly wrapped she is.

"You're so beautiful, Rose," I whisper.

God, give me the strength …

"I worked through a lot of things, Shane. A lot of things while

I was up in Portland."

"Portland?" I ask. "That's a lot farther than I thought."

"Yeah, well, I just hopped in my car and drove until I was far enough away to stop. My whole life, I was never anyone's number one. I know now that I deserve to be someone's number one."

She's so small, delicate even.

"You're my number one, Rose. You're my number one, my number two, every number that exists in my number line."

We're both raw, scared, needy. My body's vibrating, and my heart is thundering so loud in my ears, I can't hear myself think. I take a chance. My fingers caress her beautifully smooth skin, dampened by tears that are speeding down her cheeks. I feel electricity as my skin meets hers. I'm meant to do this. I'm meant to be right here, with this delicate, beautiful creature.

"You really believe that?" she asks.

"Yes. You're my everything. I'm here and will always be as long as you'll have me."

She leans into my touch before she drops her head to my shoulder, and as if I'm an old friend, a comfortable blanket, she pushes into me. Her knee, an afterthought, is pinned under us. We begin to sway back and forth, a soothing motion, trying to find the actions to mirror the fireworks taking off in my body.

I ache to heal her, to help her curb the anger that thunders through her body when she's cornered like a vicious dog, a rattler, a lion. She opens just enough to let me in.

I feel it when her body language tilts. She lets go and rests her weight across my shoulder. She's opening to me, her breathing is deliberate. Burying her face against my neck, she starts kneading her lips against my flesh.

Her words are muffled against my neck, but it doesn't matter. I hear them loud and clear. "You're so warm. Smell so good. I've missed you so much. Would it be wrong if I wanted you to kiss me?"

Tempted by her request, I want to kiss her. I want to be the one who fills every missing brick in her foundation.

"No, I think it depends on what you want. I know what I want," I whisper.

She pulls back and drops her mouth down next to my ear, and a chill surges through my body.

"This is what I want," she whispers before she pulls back from me. Her eyes, dark as the vast ocean on a moonless night, pin me.

I brush my lips lightly against the corner of her mouth. I sigh. A soft, desperate breath catches in my throat. She stops and pulls back just far enough to tickle the edge of my lips. The same lips that ache to discover every space on her body.

"Are you as nervous as I am?" she asks.

I shake my head without saying a word, and I will myself to be brave, be strong. She takes my hand and presses it against her chest. I feel her heart thundering.

"I'm so fucking nervous," she quips.

"I'm making you nervous? Why?"

"I'm still terrified there's a part of you that will turn me down. I've been gone for so long. I'm afraid I messed up so much with you." Her lips quiver, her eyes carrying the weight of her fear.

I'm breaking at her words. I need her to know I'm already hers. "You're afraid I'm not going to want you? Rose, this is all for you."

"I'm scared you don't want to share yourself with someone who messed up so bad and left you so she could find herself," she chokes out, tears streaming down her cheeks.

I take her hand and press it to my chest. "You're right here. A big part of you sits right here."

She feels my heart crashing against her hand too. Tears fill my eyes—I can't help it. I'm watching my life, the woman I want to spend all my moments with, crumble in front of me.

"I don't think you really understand, Shane ... in my entire life, you've been the only one to calm the raging sea in my mind."

My heart twists with every instinct I have to keep her and scoop her up and consume every ounce of her fear, her pain. My nose nudges her cheek. Her soft, supple lips open just enough to let my tongue trace the seam of her mouth. I close my eyes, letting the moment devour me. This is happening. I'm finally tasting the pain and pleasure of who she is.

Her energy thunders through every cell of my body as who I am and what we are dissolves in our kiss. She tastes so sweet, with a hint of bitterness. I can feel that she's just as afraid as I am.

Words have created our emotions. The act of us being together is something so much deeper. I drag my hands up over her shoulders. I feel her shiver as my touch paints her skin with love. Her lips, dampened by our tongues mingling, consume the fear and passion we've let collect in our conversations. My hands tangle in her hair as we taste each other's desires. She anchors her hands against my chest, and her warmth penetrates through to my heart.

Suddenly, nothing else exists outside of the moment we are sharing. I feel her begin to heal.

I don't push, I don't press, I don't take what I want. I hold back, and I let her decide how far she wants to take this delicate and treacherous journey of discovery. I know she needs to be in control. Her intentions are clear, and she needs to make the next move, even if it kills me. I push away the urge to have more.

God, I want more.

I move slowly, keeping my fingers tangled in her hair, my lips glued to hers. I long to drag my tongue down across her jawline. I want to taste every inch of her skin, pralines and cream. I will myself not to move too fast. I focus on the fact that she's new at this, at sharing herself with me. If it's only a kiss ... I will take it.

My world found its home, my lips found its mate, my life found its purpose. I'm filled with the moment, captured by her magic, even while knowing she owns the ability to, at any second, leave me torn, twisted, alone.

She urges me back on the sofa, her body light against mine. I feel her breasts press against me just enough to prick my body into overdrive. The heat surging below the buttons of my pants intensifies as she draws her knee up between my legs. Her lips create the perfect place to get lost. She tastes so irresistibly good, so raw and unprotected.

It's her decision if our damp clothes become the only protection between us. She withdraws from our kiss, and instantly I'm lost without her taste. I want to breathe with her until every feeling of panic filling every atom of my body disappears. I need her warm skin against mine.

She looks at me, and I see the fire raging behind her pupils. I see the inferno of confusion, defeat, fear, need, want, and love. Yes, I see that she wants to love me. *God, tell her to keep holding on to that desire to let me in. Let me love her.*

"Are you okay with this?" I ask breathlessly.

I panic because she doesn't move. Her emerald eyes are pinned to mine, her expression inquisitive enough to make me second-guess opening my fucking mouth. I just gave her an out … I've given her a free pass to choose between what she wants and what she believes she needs.

"I don't know," she says before her eyes trail down to my lips as her body hovers over mine. "I've never kissed like that before."

Her words paralyze me.

"You've never kissed like that before?" My heart falls into my gut. I know she's kissed people before. What does she mean?

"No, it was so intimate. I've never kissed someone like that, not until now."

Her eyes catching mine, I see the truth boiling behind her words. Suddenly I'm acutely aware of her firm nipples teasing my chest, her hair tickling my cheeks, and her breath mingling with mine. I'm pinned, trapped, taken by her answer, her body, her pulse thundering through the artery down the side of her neck. I need to press my lips there and feel the pace of her excitement, her desire that boils through her veins as she gives herself to me entirely.

She lowers her hips against mine and finds home.

Pressure, just enough pressure to drive me fucking crazy.

A smile crests her beautifully lonely lips. "Is this okay for you?" she asks in a delicate tone.

"It's perfect," I answer.

I rest my hands on the curves of her lower back. My fingers meet the natural curve of her ass, and I feel her desire to push down against me.

Instinctively I roll my hips and push myself up against her. Partly afraid she'll decide this might be too much, I watch her reaction. Her eyes go wide, she presses back, and I know she likes what I have to offer. Her lips crash against mine as I push up to meet hers. My hands are desperate to find some of her exposed flesh, but as bad as I want her under me, as much as I want to bury myself deep in her soul, I don't. Not yet. We are on fire, burning together, igniting something so fucking intense, something I never felt with anyone else ever before. Wordlessly, we're speaking volumes with our bodies. She loves me, and I love her.

She wiggles, adjusting herself … her hips … her legs finally straddling mine. I pull my hands from her lower back and push her hair away from her face. Both of us still dive deep into kissing each other. She backs far enough away that I can see her eyes are damp with an insatiable need. I silently ask to feel her flesh as I catch her shirt between my fingers. Six buttons—that's how many I counted when I watched her walk in. Six small buttons separate me from finally touching paradise, from dragging my mouth over her swelling breasts and tasting her milky soft skin.

She flashes a timid smile, and her hands replace mine. She teases me with her eyes as she slowly unfastens each button. She's torturing me. Her shirt is stretching open, and I do the right thing, the tough answer to her call—I wait for her to tell me it's okay to touch her beautiful body. It's taking everything I am to wait.

I take over unbuttoning the last two. I pull up off the couch a little and remove my shirt. My chest bare, my muscles tight, my heart crashes against my bones. She's not wearing a bra.

She sits straight up, and all her weight, perfectly warm and consuming, bears down on me. I buck my hips and watch her gorgeous body react. I slip my fingers behind the edge of her shirt across her shoulders. Our eyes are magically tethered to each other as her shirt slides off her shoulders. My mouth goes dry.

She moans as she grinds against me. I'm straining against my pants. I want to be inside her and feel her tighten around every inch I have to give.

"Let me in," I whisper.

"I have," she breathes.

"I want all of you, every part of who you are, all of it."

"I'll give you everything." Her words crack against my ears.

"I'm here for you. Let go and let me in, Rose."

Suddenly, as if she's been waiting for someone to ask for every part of who she is, as if the one stone blocking the rush of a river becomes dislodged … she breaks down against me.

"I never asked for this life. I just want to be free. I want to give you everything I am," she answers, her body contradicting her words. "I don't want to fear losing you to my past. I want to believe I deserve you. I want to trust your words. I want to make love to you, but I'm so fucking scared you'll never forgive me for who I was."

Her words slice deep across my heart. This woman, someone who cuts me down to the core of who I am, is still worried, after seven months of being away from each other, being separated by fear and her refusal to share herself with me entirely, that I'll leave her. Fuck that. Enough is enough. Maybe I can't tell her how much I love her. Maybe the words just aren't getting through. Maybe it just needs to be done without words, without fears dressing up like something that can save us. I can't take it anymore. I need to show her how much I love her.

I slip out from under her. Never looking away, I pull her into my chest. She doesn't fight me. Instead, I feel her melt against me. I hold her for what feels like an eternity before I speak.

"I want to show you something." I grab her hand and guide her into the bedroom.

She's nervous. Her palm is damp as we stand in the doorway.

"This is our bedroom. Yes, *our* bedroom. Our bed, our closet, and our dresser. The space saved just for you and me. You're the only woman I want here, sharing this with me."

Her eyes widen when she sees the picture of us on the dresser. Her chin quivering, her body shaking, she drags her fingers across the bed.

"When *you* decide to close this door, our pasts don't exist. Whatever was stays was. Whatever becomes … is. I've spent the last seven months discovering who I am, and I discovered that I'm deeply and madly in love with a woman who isn't defined by her past." I wrap my arms around her. "It's only you and me. No past, no future, we only exist in the moment right now. I love you, Rose Newton, more than I've loved anyone in my life. I won't leave you. I'll do everything in my power to convince you that you're worthy of being loved by me as much as I am worthy of being loved by you."

"Just stop it! Just … stop." She sniffles, wiping the tears from her cheeks, and nudges her lips up under my chin before I lower my mouth against hers. "It won't be easy. I've got a lot of baggage," she whispers against my flesh.

"I promise you, I'll carry each and every bag you have," I

answer. Dragging my hands up to either side of her face, I look into her beautiful earthy eyes.

"I complicate things, make them unbearable sometimes." She swallows hard.

"I can handle complicated things. I'm persistent, remember?"

Every excuse she flings at me, I will counter with the perfect answer. I drag my thumbs across her lips, asking without wasted words to kiss her. I lean down and brush my lips against hers. She shivers, and that's when I know she's run out of excuses.

"I love you, my Complicated Rose."

"I love you, Persistent Shane."

"Will you stay here with me tonight ... and every night after that?"

She looks up at me, her eyes beaming as silence rolls between us. Tears prick and clutter her eyelashes as I pull her into my chest.

"It's up to you, only you," I add.

She leans back in my embrace, just enough to look at me. I watch as peace floods her expression. Her eyes vacillate back and forth before forever passes between us. She pitches me a slight smile just as she gives me a slight nod, reaches behind her, and closes our bedroom door. My mind responds before my body. I believe the most beautiful woman in the entire world just told me she's found what she's been looking for her entire life ... *home*.

acknowledgements

A MOMENT OF REFLECTION AND THANKS ...

Writing a book isn't a solitary journey. There are so many hands that touch it. This book was touched by so many beautiful people. People who gave me their hearts, their talent, and their time. Nothing is work if you decide to approach it from your creative process. But man, oh, man, parts of *Broken Girl* nearly killed me, yet others made me fall back in love with the process of writing.

Broken Girl is my quantum leap into understanding how intimate, personal, damaging, and healing writing truly is. Parts of this book pull from the personal wounds that scar my soul, and other parts of this book are experiences I've plucked from the fray of humanity. I dove deep into the good, bad, and ugly, splaying myself open while letting the world take a gander.

I can never dance on the outside edge of my creative writing abyss again. Surging with love and sadness, hate and compassion, fear and strength, I had to learn how to surrender to my vulnerability in order to find out who I was as a writer. Through writing *Broken Girl*, I learned that I must be completely invested. No more teetering back and forth on the edge of the creative process and my own personal fear.

To My Family, Ed, Jared, Kyle, Nate, and Mom, this year was a tough one. Maybe it was the point where I never figured out balance, or maybe it was the point where I discovered vulnerability is something that showed up when I didn't really want to deal with it. Either way, I know the sacrifices you've made so I could follow my dream. Long days where a ghost of who I was would show up when you needed me fully present. I'm just so glad you still love me. Tough, torn apart, and rebuilt, I hope that as my journey changes, you'll still see the value in following your heart, no matter where it leads you. The whole family sacrificed even when there was no guarantee *Broken Girl* would lead to anything more than a pile of words shoved in a drawer. Your support has been my fueling cell to continue. I love you all with everything I am.

Becky Codere, "Beck", listen, do you hear that? It's you and me closing the cover on another book. I know I could leave this space blank, and not write one word here, and you'd know exactly what it would mean. We don't need words, my sister, my soul mate. We've both grown exponentially this last year, with and without this story. It was a difficult road with many days where you calmed me with words that were the key pieces to the puzzle I was trying to put together. I know Rose's story wasn't appealing to you at first, but you stuck with me, and together we created one of my favorites. I appreciate that no matter what, no matter the content of our talks, you love me with your whole heart. If I had one wish for humanity, it would be that everyone got to experience the unconditional love we have for each other. Truly, everyone should have a "Beck" in their lives. Someone who never gets spooked by what comes out of their soul-sister's mouth. I truly love you so much and thank God every day that I have you in my life.

Gail McHugh, "G", they say opposites attract, and well, I'd have to agree. I truly believe God took one look at us and thought to himself, "Why not?" And in that decision and all of his miraculous brilliance, he brought us together. I feel so blessed to have you in my life beyond the book world and all the memories I'll cherish forever, even exceeding the moments where we both learned to love unconditionally beyond our own fears. No matter if it was my reality that was bled onto the pages of *Broken Girl* or the daily posts I read aloud and sent your way, you showed me that friendship isn't defined by preconceived ideas, expectations, or what appears to be, but in fact is defined by trust, love, and understanding. There's something magical in a friendship that has been formed and placed in God's hands. I love you and all of our green hearts, dearly.

Mia Sheridan, my infatuation and author crush, I can't tell you how honored I was when you agreed to help me polish *Broken Girl*. I don't know if you really know how much I love you! Your advice was never taken lightly, and whether I spend the rest of my life writing only one more book or if I write hundreds, I will continue to ask for and honor your advice. And let it be known here that I will always keep asking to read your books before the world gets them. Thank you for being such a beautiful friend and colleague.

AL Jackson, my love, the woman I look up to in all her glory. Thank you for your words of wisdom. Thank you for investing your time in me and this book. You are such an icon in the book world, and I am so fortunate to call you my friend and colleague. I can't begin to express the gratitude I have for you. My love for you and your work will never waver.

Cassie Cox, Joy Editing, I don't know what I would have done without you! Thank you for your compassion, understanding, and ability to work under an almost unbearable deadline and pressure. I know you could have turned me away, you could have run the other way, and you didn't. I can only imagine how difficult it was to do several weeks' worth of work in less than three days. Thank you for scooping up *Broken Girl* and giving it the attention it needed. You are truly a life-saver!

Angela McLaurin, Fictional Formats, thank you so much for being there for me at the eleventh hour. You stepped up and handled what needed to be done to get *Broken Girl* formatted over again and out to the world. Thank you from the bottom of my heart.

Sommer Stein, Perfect Pear Covers, another cover down. I know I drive you insane with all the crazy I send your way. But I can't imagine having anyone else create my covers. Your vision is so amazing. Thank you for being such a giving, understanding creative. Thank you for making one of the most amazing covers ever. You truly outdid yourself with *Broken Girl!* I love and adore you.

Janett Gomez, Judith Lattin, Hannah Anderson, Jennifer Hagen, Denise Tung, Jerri Baxter, Victoria Colotta, and Mindi Lou, my proofers, the last set of eyes, who even though they're under the gun … still pulled up the pieces that needed work and found the places that needed to be tied up and put away. Ladies, your help was vital to making *Broken Girl* what it is!

Cheryl Scarborough-Wilkins, Delia Nuno, and Ashley Walczak, my beta readers, your input was invaluable. Your love for my words means so much to me. I took to heart your reactions and appreciate all the love and support you've given me. Thank you for investing your time in my words!

Holly Malgieri, thank you for working on the beginning and investing your time. I appreciate your insight to Rose and how her intention must match her words. You don't know how helpful that was to me.

Bethany Castanada, what can I say, a woman after my heart! Thank you for PM'ing me on Sunday nights for Tuesday Teasers. Your support and love has been irreplaceable. Never stop being such a beautiful and giving woman.

To My Blogger Friends, Peers and Readers, without you,

this book wouldn't exist. Well, maybe it would exist, but it wouldn't make it to people without your love and support! I've said it before and I will continue to say it, this industry exists and thrives on word of mouth. I can't tell you how grateful I am for your words flowing from your mouths regarding my books! Your love and support for me and my work is inimitable. No matter if a handful of people, or thousands, buy this book, the fact that you supported and loved me through this process means more to me than anything else. Thank you for sharing my cover, teasers, and reviews.

To those who I've missed, please know you are in my heart. I would never intentionally leave you off, so if I did, please find it in your heart to forgive me. It isn't the mountains we climb or choose to die upon that define who we are, but the quiet moments in which we choose to simply be.

With Peace and Love,
Gretchen

about the author

Gretchen de la O is a writer of romantically unique stories. A proclaimed positive-energy infuser by people who know her, she finds joy in helping those around her discover their creative process. Gretchen is a firm believer that anything is possible if you set your mind to it, and what you expect out of life always finds a way of showing up. She's authentic in her dedication to her own creative process, finds strength in her spirituality, and is always looking for the bright spot in every situation.

Gretchen released her first novel, *Almost Eighteen*, in September of 2011, the first in a three-book new adult student/teacher romance series, the *Wilson Mooney* series. In November of 2012, she followed with book two, *Eighteen at Last*, and concluded the series with *Beyond Eighteen* in October, 2013. Her fourth novel, *Prototype*, a romantic suspense and the first book in the *Possession* series, was released in October 2014. *Broken Girl* is Gretchen's fifth novel, a standalone contemporary romance released on April 29th, 2016. She'd love to hear from you. Please visit Gretchen at _www.gretchendelao.com_.

connect with me

Website: *www.gretchendelao.com*

Facebook: *https://www.facebook.com/booksbygretchendelao*

Twitter: *www.twitter.com/GretchendelaO*

Instagram: *www.instagram.com/GretchendelaO*

Pinterest: *www.pinterest.com/delaogk*

Goodreads: *www.goodreads.com/gdelao*

DO YOU OR SOMEONE YOU KNOW NEED HELP?

If you or someone you know has been a victim of sexual assault or continued abuse, there are people who can help.

RAINN: (Rape, Abuse & Incest National Network)
1-800-656-HOPE (4673)
https://ohl.rainn.org/online/

DARKNESS TO LIGHT: (Childhood Sexual Abuse)
1-866-FOR-LIGHT (1-866-367-5444)
http://www.d2l.org/

THE NATIONAL DOMESTIC VIOLENCE HOTLINE:
1-800-799-7233
http://www.thehotline.org/

Remember, you are not alone.